PRICE
TO
PAY

DAVE SIVERS

ISBN: 978-1-9997397-5-1

DAVE SIVERS

Dave Sivers grew up in West London and has been writing all his life. His books include the popular crime series featuring the Aylesbury Vale detectives, DI Lizzie Archer and DS Dan Baines, as well as the DI Nathan Quarrel series set in West Hertfordshire.

The Scars Beneath the Soul and *Dead in Deep Water* were both top three bestsellers in the Amazon Kindle Serial Killers chart. *Price to Pay* is the seventh in the Archer and Baines series.

His other works include the Lowmar Dashiel crime fantasy novels.

Dave also writes plays and other material for the amateur stage and is a founder of the annual BeaconLit book festival. He lives in Buckinghamshire with his wife, Chris.

To keep up with Dave's news and upcoming releases, subscribe to his newsletters at davesivers.co.uk.

Also by Dave Sivers

Archer and Baines
The Scars Beneath the Soul
Dead in Deep Water
Evil Unseen
The Blood That Binds
Too Long Gone
Die in the Dark

DI Nathan Quarrel
In Ink
In Ice

The Lowmar Dashiel Mysteries
A Sorcerer Slain
Inquisitor Royal

Short Stories
Dark and Deep: Ten Coffee Break Crime Stories

For Chris and Debbie

1

Detective Chief Inspector Lizzie Archer took out her phone, discreetly switched the camera to selfie mode, and checked that her hair and makeup were okay. Anyone watching would assume she was checking her emails or messages.

She was much less self-conscious about the pale, crescent-shaped scar on her cheek than she used to be, but the press and TV were waiting outside with cameras, and she really didn't need the cruel shit that social media trolls were only too willing to chuck about. She'd have been more than pleased if her boss, Superintendent Josh Stowe, had wanted to front up, but he'd brushed the suggestion aside.

"Your collar, your team's case," he'd said. "Your moment in the spotlight, like it or not."

At least her well-cut hair and subtle makeup were still doing their job. Satisfied, she put the phone away, nodded to the people with her, and stepped out onto the front steps of Aylesbury Crown court. With her were Detective Sergeant Joanne 'Joan' Collins, members of the Swain family, and their solicitor.

The big, blocky, brown brick building was an unimpressive backdrop, and the grey September day did nothing to improve the atmosphere, but none of that mattered.

Cameras flashed as soon as she and the family appeared. A few reporters started shouting questions. She stood still, impassive, waiting for them to settle down. Gradually, they fell silent. Only the shuffling of feet, the clearing of throats, and background traffic noise disturbed the quiet.

"Justice has been served today," she began, "and Dougie Upman is starting the long stretch in jail he deserves. This was a cowardly, vicious attack on a young man with his whole life in front of him. Mason Swain was seventeen years old, with dreams of university and a career in medicine, when he was stabbed to death by Dougie Upman, just for objecting to Upman's demands for his smartphone."

"What do you think of the sentence?" called Claire King, Chief Reporter at the *Aylesbury Echo*.

"Nothing can bring Mason back," Lizzie said, "and no sentence can make up for his family having to live their lives without him. They've asked that they be granted the privacy to try and rebuild their lives as best they can. Now Mason's father, Matthew, would like to say a few words."

Matthew took a step forward and, with hands and voice shaking, began to read a prepared statement, speaking of the kind of boy Mason had been, what he had meant to the family, and the impact of their loss. The media listened in respectful silence.

As he spoke, Lizzie scanned the faces in front of her. If she hadn't, she might not have spotted the figures that stood, unnoticed, a little way back from the main throng.

Gaynor Upman, mother of the teenage killer, stood with arms folded, hatred etched on her face. Alongside her, mirroring her pose, was her middle son, Archie. It was a reminder that there were plenty more Upmans where Dougie came from. Several of the extended family had been in court today, and there had been uproar when the sentence was pronounced.

Gaynor and her clan were neighbours from Hell who had been terrorising their local community ever since they'd moved in a couple of years ago, and had amassed a canon of petty crime and a couple of Community Protection Orders between them, before one young thug had finally gone way too far.

Lizzie knew that Dougie had probably never had a serious shot at a decent life, and that probably applied to the rest of the family too. But she also knew that most people in similar circumstances wouldn't do what Dougie had done just to get their hands on somebody else's property. As a DCI, she normally gave her teams space to work cases, but her anger, and her sympathy for Mason's family – robbed of a loved one forever – had drawn her in and made her vow to nail the killer.

Which, as things turned out, hadn't proved too much of a challenge.

With the possible exception of Gaynor's husband, Carl, the entire Upman family were as thick as bricks – witnessed by the murder weapon being chucked in a hedge with Mason's blood and the killer's fingerprints all over it. Dougie's bloody clothes had been stuffed in the family's own dustbin, which mercifully hadn't been emptied by the time the police came to call.

Matthew finished his statement by thanking the police for obtaining justice for his son and for their support. He looked at Lizzie, who nodded.

"Thank you for your attention," she said. "I won't be taking questions at this time."

And that was when Gaynor Upman looked her straight in the eye. She pointed her index and middle finger at her own eyes, pointed them towards Lizzie, then slowly drew her index finger across her throat. It was as clear a threat as she could make, but Lizzie wasn't afraid of her. She'd had threats from bigger, harder and uglier quarters than the Upmans.

She turned and shepherded the family back inside. They all thanked her, most of them hugged her. They all waited until the press had dissipated before they finally left the building.

Although the court was no more than five minutes' walk from the police station where Lizzie and Joan were based, she'd brought them both in her car, straight from a routine meeting on the other side of town.

They walked across the small car park to the corner where she was parked, and she had pressed the key fob to unlock her car before she saw the state of the bonnet.

"What the?"

"Oh, shit," said Joan.

Something had been carved into the paintwork. One word. 'BITCH'.

*

Even at a time when Aylesbury Vale's criminal classes seemed to be slacking, there was always one more thing to do. For

Lizzie, it was one of those days that seems to last all week. By the time she was finally able to leave the office for home, the station was almost deserted.

Yawning, she made her way down to the station car park and stalked up to her car, somehow even more affronted this time by the offending word carved into her paintwork. There were no prizes for guessing whose handiwork it was. Maybe not Gaynor herself, but Lizzie would bet a pound to a penny that it had been one of the Upman clan.

It had been Lizzie who led the raid on their home when that murdering little scumbag was taken away. Most likely someone had made a mental note of the car and its registration number even then, with payback already in mind. It wouldn't have been so hard to watch for her arrival at court, and then wait until the coast was clear, before exacting this petty revenge.

The initial shock and dismay had been quickly replaced by anger, and she and Joan had gone back inside the court to ask the security guys to review CCTV footage and pass on anything relevant – although, even if the cameras had captured anything conclusive, she was in two minds about pressing charges, or even formally reporting it.

She knew better than most that she'd need a crime reference number if she wanted to claim on her insurance, but car vandalism wasn't going to get the perpetrator off the streets. And a vindictive cow like Gaynor might just take it into her head to pull something worse next time. Lizzie wasn't sure she had the time or energy for this to turn into some stupid full scale vendetta.

She'd see what CCTV might yield and then decide what to do about it.

Right now, all she really wanted was to get home and have a glass of wine and a meal with Dominic. Doubtless her level-headed husband would have an opinion.

She unlocked the car, got in, and was closing the door when a hand gripped the frame, impeding its progress. She looked round, half-expecting to be confronted by an enraged Gaynor Upman.

Only it wasn't.

She did the maths in her head. It must be twelve years. But he hadn't changed much. Quite a few grey strands among the blue-black hair she'd liked to run her fingers through. Maybe the hairline was receding slightly. Some craggy lines in his face. A little thickening around the waist.

The man who'd once broken her heart.

"Hello, Lizzie," he said.

She shook her head, disbelieving. "Rob? What the actual fuck?"

Even the mischievous grin was the same, as he hunkered down. "Good to see you too. Your hair's different. I like it. Just going home?"

Something told her this was not a chance encounter. "What are you even doing here?"

"Ah, well…" He actually winked. "Look, I happened to notice there's a pub just around the corner. I'd love to have a catch up. Old time's sake."

She didn't know what irked her the most: his casual presumption, or his very presence. There was a difference between running into an old friend and having someone she'd very deliberately edited out of her life come casually strolling back into it.

She had to admit she was curious on one level. But her overwhelming instinct was not to go anywhere near the door he'd so cruelly closed upon her back then. Much less open it.

"What do you say?" he pressed. "Have a drink with me and I'll tell you everything that's been going on."

She sighed. "I really don't think so, Rob. I've had one hell of a day, and I just want to go home. Besides, I can't imagine what you think we have to say to each other. I seem to recall you said more than enough the day you dumped me."

He looked suddenly glum. "I know, I know. I totally deserved that. But, I also know, that was the biggest mistake of my life."

"Seriously?" She rolled her eyes. "And it's taken you all these years to… what? Have some sort of epiphany?"

"It's a long story," he said. "Please? One drink."

She found herself hesitating. She no more needed Rob Thomas waltzing back on the scene than she needed a pissing contest with Gaynor Upman. She owed him nothing. She should tell him to get lost. Yet a small, foolish part of her was intrigued.

"Look," she said, "whatever this is about, I'm married now."

"I know that."

"Yeah?" This just felt more and more off. "How exactly do you know?"

"I bumped into Sam. We had a beer. I hear you made DCI, too, so I guess double congratulations are in order."

Sam Strong had been Detective Sergeant to her Detective Inspector, back in her days in the Met before a violent incident in a pub had turned her life upside down. She still occasionally spoke to Sam. He was still in London, and they'd both been promoted in recent years.

He hadn't seen fit to let her know he'd been telling her life story to her ex.

She'd kill him.

"You had a beer," she said glacially. "That must have been nice. I suppose he helpfully told you I'm working out of Aylesbury nick, too?"

Another of those grins that had once never failed to weaken her resolve. But that had been then.

"And you what?" She knew how bitter she sounded, even after all this time. "Fancied a trip down memory lane? Wanted to see how the scar was doing?"

"I wanted to see you, yeah. Especially since I'm gonna be living and working here."

She stared at him. "Seriously?" This was turning into some sort of creepy, borderline stalking thing.

Rob sighed. "Come on, Lizzie. Just join me for one drink and I'll explain everything. And you can tell me what happened to the car. If you want."

She hesitated. Was something going on here that needed nipping in the bud right now?

"All right," she finally decided. "One drink."

Even as she said it, she knew she was going to regret it.

2

The Broad Leys was getting busy with drinkers and diners, but Lizzie and Rob found a quiet table.

"What'll you have?" he asked. "Do you still like a pint?"

"Yeah, but perhaps not when I'm driving. Make it a half of lager shandy."

She watched him walking up to the bar, his confident, striding gait still familiar after all this time. She had a husband who she loved, and who adored her. She had good friends, especially her close colleague, Dan Baines. She had a career that was finally back on track, and a good life here in Buckinghamshire.

She even had a cat.

These days, it was rare for Rob Thomas, and too many bad memories, to even cross her mind.

And now he was bringing them all back.

*

2011
Rob sits on the edge of the bed, his head in his hands. Lizzie watches him with the covers drawn up to her chin. Every time lately, when she's looked in a mirror, or otherwise caught a glimpse of her reflection, she's thought she couldn't feel any more hideous or undesirable.

Now she finds she was wrong.

"I'm sorry," he says, still not looking at her. "I don't know why. I can't, that's all."

"It's the scar, isn't it?" She says it as a statement, not a question.

"It's more than just that."

7

Everything has changed since that lunchtime in London, an off duty drink when they were happy and she couldn't imagine a future without this man.

She has dreams about that altercation at the bar. Sometimes she doesn't intervene and the guy with the broken bottle stabs the other man in the neck; lifeblood geysers while she calmly calls it in for someone else to deal with. Sometimes she is the one stabbed in the throat, dying on the floor while Rob beats the shit out of the man who has killed her.

Sometimes, she disarms him and gets the cuffs on with no harm done.

But mostly, it plays out exactly as it did in reality. Screams and commotion at the bar, Rob reminding her she's supposed to be off duty, and her going in anyway, holding up her warrant card and urging everyone to calm down. The guy with the bottle, fired up on booze and drugs and attitude, turning on her. The self-defence skills she's been taught kicking in, her assailant face down on the floor.

Then the coppery taste of blood in her mouth, even as she cuffs him.

The aftermath, the mess made of her cheek, the post-traumatic stress, has been a time when she would have sworn Rob would be there with the love and support she needed to help her through. Instead, he's become ever more and more distant. Avoiding physical contact, avoiding sex. Often not looking at her when she's talking to him.

Now this.

Was she too needy in trying to instigate sex? Has she been naive in thinking it might somehow get them through the roadblock in their relationship?

She certainly hadn't anticipated impotence. Even now, her face burning with rejection and humiliation, she feels for him, an alpha male fireman and a real hero in her eyes. How must he feel, not being able to get it up?

"More than that?" she says as gently as she can. "So talk to me."

He sighs. Still won't look at her.

"Okay," he says. "Yeah, it is partly the scar. Every time I look at it, I can't stop thinking about that day in the pub."

"Me too."

"I wish you hadn't. I begged you not to. You were off duty."

"I'm never completely off duty. Nor would you be, Rob, if you could help someone."

"Yeah, sure, and what did I do? Just sat there and watched my girlfriend get in a fight with that piece of shit with the bottle. Get her face ripped open. I should have come with you. Backed you up. I just sat there."

She watches him starting to pull on clothes, still with his back to her.

"Oh, Rob," she says, "you can't be blaming yourself. I don't blame you. It was my job, not yours."

"Easy to say. Except I can't help feeling I let you down. That scar is a constant reminder of what a coward I was."

She can't not laugh. "A coward? This from the man who pulls people out of burning buildings? Seriously?"

"You don't understand."

"I think I do. But you don't seem to get that this is about me, not you. I'm the one who'll probably be marked for life. I'm the one who can't even think about going into another dangerous situation without feeling like I'm going to be sick, or pass out, or both."

"And I'm sorry, Lizzie. But this..." He seems to grope for the words. "This embarrassment just confirms what I guess I already knew. I can't give you whatever you think you need from me. I can't do this any more." He finally turns to face her, making an open-palmed gesture of despair. "Any of it."

She stares at him, hurt and panic and anger mingling. "You're dumping me?"

"If you want to call it that."

"You're dumping me?" Anger wins out. For now. "Because my face makes you feel bad about yourself?"

"I'm sorry," he says again.

"Don't give me your pity. Get out."

"We're in my house." He gives her an eye-rolling grin that angers her more.

9

"So we are. At least get out of the room while I get dressed."

He holds his hands up again, this time in a surrender gesture, and heads for the door.

"You were right, though, Rob." Her voice breaks as the tears begin to flow. "You were right after all. I just never knew until just now. You really are a fucking coward."

*

Rob had returned from the bar with Lizzie's half of shandy and a pint of some sort of bitter for himself. There were four chairs around the table, and he chose to seat himself next to her, rather than across.

"Cheers." He held up his glass for her to chink.

She disappointed him, merely shrugging.

"Here we are, then," she said, although she still wondered why she'd even agreed to come with him. "So say what you have to say. But first, what did you mean when you said you'd be living here?"

"I quit the fire service," he said. "I'm pushing on fifty, and I've had enough. There are plenty of jobs that pay more, aren't so dangerous, and keep more civilised hours."

She digested this. They'd first met in the course of a very nasty serial arson case down in London, in which three people had died in one of the fires. Tony Noakes, ostensibly a respectable family man, had been caught and jailed for life. Lizzie had been the arresting officer and Rob had given evidence at the trial. There had been a spark from the moment they met.

He'd been passionate about his job then. But that had been a while ago. Times changed, and so did people.

"Okay. I get that. A change of career direction. But why *here*? What are you going to be doing, anyway?"

"Dunno yet. Still weighing my options. But I'm staying at the Travelodge while I look around." He smiled. "As to why here? That's all about you."

If she'd been suspicious about his motives before, now she was on high alert. Yes, she'd loved Rob Thomas once. She'd been broken when he deserted her. It hadn't been the only reason she'd transferred to Aylesbury Vale in search of the new life she'd made for herself here, but it had been a big part of it.

Despite the hurt, she'd never allowed herself to waste energy on hating him. Rather she had exorcised him from her system.

She'd never expected to see him again. She'd certainly never expected him to make her skin crawl like it was now.

"You're saying you're coming here for *me*?" There was no mirth in her laugh. "Word to the wise. Don't waste your time. Change your job, your home, your whole life for all I care, but don't imagine for a moment that I'll ever be part of it."

He held up his hands. "Hear me out. Please." There was a desperation in his voice. "After we split up—"

"After you chucked me away."

"That's fair. I only saw my own feelings. I acted like a shit. As I said, it was the biggest mistake of my life. Nothing has really worked since. Oh, I dated a few times, was even married for all of eighteen months, but no relationship has worked. Because none of them was you. In the end, I realised that. Maybe that kind of made me disillusioned with my whole life, I don't know."

She took a sip of her drink. He was trying to tell her everything had changed, but every word that came out of his mouth convinced her that he was the same self-centred individual he'd always been. Even before their split, the signs had been there, but she'd been too much in love to recognise them.

"Anyway, I'd already decided to change my job and get out of London. And that's when I literally bumped into Sam, next to me in the queue at McDonald's. I mean, what are the chances? So we grabbed a table with our burgers and coffees and had a bit of a general chat and catch up. I asked after you, and he said you were happy, and... look, you said epiphany, and it was. I mean, that had to be a sign, right?"

She barked another mirthless laugh. "So Sam told you I was happy and you took that as a sign that you should come here and try to mess it up, or something?"

"No, darling."

Her irritation turned to hot anger. "Don't you dare call me that. You don't get to call me that."

"Your husband. Dominic, right? You're Lizzie Newman now, but Sam says you still use Archer for work."

"You and Sam had quite the chat, didn't you?" She would definitely kill Sam. Slowly.

"You must have squeaked the wedding in just before the pandemic lockdown."

"So?"

"So will you tell him? About…" He gestured vaguely at the table, the drinks. The two of them. "About this?"

She rolled her eyes. "There is no 'this'. And, yes, of course I'll tell him. We don't do secrets."

He took a slurp of his own drink. "Well that's good. But be honest with yourself."

She stared at him, bemused. "Honest?"

He nodded. "It's not as good as it was with me, is it?"

Now he was really getting under her skin. "Oh, it's so much better than it was with you. Ultimately you did me a favour. I love my life. I love my husband. I came to realise what a selfish prick you are. If the scar hadn't happened, if we'd got married, or moved in together? I think either I'd have realised what you are and it wouldn't have lasted; or, worse still, I'd have lost myself, piece by little piece."

"You're so wrong. And I haven't come here to mess up your life. I've come to make it better. I've come to win you back."

She was in mid-sip, and that last phrase was so ridiculous that she snorted and shandy went up her nose, leaving her sneezing, dribbling and coughing all at the same time.

"Now I know you're winding me up," she chortled when she'd recovered. "*Win me back?* Jesus. I know we're not characters in some sort of reality romcom, because I don't see any cameras. So this has to be some terrible mid-life crisis you're having. Please tell me you didn't buy a red sports car."

He smiled. "It's a bit much to take in, isn't it? I get that."

She realised he was completely serious, and she didn't know whether to be even more amused, or even more worried.

"I mean," he went on, "I'm happy for you. That you're happy with that guy. But he's not me, is he?"

That did it.

"You got that right," she said icily. "No, he's not you. He's not 'that guy', either. He's my husband, and I love him, and he's more of a man than you'll ever be."

"You need time..."

"No, Rob. You need to stay away from me. Starting now. Please, please, forget any mad idea you have of us getting back together. And, for Christ's sake, don't waste your time moving here on my account. Never going to happen."

Even now, something inside wouldn't allow her to continue her rant. Some crumb of pity for him.

"Look," she said gently, "I'm genuinely sorry your life hasn't turned out so well, but you can't turn the clock back. You say ditching me was a mistake, and I believe you think that. But it was your mistake to make, and you made it. Don't make another one by pursuing something that was over a long time ago. It won't end well."

He sat back in his chair. "Is that some sort of threat?"

"Call it what you like. I've seen stalking in this job, I know what it looks like, and I know the law. Having to go down that route will be painful for us both, so please let's avoid it. You want to leave London and the fire service? Fine. Whatever you decide to do with the rest of your life, just do it somewhere else. Please?"

Rob shook his head. "I don't think I can do that."

She stood up, grabbing her bag.

"You've barely touched your drink," he protested.

"You're lucky you're not wearing it." Just before she swept out of the pub, she looked him in the eye. "Just stay away from me, Rob."

13

3

Detective Inspector Dan Baines looked at his sleeping daughter, knowing he had only felt such love once before, and that had been some twenty years ago. Back then, he'd silently sworn to keep his son, Jack, safe, and he'd failed to keep that vow. It made him all the more determined to look after this beautiful little girl, and her mother. He'd die before anything happened to them.

Karen had slipped quietly into the room, and he only became aware of her presence when she slipped her arms around his waist and laid her head on his shoulder.

"I'm going to dish up dinner," she said, "if you can tear yourself away from the other woman in your life."

"It's tough," he admitted, "seeing as she's so fabulous. But then, so are you. I'll come and pour us some wine."

He bent and planted the lightest of kisses on Ellie's forehead. She stirred slightly, snuffled, and then resumed the rhythmic breathing that he never tired of hearing. He checked the baby alarm was on, then followed his wife downstairs.

"Smells good," he said, "and I'm hungry. Red?"

"I think so."

Dan sometimes felt slightly guilty. Karen had found a job that she could do from home, with hours to suit, and she juggled it with looking after a toddler and cooking the meals on weekdays. On weekends when the job gave him time off – which were mercifully more frequent at the moment – he did his best to do his share of the catering and household chores. He wasn't a domestic god like Lizzie's husband, Dominic, but Karen seemed to appreciate him at least trying.

He poured the wine and laid out cutlery while Karen served the food, a chicken and leek pie she'd made herself.

"Christ, this is good," he said after the first mouthful. "WI recipe?"

Joining the WI a few years ago had found Karen a circle of local friends, but also unleashed her inner baker, and she had moved on from cakes to pastry this year.

"One I found on the Internet."

"It's great."

They made some small talk as they ate and drank. One subject Dan knew was coming, but they both avoided it, as if by mutual agreement, until they'd finished eating. Dan told her about the Upman case result, and he inevitably included the subsequent vandalism to Lizzie's car.

"I suppose it might have just been some opportunist yob," Karen suggested.

"Who just happened to be passing the court, and just happened to pick on Lizzie's car? I don't think so. I just hope that's as far as it goes. They're nasty bastards."

"Is she worried?"

"Pissed off about the damage, but inclined not to go after them for it. We've all had threats before from time to time. Mostly it's just words. Gaynor Upman's probably as full of shit as the others. And, boneheaded as she might be, I doubt she wants to follow her boys into prison."

Karen swirled the wine in her glass and took another sip. "Speaking of prison. Did you confirm your visit to Peter for Saturday?"

He put his own glass down, picking up on her change of tone. Her change of subject.

"Yep. It's on, if work doesn't get in the way." He looked at her. "You're really okay with it?"

"Sure. He's your son. My nephew. My stepson too, now."

Her calmness on the subject never ceased to astonish him. She'd even readily accepted that Jack Baines wanted to go on being called Peter McNeil, the name given to him by the serial killer who'd raised him as his own after murdering Jack's mother and Dan's first wife. Karen's identical twin sister, Louise.

In a hideous postscript, Duncan 'Mac' McNeil, Dan's former colleague – aka the Invisible Man – had returned to Aylesbury Vale two years ago and attempted to get Jack/Peter to kill Karen. Only Dan's intervention had saved his wife and their unborn daughter. Duncan McNeil was serving life in a high security prison, while the young man he'd tried to make a killer was in a young offenders wing nearby in Aylesbury prison, sentenced to eleven years for his part in the attack, with a recommendation that he serve at least five and a half.

Peter had willingly enough submitted to a DNA test, and had accepted that he was Dan and Louise's biological son. What he had been unwilling to do was accept that Jack Baines could be his identity henceforth. He'd said as much in the letter he'd sent to Dan, explaining that he wasn't about to accept any visits from the man who had fathered him.

'I know what my father – I mean the only father I've ever known – did,' he'd written, *'and I know there's something badly wrong with him. Maybe it's wrong with me, too. I'm still trying to get my head around that. But as far as I'm concerned, he's still my dad.*

'Forgive me, Dan, but I don't know you, and I don't know Karen. I don't remember my birth mother. I'm still Peter McNeil and, until I can think everything through, that's all there is. I can't have you coming and trying to make me the son I'm not. So I won't be putting you on my visitors' list, and I won't be accepting any letters from you. Please try to understand.

'Once I've had time to think, if I decide I'd like us to meet, I'll write to you again.'

He'd signed it, *'Yours sincerely, Peter McNeil'.*

Dan had been devastated, but he'd bottled up the hurt, put it in a box, locked it, and consigned it to a dusty attic in his mind, just like he always did when he couldn't cope. Karen had been through a terrifying trauma and then given birth to Ellie. His current family needed him, and he couldn't let the past interfere with what he needed to do for them.

There was only so much of him to go around.

Then the Covid-19 pandemic had come and access to prisons had been suspended anyway under lockdown. By the time visits were possible again, Dan had more or less resigned himself to his son being alive but wanting nothing to do with him.

Then, out of the blue, he'd been advised that he was now on the approved visitors' list for the prisoner known as Peter McNeil. What he guessed was a very short list. If there was any other name, it was probably his lawyer.

He still didn't know what he was going to say.

"Will you ask him?" Karen said softly. "About what Mac said that night?"

McNeil had implied that there had been other murders since the Invisible Man's original reign of terror in Aylesbury Vale, and that Peter had played some part in them. Neither of them had said anything further on the subject since, to the best of Dan's knowledge.

"I don't know," he admitted. "I don't know why the change of heart, or what he might want to talk about. I think I'm going to just have to play it by ear."

He put down his glass and looked at her. "But what about you? You say you're all right with it, but it can't be that simple, can it?"

"Yes. And no. I thought I was going to die, Dan. He did almost kill me. I still have nightmares. Panic attacks. You know that. But we can't pretend he doesn't exist, and that he isn't a part of this family, even if he has no wish to be. So go and see him. Maybe he's looking for some sort of closure too."

*

Lizzie pulled up on her drive, sliding her car in beside Dominic's, and cut the engine. The lights shining in the windows raised her spirits, and she was pleased all over again that they'd got this place together.

They'd started off as neighbours, become close friends, then lovers. By the time they'd decided to make it official, the two houses in Great Marston were already serving as one idiosyncratic home, possessions randomly divided between the two. It hadn't been the most convenient arrangement. Selling both and buying this four-bedroom detached in the village of Long Lees had made perfect sense.

The only disgruntled party was Barney, the ginger tom they had jointly adopted when they were still at the friends stage. He'd been used to coming and going between both cat flaps and conning each of them into feeding him. These days, with no more double rations, he was slightly more sylph-like, and doubtless healthier, but Lizzie doubted he appreciated the benefits.

She'd phoned Dominic three times this evening: once to say she was calling it a day; once to say she'd been waylaid by an old friend; and once to say she was finally coming home. He'd promised to rustle up a risotto, and she salivated at the thought of some proper food. Since breakfast, she'd had a pretty ghastly sandwich out of a vending machine and three chocolate bars. Too many days like this, and she'd be pale and bloated.

She'd barely noticed the dark Mercedes that had turned into her road behind her, nor did it register when it parked across the road from her house. She was out of the car and heading for the front door, fumbling in her bag for keys, when a male voice behind her brought her up short.

A voice she hadn't heard for over three years, but one that still sent chills through her.

"Just a moment, Lizzie. I'd like a word."

Her overwhelming instinct was to run for her door, let herself in, lock it and put the chain on. But one thing she'd never done, and was not about to start doing now, was show Cameron Connolly she was scared of him.

Even though anyone who didn't fear him was either much braver than she was, or a fool.

Reluctantly, she turned to face him. He was in a dark suit. White shirt, black tie. She didn't recognise the woman hanging back behind him, her dark coat similarly sombre. She was a little shorter than Lizzie, and boyishly slim.

Leaning against the car was a black, bullet-headed man: Cal Dougan, ostensibly Cameron's 'assistant', but actually his enforcer. His height and build were unremarkable and, unlike his late, unlamented predecessor, he wasn't an unstable and violent lunatic, but his reputation was still frightening.

Lizzie looked Cameron Connolly in the eye.

"Don't say you've been following me, Cameron," she said.

"All right." There was no humour in his voice. "I won't say it, even though it was pretty tedious waiting around while you had your illicit meeting with your boyfriend. Not that I'm judging. Hardly surprising a woman like you isn't content with just the one man."

She wasn't going to give him the satisfaction of correcting him.

"Still," he said, "it was good to observe you. I like knowing things."

She sighed. "Glad to have been of service then. But you wanted a word. Can we move it along, so I can get indoors and eat something?"

"Please, Cam," the woman with him said. "I told you this was a bad idea."

This softly-spoken woman had a little more of a Scots burr than Cameron who, to Lizzie's ear, had not a trace of the accent that would have hinted at his ancestry.

"I'm forgetting my manners," he said. "Lizzie, this is my sister, Grace. She's down for the funerals."

Lizzie suddenly understood the significance of their attire. Murray and Desmond Connolly. Their deaths on the same day had been the talk of the office at the time, but her mind had moved on since then.

Cameron's father, Murray Connolly, had started to build what he called his business empire many years ago, when Glasgow had been his playground. Before he'd decided that even Scotland's second city wasn't big enough for him.

Even in those early days, philanthropy had been all part of the legend, a respectable mask that had hidden something far uglier. Later, Glasgow had been the boiler plate for what he'd achieved down south. Splashing the cash on good causes, investing in companies that created wealth and jobs. Spinning a financial web that looked immaculate on the surface and kept the auditors happy.

As for the drugs, the prostitution, the money laundering and the people smuggling, the National Crime Agency had been trying to build a case against the family for years. And if anyone fancied they glimpsed what was beneath the façade, and perceived that it was rotten to the core, there were plenty of ways to shut them up.

A well-greased palm.

Top lawyers who could play terrifying hardball when it came to a whiff of slander or libel.

The odd unfortunate, but timely, accident.

Murray Connolly appeared to have it all. The gorgeous, white-walled, Georgian-style house on the outskirts of Hampstead, tucked away behind high walls and electronically operated steel gates. Several cars, any one of which would be the envy of any mere mortal, with someone to drive him when he didn't feel like it, or perhaps when he was going somewhere that would involve drink. Acquaintances bordering on friendship with some big names in the sporting, music and acting worlds.

Lizzie knew it hadn't all been easy. His wife had passed away just over a year ago, and it had turned out his health was no longer what it had been. And then there was his youngest son, Desmond.

His other three children were very successful. Even Grace, who'd apparently eschewed the family business in favour of a career as an artist back in Glasgow.

But Desmond had been a fuckup almost from the get-go. His bigger attempts to show how clever he was had backfired spectacularly. He did time for some independent drug dealing and hadn't been out long before he went back inside, this time for conspiracy to murder.

Officially, Desmond's actions had been his own, unconnected with the Connolly business interests. Officially, those interests were wholly legit, and Desmond had admitted in court that he'd acted entirely of his own volition.

But it seemed there was some justice in the world after all. Lizzie kept a professional eye on what the Connollys were up to and, since Desmond's conviction, Murray no longer appeared in photographs taken at charity galas. She suspected that his phone rarely rang these days. Shit sticks, and maybe too many scales had fallen from too many eyes.

And now he and Desmond were gone, departed this world within a few hours of one another.

"The funerals were today?" she asked. "Well, I was sorry to hear about what happened."

He barked a laugh. "I'm sure you were. Two Connollys down, eh? I'm sure you were all weeping buckets."

She shrugged. "I still don't understand what I owe the pleasure to."

"I think you do. See, I told you when you put Desmond away that I make a bad enemy. You put my little brother in Newlands prison, where people with a grudge against my family could get to him. Stabbed with a shiv and no one saw or heard anything. And my dad... well, the news finished him off, didn't it? Massive heart attack, right there and then. I never saw that coming."

There was an ugliness to his tone and his expression. She remembered a moment, a long time ago, when, just briefly, she had come close to falling under his spell. Close to forgetting what a dangerous reptile dwelt beneath his handsome exterior. It made her shudder with shame, but that wasn't her overriding emotion now.

She could feel her fight or flight mechanism kicking in, cold sweat breaking out, her heart beating faster. Controlling her breathing was a challenge, but one she was determined to be equal to.

No way was he going to sense her fear.

"And I've said I'm sorry," she said firmly, "and I meant it. But you seem to be blaming me. And threatening me."

"Who's threatening?" He was grinning. "We're just talking here."

"Look, the person to blame for your loss is whoever killed Desmond, and whoever put them up to it. Assuming it wasn't just a falling out among prisoners. And your crooked family business is the only reason he was there in the first place."

He wagged a finger at her. "You need to be careful of slanderous allegations. We've talked about this before. Our business is legitimate, as well you know."

"Of course," she said with irony.

"Des was a bloody fool who went in for a bit of illegal enterprise and got caught. But he was a young, naïve bloody fool. You were still the one who nicked him, charged him."

"I was supposed to have turned a blind eye?"

He shrugged. "All I'm saying is, as far as I'm concerned, this is on you."

With deliberation, she shrugged back. "What's your point?"

She heard the first actual tremor in her voice, because she had a pretty good idea what his point was.

"Oh," he said, "you know. I just wanted to tell you to your face that I hold you responsible for the tragedy in my family. That I hold grudges for an awfully long time. And that one day you'll find out what it's like to lose someone you love."

"I've already found that out, thank you." Irritation briefly trumped fear. "Both my parents are dead."

"Yes, I know that. As I said, I like to know things. But there's still your lovely husband, Dominic. Your brother. Adam? Your nephew and niece. Not forgetting your adorable goddaughter, Ellie. I can't imagine how you would feel if anything happened to any of them."

"Please, Cam," Grace protested. "Enough now."

"You should listen to your sister," Lizzie said, heaving as much conviction into her voice as she could muster, even though terror was gnawing at her guts. "It really does sound like you're making all manner of threats against a police officer."

"That's just your paranoia talking," he retorted. "I've said my piece. Told you how I feel. And given you advice. Make the most of loved ones." He snapped his fingers. "They can be gone just like that." He gave her a bleak smile. "See you around."

He turned away, striding towards the car, his sister hurrying to keep up. She watched them get in. Heard the engine start. Watched them drive away.

Only then did she turn towards her door, her hands shaking so much she couldn't find her key.

4

A product of the Direct Entry Superintendent Programme, Josh Stowe had soaked up knowledge like a sponge in his first few months as Divisional Commander at Aylesbury Vale. Newly promoted herself, Lizzie applauded his drive to understand everything about his teams, the job, the local area and its criminal classes – but at the same time, he'd driven her mad, stepping on her toes and getting in her way as she got to grips with the challenges of higher rank.

Fortunately, he'd backed off quite soon, and he showed every day why he was going places. Josh was definitely an acquired taste, but one she'd learned to appreciate.

He was still young for his rank. Throw in the obvious fact that he was from an ethnic minority background, and she supposed some of the less desirable coppers still to be found in pockets around the force might make the mistake of dismissing him as some sort of poster boy.

But that would ignore the high-flying career he'd been enjoying at the Home Office, where working closely with police forces had attracted him to the service. The simple reality was that Josh Stowe was very, very good. Good with people. Good with the media. Sharp and insightful. And a fabulous leader, one who was very comfortable with delegation, but at the same time unstinting in his support for those working under him. Not that he couldn't be hard when he needed to be, but he was very rarely unfair.

Lately, rumours had been circulating that a Chief Superintendent opening was coming up at Thames Valley's headquarters in Oxfordshire, and that Josh was in pole position. Lizzie wasn't altogether surprised, but she would be sorry to lose him as a boss, and was also apprehensive about what they might get in his place.

It had been Dominic who'd persuaded her to talk to Josh about yesterday's events. She'd tried to laugh off both the crude threat from Gaynor Upman and the darker variety made by Cameron Connolly on her own doorstep, but he hadn't let her get away with that. He'd taken her hands in his own, looked in her eyes, and shaken his head.

"Stowe needs to know," he'd said. "You might well be right – I hope you are. Upman might have done her worst with the car, and Connolly might have just been letting off steam at the end of an emotional day. But what if you're wrong? Your boss needs to be in the picture before it escalates."

"And what's he going to do? Warn them off? I can't see anything getting through to Gaynor if she wants a fight, and Cameron will likely deny that the conversation even happened. It could make matters worse."

"It could," Dominic conceded. "But let Josh decide. You're always singing his praises. So tell him. I'm sure handling this sort of shit, however he thinks it should be handled, is part of his job description. Think how pissed off you were a few years ago, when Dan was having some sort of meltdown and didn't talk to you."

He was right, of course. As usual. She'd promised to do as he suggested.

She'd also told him about the encounter with Rob, not sure how he'd respond. In typical Dominic style, he'd kept his cool.

"So I've got a rival," he'd said, half smiling. "Not so surprising, given how wonderful you are. Even if I am biased."

"He's twelve years too late," she'd assured him, "and frankly a bit pathetic now. I'm sorry for him. But he's no threat to you. You're worth ten of him."

"Only ten?" He feigned disappointment. "Well, with us both being so wonderful, let's hope he buggers off and doesn't hang around trying to 'woo' you. It would be a terrible bore having to challenge him to a duel."

She'd laughed. "You'd need to choose your weapons carefully. Hunky ex-fireman, remember."

"I'm sure I can take him. Well, at something like Scrabble, anyway."

"But seriously." She sobered. "I hope he's not going to be trouble."

"What does your gut tell you? You've seen a few obsessive males in your time."

"True." She considered it. Stalkers, domestic abusers, dangerous narcissists: she'd seen them all. "Honestly?" she said. "I don't quite know. They're usually in the victim's life, not out of it for so many years. And I know Rob. Used to," she amended. "The Rob I saw last night was weird. The one I knew turned out to be an arse, but he wasn't weird. Maybe I was too hasty telling him to sod off. Maybe I should have heard him out properly. I'd maybe have a better idea of what's going on with him."

"That might just have encouraged him," said Dominic. "Maybe he came here with some daft idea of rekindling an old flame and, now you've put him right, he's gone back to London feeling a bit of an idiot."

"I hope so."

"Look, if I'm wrong, we can deal with it, can't we?"

"Yeah." He was right. It had just been a tough day. She was probably making too much of it.

She'd gone to bed a little happier for having talked everything through with him, but that hadn't stopped her lying awake into the small hours with the day's events running through her mind.

And now here she was, in Josh Stowe's office. She'd told him about the two threats she'd received yesterday, and he'd listened with his usual stillness, only asking the occasional question to make certain he understood.

"Okay," he said finally. "Here's what I think. You may be right your car. If you can stand not to do her for criminal damage, that might be the end of it. But it might not."

He scribbled a note to himself in the A4 notepad that sat on his desk. "I'll send some suitably intimidating uniforms round to see her. Let her know that you've magnanimously decided not to follow up on it, but make it clear that any more messing with a police officer is likely to land her and her family in a whole world of hurt. If one of them so much as farts in the wrong key, we'll find the most serious thing we can to charge them with. Over and again."

"Okay. Thanks, boss. And Cameron Connolly?"

"You say he's threatened you before?"

"Yes, when I first nicked his brother. I'm not going to lie. I was worried at the time, but nothing's come of it until now. Maybe it's just words again." But she knew that, when people crossed the Connollys, they often paid a price in blood.

"Maybe," said Josh, "but, in any event, do we really want to poke that sort of hornet's nest unless we're sure he's posing a serious danger?" He frowned. "Look, don't spread this around, but I was at a meeting last week. Word is that Murray Connolly's death has left a bit of a vacuum in the London underworld and other players are already scrambling to try and fill it. At the same time, it's not yet clear whether Cameron or his brother, Fraser, will be assuming the reins at the Connolly family firm."

On the face of what she knew, Murray Connolly's eldest son, Fraser, and Cameron, his second son, were more than capable of running everything. Chalk and cheese, by all accounts, but both brilliant in their way.

Fraser was known to be solid as a rock, the real business head, the numbers man, the diplomat when one was needed. For a long time, it had been assumed that Fraser would one day succeed Murray at the head of the family business. But one of her contacts at the National Crime Agency weren't so sure. He seemed to have no obvious aptitude for getting his own hands messy. He was good at wielding his father's power, up to a point, when a nasty job wanted doing, but that only got you so far.

Cameron was more of a chip off the old block, a throwback in some ways to the hard man Murray had needed to be to claw his way to the top on the mean streets of Glasgow. He was living in Buckinghamshire now, where the expanded business had become firmly established – indeed, still growing, despite the bad headlines Desmond had generated here.

Whatever Murray's plans were, perhaps Cameron had other ideas.

She saw where Josh was going with this.

"You're thinking he's going to have enough on his plate as it is, without targeting me and likely bringing the whole of the Thames Valley force and the Met down on his head?"

"I mean, we can look at protection, if you'd like. You could consider a temporary change of address…"

"Screw that," she said, without missing a beat. "Dominic and I have worked bloody hard for the life we have. I mean, I'll ask him – he has a voice in this too. But I'd be surprised if he felt differently. If Cameron Connolly drives us out of our home, he'll feel he's winning. I also think he's less likely to stop if I do that than if I just leave it be. I'm not saying I'm entirely comfortable with it, but…"

He nodded. "I tend to agree, but talk to Dominic as you say. And if you have any more concerns, I want to know immediately, are we clear?"

"Crystal. Thanks, Josh." She hesitated. "It's not just me he's hinted at harming though, is it? There's my brother and his family, even Dan Baines's daughter, my godchild."

"So speak to your brother. Let him know to call the police if anything at all seems amiss. Talk to Dan too, if you haven't already."

She hadn't. She'd wanted this meeting first. She wasn't entirely happy with the outcome but, short of arresting Cameron Connolly on some trumped up charge, she couldn't think of a better plan.

She was about to rise from her chair when he raised a finger. "While I've got you here, there's something else."

She eased herself back in the seat.

"I know what the rumour mill's like," he said. "You may have heard something about a Chief Super role at HQ."

"There's been a bit of talk, yes, sir."

"Well, keep it under your hat, Lizzie, but the job's mine if I want it. I've been given a day or two to decide but, in all honesty, I'd be crazy to turn down a promotion like that at this stage in my career."

Even though she was genuinely delighted for him, and thought it was richly deserved, her heart sank. "Congratulations.

They'd be just as mad not to choose you." She swallowed. "I suppose it's too soon for any word about a successor?"

He gave her a half-smile. "Well. Yes and no. There are names being bandied around, I gather, although I genuinely don't know whose. But I've been asked if I've got any thoughts and, well, I wondered if *you*'d be interested?"

Her overwhelming reaction was shock. In fact, she wondered for a moment if she'd heard correctly.

"Me?"

"Why not? You know the place like the back of your hand. You're liked and respected. You have all the instincts and leadership qualities."

"But... it's not like I've been DCI that long."

He gave her a rare chuckle. "Come to that, I've not been a Superintendent, nor a police officer, that long, either. You've got the competencies, and you've got experience in spades."

She found herself looking at his pristine uniform. Her own only came out on high days and holidays when there was some formal requirement to wear it.

"I'm flattered, sir, I really am, but I'm a detective. I was sort of imagining *Detective* Super, if I was ever lucky enough to get another promotion." She mentally kicked herself. He was talking about a possible step up, and she wasn't exactly selling herself.

But he simply nodded. "I do get that, but think about it. We both know you were going places in the Met, before you had that bit of bad luck." It was an interesting way of describing her encounter with a broken bottle. "It put you back, but I could still imagine you going on to have a decent shot at ACC. I reckon you'd be a far more convincing prospect for that level with proper management experience under your belt."

She felt a little giddy. She still had ambitions to take her career as far as she could, but she'd imagined Assistant Chief Constable to be out of her reach.

"I don't know what to say." And Lizzie Archer was rarely lost for words.

"As I say, keep all this to yourself for now. I haven't definitely decided to take the Oxford job yet and, if I do, the most I can do is put your name forward. So have a think and let me know. Is tomorrow too soon? One more thing to talk over with your husband."

She'd walked into his office with worries on her mind. They hadn't entirely gone away, but she walked out feeling at least a foot taller.

One way and another, this was turning out to be quite a week.

5

Dan Baines sat in Lizzie's office, taking in what she'd just said. "He actually threatened to harm Ellie?" he growled. "I'll kill him."

"Take it easy, Dan. You know, and I know, you're not about to go rogue."

And yes, he did know it. Of course he did. The knowledge did nothing to calm him.

"My family has had more than enough," he said bitterly. "And now it's the bloody Connollys. Again." He shook his head angrily. "It must be what? Six, seven years since they first started nosing around our patch? And a good deal longer they've been operating in London. They got me shot. They nearly started a turf war on our doorstep. Cameron's threatened you more than once. And still they're Teflon-coated. Nothing has their fingerprints on it, and there are never any witnesses. Not alive, anyway. No one who does their dirty work will speak out, for fear of what will happen next."

"They'll slip up one of these days," Lizzie assured him. "When they do, I hope it's here, so I can have the satisfaction of arresting that scumbag."

"Yeah," he said, "but that's not today, is it? And he actually said Ellie's name?" He felt compelled to check again. Just the thought made him feel sick.

"He did, but I don't know, Dan. Targeting babies and children? It's not really Cameron's style, is it?"

"You think he draws lines? He seems to have no qualms about catching kids as young as eleven up in his county lines pyramids, trafficking drugs and even weapons. Maybe you're right, and he'd draw the line at babies. I bloody well hope so. But Adam's kids? They're at least of an age with some of those at the bottom of his food chain. So what do you think makes them immune?"

"I know." She chewed her lower lip. "That's not a conversation I'm looking forward to with my brother."

He looked at her. "Do *you* think he was serious?"

She sighed. "Honestly? He's wounded and lashing out, that much is clear. And yes, he was suggesting I'd hurt his family and now he was coming after mine. But I don't know. I'd expect him to be more direct. If anyone's got a target on their back, it's more likely to be me. I think the Super's right. Vigilance makes sense, but not blind panic."

"Like there's much we can actually do anyway, if he decides to pull something. We won't know where or when it'll come. We could go into hiding, but for how long? As you said, that gives him a victory without him doing anything. Plus his grudges last a long time, and his reach is even longer. He'd most likely find us."

At least he was thinking more clearly, the red mist that had been rising beginning to dissipate. It didn't help his feeling of helpless impotence.

"I think you're right," she agreed. "Anyway, maybe his sister will manage to talk some sense into him. She was clearly embarrassed by the whole confrontation. I'm sure she would have rather been mourning her losses than watching her brother trying to intimidate me."

"Let's hope so," he agreed. "Christ, how can I tell Karen any of this? I think she's still more fragile than she's letting on. Did I mention I'm seeing Jack – I mean Peter – at the weekend?"

"You said you might be."

"Well, it's confirmed." His stomach lurched.

"And Karen's okay with it?"

"So she says. I don't know. I think she *would* say that, for me. Obviously, the whole thing is just totally messed up. I'm not even sure how *I* feel." He threw up his hands as he groped for a way to explain. "It's like, my son turns out to be alive, but he's not really my son any more. For year after stupid year, I kept a toddler's room exactly as it was, even though I knew that, if he was alive, he'd have long outgrown it."

"Of course you did. I can understand."

He laughed hollowly. "I'm not sure I do. And now he's in prison and calling himself Peter McNeil, and for all I know he's been involved in actual murders – not just trying to kill Karen. It's like losing one of your favourite things and then, when you finally find it again, it's broken."

"At least he's said he'll see you. Maybe that's the first step towards building a relationship and getting some answers."

"Maybe." His mind ticked back to Cameron Connolly. "But I swear one thing, Lizzie. I've lost one family to a psychopath. If the Connollys harm Karen or Ellie, I really will have nothing to lose. I *will* kill them," he said for the second time.

He read the dismay in her eyes. "You don't mean that. You're upset, that's all."

"I do mean it, Lizzie," he said softly, and he did. "I believe in the law and I believe in justice, you know I do. But the law and justice have failed over and over with the Connollys. I'm not going looking for trouble but, if Cameron comes after us, I'm not going to rely on the law to make him pay."

She held his gaze for a long time, neither of them speaking. Then she nodded tightly.

"Then let's hope it doesn't come to that."

*

Before speaking to Dan, Lizzie had called Dominic and relayed the conversation she'd had with her boss. As she'd expected, he'd rejected the notion of changing address, even on a temporary basis, out of hand.

"I agree with you one hundred per cent," he'd said. "I'm not living my life in fear of anyone, especially as we don't know how long it would last. I mean, he's already shown how good he is at following you. Unless you give up the job, all he or one of his minions need do is wait for you to leave the station."

"So long as you're sure."

"I'm sure. Look, he was angry. He'd just buried his dad and his kid brother. I've even got sympathy for a piece of shit like

Cameron Connolly in those circumstances. I bet he woke up this morning and regretted what he did last night."

Lizzie doubted Cameron knew the meaning of the word regret, but Dominic's words reassured her somewhat. She mentioned the possibility of a promotion, and he was enthusiastically encouraging.

"You should definitely go for it. You could be waiting around years for a Detective Superintendent opening and, as Josh says, taking over his job needn't keep you out of detective work forever."

Her next call would be to her brother, Adam, and she dreaded it. The rift that had opened between them during their mother's illness, and after her death, had healed, and there was a closeness that had never been there before. She'd even grown fond of his wife, Nic, and she loved her niece and nephew, Ruby and Luke. The latter was even talking seriously about a career in the police force, much to his dad's horror.

She wondered if this was a conversation she should have face to face. Maybe he could get out of work for an hour, and she could buy him a coffee and a sandwich.

She'd called up his number, and her thumb was hovering over the 'call' button, when the phone rang in her hand, making her jump and almost drop it.

"Archer," she gabbled.

"Is that DCI Archer?" A woman's voice, soft, a Scots burr. "This is Grace Connolly. We sort of met outside your house last night. I don't know if you remember."

Lizzie wasn't about to tell her she'd thought of little else since Grace's brother's hostile rant. "I remember."

"I just phoned up to apologise."

She stared at the phone. "I don't think it's you who needs to apologise."

"Oh, no," Grace said quickly. "He would, I know he would. But Cameron... he's not the sort to climb down. Not even when he knows he's in the wrong."

"And he says that, does he?" Less than a minute into the call, and Lizzie was already finding Grace Connolly's words about as believable as her brother's. "I mean, he actually admitted it?"

"More or less."

"What does that mean?"

"Well, I was so worried after what he said that I spoke to our other brother, Fraser. And he came over and had words with Cam. I mean, Cam takes no notice of me, but Fraser... When Fraser gets serious, Cam listens."

Grace heaved an audible sigh. "Look, it's been a horrendous time. Des was the baby of the family, and he always did go the wrong way about trying to get attention. But we're also really close as a family. So losing him and Dad on the same day... We're all coping in different ways. I've been painting as usual. Fraser's thrown himself into work. Cam's just angry and wants someone to have a go at. He shouldn't have picked on you, and he knows it. Threatening your baby goddaughter? He's a lot of things, but he's really not like that."

"If you say so."

"I do. I'm only sorry it's me having to put it right, and not him."

"Well," Lizzie said, still having doubts about Cameron, but having a bit more faith in this woman's motives, "thank you for calling, at least." A thought struck her. "By the way, how did you get my number?"

"Cam gave it to me. All I had to do was ask."

"And he knows you're making this call?"

"He does."

"I see." She found herself smiling. "Can you do something for me, then?"

"If I can."

"Tell Cameron I accept his apology."

"Oh, I..." Grace faltered, then burst out in a giggle. "I might, but that might set him off again. He doesn't like people taking the piss out of him, so naturally I do it all the time. Best we just take the apology as read, if that's okay."

"I suppose. Sounds like it would save a lot of trouble all round."

"I think so."

"I really am sorry for your loss, Grace. I meant that when I said it."

She was still thinking about the difference between siblings when her phone rang again.

Five minutes later, she had one more worry on her mind.

6

Dan Baines had spent much of his afternoon on a depressingly familiar domestic abuse case. The victim, Caitlin Squire, was in hospital, and not for the first time. She was probably only there because neighbours had heard her cries as her partner attacked her, and had called the police.

Her partner, Lewis Lawton, had stuck doggedly to his story that, yes, he'd dropped in for lunch, but Caitlin had been fine when he'd gone back to work. Caitlin herself seriously expecting them to believe that she'd sustained so much damage standing on a chair to get something from the back of a cupboard and losing her balance.

It was no great surprise that there was no sign of a fallen chair when, barely able to stand, she'd somehow managed to get to the door and let the officers in. She claimed that she had picked it up and put it back in its proper place at the kitchen table, despite her injuries, because 'Lewis likes things tidy'.

She hadn't wanted to go to hospital, clearly more terrified of the consequences of making a fuss than the risks of not getting herself checked out for serious damage. And, no matter how many times she'd been asked, she'd persisted with the line that Lewis loved her and would never hurt her.

In the end, Dan and Joan Collins had been forced to admit defeat. Both had come away filled with impotent rage. One day, and possibly sooner than later, they were likely to be questioning Lewis Lawton again, in connection with Caitlin's death. Around 150 women in the UK were killed by men each year, and about two thirds of those were killed by a current or former partner.

He'd just about finished writing up his notes when Lizzie put her head round the door and asked him to join her in her office.

There was something awkward in her demeanour, he thought, when she closed the door and offered him a seat.

He caught her up on the Caitlin Squire case, and then she related a call she'd had from Cameron Connolly's sister, who claimed she and her other brother had talked some sense into him.

He blinked. "Do we believe her?" He'd never met a Connolly he'd believe if they were standing in a field and they told him it was raining. Although he'd only ever actually met Cameron and the late, frankly unlamented Desmond. That was more than enough for him.

Lizzie waggled her hand. "Who can tell? I'm about sixty per cent confident that she, at least, believed what she was telling me. I don't know how much real influence she has, of course, but I suspect Fraser has some."

He shrugged, not greatly reassured. "Well, let's hope the kid sister knows what she's talking about." He didn't like it, but there wasn't a lot he could do. "So what's the other thing?"

Suddenly, something on her desk seemed to fascinate her. She picked at imaginary lint on her jacket.

"Lizzie?" he prompted.

"Yeah, sorry." She looked at him. "I just had a call from Police Scotland. Apparently they started with the Super and he told them to contact me, as your line manager. Why they couldn't just come straight to you is anyone's guess."

"Police Scotland?" A shadow seemed to fall upon the room. His palms felt clammy. "What do they want?"

"You can guess, can't you?"

"It's about Mac? And Ja… Peter?"

She looked uncomfortable again. "I really hate dredging all this up again, but…" She sighed heavily. "You said Mac taunted you about more killings after the Invisible Man murders ended. Hinted that Jack was involved in at least some."

He held up a hand. "Peter. I've got to start thinking of him as Peter. It's what he wants me to call him. Right now, anyway."

"Peter, then," she conceded, maybe dismissing what they called his son as a minor detail. It wasn't to him. "Anyhow, the thinking was that, unless it was a load of old bollocks aimed at winding you up, any such crimes are most likely to have happened in Scotland, or possibly the north of England."

"Yep, we know all that. We know forces up that way have been reviewing unsolved cases, separately and collectively, to see if there are any that might be connected and which appear to bear at least some of the hallmarks of the Invisible Man." His sense of dread deepened. "And what? They've found something?"

"They think it's a possibility, yes." Her voice was soft. "They didn't give me many details, but there are quite a few cases, all in different locations, that you wouldn't necessarily connect unless you were already looking for a particular signature."

He fought down a rising sense of panic and helplessness. Reached for some kind of calm and found it.

"But I'm guessing it's not the identical signature? The victims suffocated with cling film, toddlers abducted, only to be murdered at the next crime scene?"

"I did ask that, and no, it's not identical. I don't think they wanted to go into too many specifics. Maybe they'll fill you in when they call you. They thought the news would be better coming from me. They'll call you in less than half an hour."

He rubbed his eyes. "So, is it just a courtesy thing?"

"No, Dan, it's not that. Look, you remember why Mac came down here in the first place. Claire King was writing that bloody book about the Invisible Man, and wanted someone who'd been involved in the original case to help with the research."

Ironically, Mac's attempt on Karen's life, the news that Dan's son was still alive, and the subsequent trials, had all conspired to make *Invisible* a bestseller. Dan was surprised Claire was still wasting her time working for a back of beyond local rag.

Now he saw where this was going. "No," he said flatly.

"It makes sense, Dan, you know it does. You're the only detective who worked the case who's still alive and serving, and you have the added insight of being the only person Mac has ever really talked to about his crimes. Of course they want you to look at what they have."

He got out of his chair and paced, nervous energy pulsing through him.

"Shit," he said. "The timing couldn't be worse. I told you I'm seeing Peter on Saturday?"

She nodded.

"Three years and he's refused any contact with me. Now suddenly I'm an approved visitor. Of course I want to know whether Mac was speaking the truth about him being an accomplice to later murders. But I can't just go in there interrogating him about that. He'll run a bloody mile. I was going to take it slowly. Try to build a relationship. Do you think the tartan brigade will be happy with that?"

"I wouldn't," she admitted.

"No. Nor would I." He returned to his chair and sat down heavily. "I'm never going to be free of Mac, am I?"

"I get what you're feeling." She reached across the desk. After a moment, he leaned forward and took her hand. She squeezed gently.

"I get it," she said, "but you're not free of him now. You never will be until you know exactly what happened in the years between Jack's abduction and... Peter's arrest. You'll always be wondering. Maybe you'll finally get some answers. You know I'll support you if you need to go up there."

"Thanks. I do know. It doesn't help."

She nodded, sympathy etched on her face. "Then let me say this. He's your son, even if he thinks that's just biology at the moment. No one can force you to interrogate him, question him, or otherwise try and get information out of him, unless and until you feel ready to. We've worked together the best part of ten years now. I know you, and I know no one can make you do anything you don't want to. So see what they have to say, help them with their unsolved cases if you can, but you don't let them push you around."

He smiled, even though he didn't feel like smiling, and he squeezed her hand back before releasing it. "Thanks, coach. I won't."

"I wouldn't let Jason hear you calling them the tartan brigade though."

DS Jason Bell was a red-haired Scot.

"I won't," he said again, allowing himself a chuckle this time. "I don't want him running to HR."

"Like he would. But he might set Holly on you."

Jason's girlfriend, Holly, was a nurse, lovely most of the time, but fiercely protective of her man, whose fragile confidence had come on in leaps and bounds since they'd been together. It was one of the reasons he'd finally made DS about a year ago, after Amir Rashid had gone to Milton Keynes on promotion.

Dan was about to respond when there was a tap on the door.

"Come in," called Lizzie.

The door opened and Jason himself walked in. He was carrying a large bouquet of flowers.

"Why, Jason," Dan said. "For me?"

Jason may be more confident, but he still occasionally blushed to his red roots, as he did now.

"These are for Lizzie, actually," he said. "Delivered to the front desk just now." He looked at her slyly. "What's Dominic done that deserves such a big apology?"

Dan saw only puzzlement on her face as she took the bouquet from him, laid it carefully on her desk, and found the small white envelope containing a card. She took the card out and read it, and her expression changed. He wondered if Jason could read how angry she was.

She stuffed the card in her pocket, picked up the flowers, and dumped them in the bin with a savagery that caused petals to fly.

"Wow," Jason said. "He must have really pissed you off."

She looked at him as if she'd forgotten he was there. "Anything else, Jason?"

"No," he mumbled, reddening again.

"Shut the door on your way out."

"Everything okay?" Dan asked when he had gone.

"They're not from Dominic," she said.

"Oh." He gaped at her. "Not Cameron bloody Connolly?"

"What?" She laughed without humour. "By way of apology? No. I'd keep the flowers and frame the card."

"So…"

"They're from Rob. As in my ex."

"Whoa. After all this time?"

"Yeah, I should have said. He's quit the fire brigade and now he's come here, looking for a home, a job and a new start."

"Seriously?"

"Well, he thinks he's serious. But here's the best bit. He's decided he wants me back."

"You're joking."

"I wish."

"When did all this happen?"

"He ambushed me in the car park. Persuaded me to go for a drink. Shared his mad plan with me. I mean, he knows I'm married, but he thinks he and I are 'meant to be'."

Dan puffed out his cheeks. "Why didn't you say anything before?"

She looked as if it was a hard question. "I didn't think I wanted to. I don't know why. Obviously I told him to push off, but…" She pointed at the bouquet in the bin. "It doesn't look like he's taking the hint, does it?"

7

The call came from Detective Inspector Alec McGivering in Glasgow. With an accent so thick that Dan had to concentrate to understand him, he'd asked if there was somewhere they could do a video call without being overheard.

Dan had slipped into an empty meeting room, closed the door, and sat down, a fearful coldness settling over him.

"Thanks for agreeing to talk to me," McGivering said. He turned to be bald and bearded, with a nose like a potato. "You know that Police Scotland, liaising with Northumbria Police, were looking at eleven cases between 2005 and 2018 that bear certain similarities. I'd imagine you're as hopeful that we get some answers as we are."

Nothing could be further from the truth. Dan knew he'd give anything to know that Mac had just been playing mind games with him. That his son wasn't a killer. Those were the only answers he was interested in.

He honestly didn't know what he'd do if it turned out that Mac had spoken the truth.

But of course, he said nothing of this.

Instead, "I'll do what I can," was the best he could offer.

Maybe McGivering had expected a little more enthusiasm, because he looked nonplussed for a moment.

Right," he said finally. "Let's talk about how the cases *aren't* similar to your Invisible Man murders. For a start, I can tell you not all the victims are women, and their ages range from twenty to sixty-three. And there are no children involved."

"So a totally different victimology from the Invisible Man. Different across the cases, too, by the sound of it."

"Yep. Then there's the method of killing. No cling film involved. Three suffocated with cushions, two with pillows, two with plastic bags over their heads. Three strangled with

42

garrottes – an apron string, a pair of tights, even another plastic carrier bag, rolled up. One forcibly drowned in a sink. One manual strangulation. They'd all been tied up first."

Dan took notes as he listened. "So far, there's not that much of a pattern, is there? How sure are you that they're connected, let alone Duncan McNeil's work?"

"Well, good question. We started off looking for any cling film murders, found none, so we started looking for methods that denied the victims air to breathe. There were a lot of those, as you can imagine, but we further narrowed it down to victims killed in their homes where no one saw the killer come or go."

"Okay. That's exactly what gave rise to Mac's nickname."

"Then we noticed that these eleven were killed with items found in their homes – the killer hadn't brought anything with him."

"The Invisible Man always used the victims' own cling film. I see where you're coming from. But manual strangulation doesn't fit at all."

"No, it could be an outlier. Or something went wrong and he wasn't able to get their hands bound like he did with the others. Perhaps he tied them after death. Of course, in your original cases, you speculated that McNeil threatened the children and made the victims wrap the film around their own heads."

It conjured mental images he'd been trying to forget. "We'll never know for sure. He's said nothing since his arrest, and he didn't elaborate in the time before that when he was being chatty to me."

"Understood. But, if some or all of these cases are connected, then he was deliberately avoiding his old signature, especially the no kids bit. So he had to subdue them another way. Some had been knocked out. A couple injected with substances or made to inhale chemicals. Some, it's just not clear how it was managed."

"Sounds like you've just got eleven separate murders to me," he said, even though he could see the other man's point. "Do you think maybe you're reaching?"

"Could be," McGivering conceded. "Especially over so wide a geographical area. You could easily be right. Or it could be that he's been having fun doing the opposite to what he did with your lot."

And, much as Dan didn't want to believe that any of these killings had anything to do with Mac, and possibly his son, he knew it was a theory that couldn't be dismissed out of hand.

"With the original killings, he was certainly having a laugh at the very force he worked on. He was even being part of the investigation," he conceded. "Murder was all a big game for him. Maybe this time he was laughing at us because he thought he was committing perfect murders that wouldn't even be connected."

"And he'd have been right," McGivering acknowledged. "We might never have looked for dots to join if he hadn't said what he did."

"It's a way of looking at it," Dan mused. "But even now, you don't really *have* any dots, do you? Some or none could be connected. Maybe you're trying too hard to make the pieces fit. Maybe they're not all parts of the same puzzle at all."

"You almost sound like you want that to be true."

"Yes," he said. "And no. Let me level with you. Most of this, I'm sure you know. Duncan McNeil took my son when he was just two years old and brought him up as his own. I don't know if he expected to gain paternal feelings for him, but I think he did. That's not the point though. The point is, the only people who knew for sure what happened over the next seventeen or eighteen years are those two."

He paused for breath, realising that his voice was shaking. This was almost unbearable territory for him. "So you ask me if I want these cases to be unconnected, and certainly nothing to do with McNeil – or, more to the point – nothing to do with my son. And the answer is, of course. I want McNeil's claim that my son helped him to kill to be lies."

"So you're not sure you want to help us." McGivering nodded. "I get it."

"No, you don't. Because the only thing that's going to give me, my wife, probably my son too – although I can't be certain about that – any peace is to finally get to the bottom of this. For the truth to come out, however bad it is."

44

"So you *will* help?"

"What do you need?"

"I could fly down from Glasgow next week. Monday, if I can get a flight? Maybe stay a couple of days? I've read the original case files, but there's nothing like a cop who worked the case to help fill in the blanks and tell us what's not there in black and white."

It wasn't what he'd been expecting. Now the request had been made, he knew he'd have asked the same. But he hesitated.

"I'd have to clear it with my boss." He knew Lizzie would agree, but that wasn't the only thing troubling him. His impending visit to Aylesbury prison was causing bad memories to resurface as it was, without him immersing himself in a whole new series of potential Invisible Man cases. And did he really want the distraction now? A ruthless gangster – ironically Glasgow-born – had threatened him and his family, through Lizzie. His sister had given assurances that the threat had been withdrawn, but could she be trusted?

"It's only a couple of days maximum," McGivering pressed.

And he knew it was the right thing to do. The only thing truly holding him back was a fear of what he might find. That it would turn out that his son was at best an accomplice to murder and at worst an actual killer.

But the not knowing was even worse.

The time it would take was not a major problem. Things were quiet at work, Joan Collins and Jason Bell could easily hold the fort if need be.

"I'll get back to you," he decided. "There's one more thing you should know though. I'm actually seeing my son on Saturday, for the first time since his trial. I'm telling you in the interests of full disclosure, and to make it clear I won't be raising any of this with him."

"I wouldn't want you to, Dan. It does none of us any good for you to start quizzing him on what I freely acknowledge are half-baked theories at the moment. When they're baked enough for us to take them seriously… well, then I'll be the one asking him the questions. Do we have an understanding?"

He mentally counted to ten, just to give himself time to think. Knowing there was really nothing to think about.

"We do," he said.

8

Dominic was upstairs in the small bedroom he used as an office when Lizzie got home. She called up the stairs and he came down, eager for a hug and a kiss.

"So how was your day?" he asked as they broke apart.

She kicked off her shoes and shrugged out of her jacket. "Oh, you know. This and that."

"Did you ask Josh to put you forward for that promotion?"

"Didn't get around to it. Or maybe I'm procrastinating. Anyhow, I'll sleep on it and give him an answer first thing tomorrow."

He gave her a sidelong glance. "You know, I quite like the idea of you wearing uniform every day."

She laughed. "Do you now? Maybe I should get Holly to loan me a nurse's uniform."

"I dunno. Nurse attire isn't quite what it was."

"Jason doesn't seem to be complaining." She slung the jacket over her arm. "I'm going to get changed. Are you cooking, or am I?"

"If you call shoving a ready-made lasagne in the oven cooking, I'll get it started."

"Maybe I could fancy *you* in chef's whites."

As she made her way upstairs, she realised she hadn't actually told Dominic about Rob and the flowers. She'd rectify that after she'd changed out of her work clothes.

She was just coming out of the bedroom in jeans and a jumper when the doorbell rang. She started walking briskly downstairs, but Dominic beat her to it. The voice she heard caused her heart to sink.

"Hi, you must be Dominic. Good to meet you, mate. I'm Rob, an old friend of Lizzie's."

47

She reached the foot of the stairs and strode across the entrance hall to stand at Dominic's shoulder. Her husband looked tense and confused at the same time. Rob was holding out a hand for him to shake, and Dominic was staring at it like it was a threat.

Rob looked at her with a delighted smile on his face.

"Rob, how the hell did you get my address?" she demanded.

"Ah," he said, a little sheepishly, but only a little. "Yeah. Well, I have to admit, I, um…"

"Please tell me you didn't follow me home." This was getting to be a trend, and not a pleasant one.

"Guilty," he admitted. "Sorry, I know it was a bit out of order."

"A bit?" Dominic was clenching his jaw. And, Lizzie noted with dismay, his fists.

"Rob." She took a step forward, casually inserting herself between them, before things got any worse. "I don't know what's going on with you, I really don't. Mid-life crisis, whatever. But this has to stop right now."

"I can't."

"You'd better. I mean, you turn up at my work, I join you in a drink for old time's sake, and you talk a lot of crap about winning me back. I tell you I'm happily married and it's never going to happen. I tell you to stay away from me, and what do you do?"

He grinned mischievously. "I sent you flowers. Did you like them?"

Dominic glowered. "You sent her flowers?" He leaned in to Lizzie. "When was this?"

"This afternoon. I binned them. I was going to tell you, and then he turns up." She returned her attention to Rob. "And now you've followed me home. This is not normal."

"It's not normal at all. Mate." Dominic said icily. "You need to leave. Now."

"What's the rush?" Rob drawled. "*Lizzie*'s not asking me to leave, and it's her I've come to see."

"You'll leave when I tell you to."

Rob's grin broadened. "Or what?"

"For God's sake," Lizzie said. "I'm pissed off enough for one day, without you two having a handbag fight. I'll deal with this, Dominic."

He folded his arms. "Fair enough."

She knew she ought to be at least slightly anxious about this situation, but she could only feel ice-cold fury. In the past two days, she'd received threats from more than one quarter and her car had been vandalised. Now, for the second night running, someone had followed her home from work and now there was a punch-up brewing on her doorstep.

"Right," she said. "Here's what's happening, Rob. Like I said, I've no idea what's going on in your head. I think maybe you need professional help. But I'm not having this. Keep it up and, trust me, you're the one it's not going to end well for. Do you really want a criminal record, even jail time?"

He sighed and looked down at his shoes. "I can see this wasn't the right way to go about it. You need a bit of thinking time."

"There's nothing to think *about*, you sad bastard!" she finally exploded. "You're ancient history to me and, frankly, I'm well shot of you. I am not going to 'come around', or whatever your crazy delusions think is going to happen. Please get off our property and never come back. Any more of this and I'll get the police involved."

He smirked. "You'd arrest me?" He thrust his arms out in front of him. "Snap the cuffs on. I'll come quietly."

"Can I slap him now, please?" Dominic murmured, squaring his shoulders again.

"No one is slapping anyone, okay? On your bike, Rob," she said. "I mean it. I'll call the police and that'll be grief for all of us."

He looked about to make another smart remark, then he shrugged.

"Okay," he conceded. "Okay, I'm going for now. I'll drop by in a day or two."

"No you won't. You come near me again and I'll make it my mission to make your life a misery. Are we clear?"

"Whatever. I'll see you around." He looked at Dominic. "Nice meeting you. I wanted to size up the opposition."

"There *is* no opposition!" She got right in his face. "Now, are you going?"

He held up his hands in surrender. "Yeah, yeah. Have a good night."

He turned and walked away.

She almost laughed with relief, but it was no laughing matter.

She ushered Dominic inside and closed the door.

"*Can I slap him now?*"

He had the grace to redden, but his jaw still jutted. "He can't just come round here—"

"That was painful enough, without the pair of you getting into a pissing contest. What are you, a caveman protecting his territory?"

He opened his mouth. Closed it. Then visibly relaxed.

"Ug," he said, beating his chest.

She couldn't help laughing, and he joined in. "My hero. But you'd have come off worse, and I'm too tired to spend half the night in A&E."

"I could have taken him."

"Yeah, right. In your itty-bitty dreams."

He didn't pursue it any further. "Is he safe?"

"Christ, I don't know. One more stunt and I'm reporting him."

"He sent you *flowers?*"

"Yeah. The office assumed you'd screwed something up and sent them as an apology."

"Nice of them."

"Well, I assumed they *were* from you until I read the card."

"Have you still got it?"

"The card? Yeah. I didn't want to leave it lying around in the office to start tongues wagging."

"I can see that. Because binning a mysterious bunch of flowers won't do that, right?"

"I told you. I didn't want them."

"Can I see the card?" he asked after a moment

"It's still in my jacket pocket. Hang on."

She went upstairs and retrieved it. Dominic read it:

"Bloody hell. *'I'm not giving up. I know you'll come back to me. I'll wait forever.'*"

"It sounds like some horrible pop ballad, doesn't it?"

"It's really not funny, Lizzie."

"No," she agreed. "I'd better keep it. It's evidence."

"You think he'll keep it up?"

"I think there's something wrong with him. I almost wish I'd been kinder now."

Dominic stared at her. "Seriously?"

"Seriously. I mean, yeah, it's been a long time, and I know people change. But he was never weird like this. Not even a little bit. I really should have urged him to get some help."

"You sort of did."

"Mm. Not in a nice way."

"What he did wasn't nice."

"Well, maybe he'll get the message now."

"Didn't sound like it."

She was suddenly weary of the subject. "Is that lasagne in?"

He blinked. "I just about managed it before lover boy showed up."

"Well, I'm going to get a beer while we're waiting."

He smiled. "Now you're talking."

She got the beers. They sat on the sofa and clinked bottles.

Dominic looked uncharacteristically gloomy. "We seem to have a lot to worry about, don't we? Threats from all sides, and now a possible stalker. I'm not even sure which is the worst. Probably your obsessive ex, though. If he's really gone a bit bonkers…"

She chugged some beer. "If he has, I can deal with it. Trust me."

He sighed. "All right. You're the police officer, I suppose. But he'd better stay away from here. Underneath this mild-mannered exterior…"

"…beats a mild-mannered heart," she completed for him. "Seriously, I love you wanting to defend me, and I know you would, but I've got this. And who knows, he might realise in the cold light of day that he's being a dick and piss off back to London."

"Let's hope," he agreed.

She leaned across and kissed him. There was no way she was going to worry him further by showing how agitated she really was.

She'd been in love with Rob Thomas until he'd dumped her. Or she thought she had. The circumstances hadn't been great, but she'd never thought she'd ever have reason to be afraid of him.

She really hoped that wasn't about to change.

9

For all that Lizzie tried to make light of it all, telling herself she wasn't afraid of anything was easier in the light of day than it was lying in the dark.

She worried about Dominic too. He was probably the most laid back person she had ever met. It was one of his great strengths, and it made him her rock. In times when she was under pressure, or when the horrible things she saw in her job got too much to bear, he was a calm, reassuring presence she could always turn to. He'd put his arms around her and things didn't seem so bad any more.

Even so, she knew him well enough to know he was on edge too. She doubted it was because he felt threatened by Rob coming back on the scene. She knew Dominic trusted her completely when she said her ex was firmly in the past, just as he'd been content to wait when she wasn't sure about progressing their friendship to something deeper. In fact, it had been Rob's rejection, and some bad rebound decisions afterwards, that had made her so cautious. Another man might have become impatient and moved on, but Dominic had been happy to bide his time.

So, no. She thought it was everything coming at once that was getting to him now. She could just about imagine him actually getting in a fight he couldn't win with Rob if he thought he had to, but threats from a nasty, unpredictable family, and from a dangerous gangster... he must be doubting that he could protect her, however much he might want to.

But her concern about Dominic just added to her own worries. She had a promotion opportunity on her mind too. All the arguments for grabbing the chance with both hands made complete sense, yet still she hesitated.

It all went round and round in her mind, running through scenarios, rehearsing what she might say, what she might do. In those periods of wakefulness, she knew Dominic was awake too. Neither of them spoke though. As if speaking would confirm that there would be little or no sleep tonight.

On the fleeting occasions when she did nod off, what sleep there was seemed to be accompanied by weird, kaleidoscopic dreams where she was being chased by Rob, Gaynor Upman or Cameron Connolly. Or all three.

It was one such nightmarish dream that was interrupted by the shrill shriek of a smoke alarm.

"Shit," she mumbled as the noise filled the house and pierced her ears.

"Bugger," Dominic said. "That's all we need. Probably the battery wants replacing. You stay there."

He got up, padded across the bedroom carpet, muttering inaudible curses that could barely be heard above the din, and stepped out onto the landing.

"Oh, *Christ!*" he said, a note of alarm in his voice.

"What?"

He didn't reply. She heard him hurtling down the stairs. Wondering what on earth was happening, she climbed out of bed herself and followed him.

She could feel the heat from the top of the stairs, the smoke already in her nostrils and tickling her throat. She could hear Dominic coughing somewhere downstairs. She screamed his name as she started down, her eyes fixed on the flames that were roaring around the front door.

Dominic dashed out of the kitchen with the fire extinguisher, turning his head her way as he did so.

"I dunno if this'll be enough," he yelled above all the noise.

"I'll get the fire blanket." She half-stumbled down the remaining stairs, trying not to breathe in smoke, then sprinted into the kitchen, where she grabbed the woven fibreglass blanket. Back in the hall, Dominic was still spraying the area of the fire. Mercifully, the powder had already smothered most of it.

Moments later, he looked up at her. "The spray's run out."

A few tongues of flame still danced on the tiled floor. She hurried to his side and together they opened out the blanket and threw it over the remaining flames. Some half-hearted wisps of smoke briefly seeped out from under the material, but Lizzie was confident that the fire was out.

Only then did Dominic turn and meet her eyes. His eyes were red and watery, and he was coughing horribly.

"Jesus," he hacked. "Thank Christ the alarm *is* working."

Its shriek continued, a white hot needle in her brain.

"Yeah," she agreed. "But it can pack up now."

Then they were clinging to each other, the horror of what might so easily have happened too real to ignore.

If they hadn't managed to put the fire out, they'd have had no choice but to escape by the back door, but God knew how much of their home would have been saved once the flames really took hold. She'd seen a few arsons in her life and had seen at too close quarters what fire could do.

No way had this one started by itself.

"I need to call this in," she said, "but first I'll get us some water. Best keep an eye on it in case it wakes up."

"It's not a living thing," he said.

"Fire?" she coughed a laugh. "Oh, believe me, it is. You ask Rob."

"I don't want to ask Rob anything," he muttered as she walked into the kitchen.

They found Barney cowering in a corner, his usual swagger at least temporarily departed. Dominic picked him up while Lizzie filled two glasses of water. They each drank theirs in one, and she got two more.

"I'll take mine over to the phone," she said. "You were coughing a lot. Smoke inhalation can be nasty. Shall I ask for an ambulance?"

"No, that'd be overkill. If I'm worried in the morning, I'll see the GP."

She asked for both fire and police services. She also rang Dan, even though the clocks on the cookers told her it was just after 3am. As soon as she told him what had happened, and assured him they both seemed okay, he told her he was on his way.

She rejoined Dominic in the hall.

"What did you mean?" he asked. "About it not starting itself?"

"I think you know exactly what I mean," she said. "You know as well as I do that something like that, right by the front door, has to be someone pouring petrol through the letter box and chucking a match in."

"Yeah," he agreed. "Of course I know. I was just hoping it might be something else."

"Spontaneous combustion?" She gave him a quick hug. "That'd be something."

He looked at the blackened door, the sooty ceiling.

"Jesus. Who, though?"

She regarded him seriously. "Take your pick. But we both know I'm the one with the enemies."

*

Lizzie's call had jolted Dan and Karen awake, but her news had shaken the sleep off him like a cold shower. Karen had got up and made him a coffee while he threw some clothes on, and then made him drink it before he left, so he wouldn't be driving groggy.

The drive from Little Aston to Long Lees was less than a quarter of an hour, but the uniforms had still narrowly beaten him to it. Lizzie and Dominic stood outside the house in coats, talking to a couple of officers, while another put blue and white police tape in place. A small crowd had gathered in the road outside the property, while a number of other neighbours were on doorsteps, some in dressing gowns, watching the show.

"Are you two okay?" was his first question.

"Think so," Lizzie said. "Dominic might have breathed a bit more smoke than was good for him, but he insists he's okay. I'm sending him to the GP tomorrow, just to make sure."

"So what happened?" was his second question.

"The Fire Scene Investigators are on their way and can probably tell us for sure, but my money's on someone starting it. You know – accelerant through the letter box."

"Christ." He glanced over at the house. "How bad is it?"

"Could have been a whole lot worse," she said. "The smoke alarm woke us and Dominic was brilliant."

"Well," Dominic said modestly, notably hoarse, "I managed to use the extinguisher without spraying it straight in my own face. I guess that's a bit brilliant."

"You were calm and did what was needed," she told him. She looked at Dan. "As it is, we stopped it before it got too much of a hold. We'll need a new front door and some redecoration. The hall was due it, and now the insurance will pay. A result, of sorts. I suppose it could have been much worse, for us as well as the house."

He noticed that her voice shook a little.

"No CCTV, I don't suppose?"

"Not us, no. We keep talking about getting one of those doorbells with a camera, but talk's all it's been. I don't know if any neighbours have anything that'll help."

"We'll ask," he said. "I take it you'd like my team to follow it up?"

"I don't know." She grimaced. "I probably shouldn't have bothered you. I mean, the fire investigators will establish cause and any evidence. The enquiry is probably a uniform job. You know, a bit of door to door..."

He held up a hand. "Don't treat it like a small matter, Lizzie. Someone's targeted a senior police officer. As you say, it could have been worse. If it wasn't for the smoke alarm, chances are the carbon monoxide would have ensured you never woke up. We might have been looking at murder here. As it is, I'd call it attempted murder. That sounds like a major incident to me."

She blinked, then her shoulders slumped.

"Yeah," she said. "Fair enough. Although I'll ask the Super if you can report direct to him on this one. I'm the victim here, so the last thing we need is a conflict of interests."

"I'll speak to him myself," he said. "As to who's behind it, I know who my money's on."

"Me too," she admitted. "I seem to be particularly unpopular this week but, even if Cameron Connolly's withdrawal of his implied threat was totally insincere, this feels a bit small time for him."

He thought she was right, but didn't want to dismiss it out of hand. "Unless he wanted it to look that way," he pointed out.

"Yeah, except it was pretty bungled."

"Maybe he just wanted to scare you?"

She shook her head. "Nah. When he came round here the other night, he was holding me responsible for two deaths in the family. If he does still want to get even, he's going to go for more than just a little scare."

"I'm inclined to agree." He shoved his hands deeper into his coat pockets. "The Upmans then. This sort of shit is right up their street, don't you think?"

"I think so."

"Bit obvious, though, isn't it?" Dominic suggested. He'd been quiet up to now, probably trying not to strain his voice unnecessarily. "I know they're supposed not to be the sharpest tools in the box, but first the car, now this…"

"They're obvious people," Lizzie said. "But we can't arrest anyone just because Gaynor made a few intimidating gestures at me."

"Pity we lucked out on CCTV at the court," Dan remarked. Lizzie had managed to put her car in a spot where it wasn't covered by a camera. CCTV had probably picked up everyone who came to the site that day, but that didn't help identify whoever carved up her car.

"The Upmans still have to be the favourites," he continued. "As you say, the family are thick enough to have done both. They might get away with the car, but maybe someone across the road has a camera or happened to see something."

"Cameras are the best bet," Lizzie said. "They'd have to be insomniac to be looking out the window at that time of the morning."

"We'll still ask. We'll check CCTV around the village too. See who was driving around Long Lees around the time the fire started. There can't be that many. We'll ask every one of them

58

to account for their movements." He looked around. "You mentioned fire investigators. What about CSI?"

"Yeah, I asked for Phil Gordon to be knocked up. He'll be thrilled with me."

"He'll be angry with whoever did this," Dan countered. He knew as well as she did that the Geordie crime scene manager wore his heart on his sleeve and would leave no forensic stone unturned here.

Lizzie yawned and suppressed a shiver.

"Cold?" he suggested.

"Probably a bit of shock. I suppose we'll have to find a hotel until Phil releases the house."

He hadn't thought of that. "Let me call Karen. I'm sure we can put you up at ours."

"We can't impose," Dominic protested.

"Don't be daft, mate. Of course you can."

As if on cue, a woman in a dressing gown appeared with two thermos flasks and held them out to Lizzie and Dominic. She looked as if she'd taken the trouble to straighten her hair before she came out. Dan judged she was in her seventies.

"Tea," she said. "Hot and sweet. It might not be what you like, but it's what you need. At least," she added, "that's what my mum always recommends for any sort of shock."

They took the flasks without protest. "Thanks, Margaret," Lizzie said.

"How bad is it? Where did it start?"

"In the hall." She barely missed a beat and Dan appreciated the vagueness.

"What was it? Faulty wiring?"

"Can't say for sure. Anyway, thanks for the tea, but we're busy with the police."

She nodded. "Oh, of course. I'll get out of the way."

The three of them watched her drift back across the road.

"I thought you hardly knew your neighbours," Dan commented.

"We don't."

"*You* don't," Dominic corrected. "But then I lived next to you in Great Marston for two months before you realised your old neighbours had even gone."

"Yeah, well." She smiled. "Maybe I'm a crap detective after all. But we both know Margaret. When we moved in, she was on the doorstep with cake before we could unpack the kettle. She makes it her business to know everyone in the street."

"If not the entire village," Dominic added.

"Sounds a useful person to interview," Dan said. "It doesn't sound as if much slips by her."

"Here's Phil," Lizzie said.

Dan turned to watch a dark van pulling up, blocking next door's drive. Men and women climbed out. One of them went to the back and started handing out white paper overalls, but the man from the front passenger seat came straight up to join Dan, Lizzie and Dominic.

Phil Gordon asked most of the same questions as Dan had about Lizzie's and Dominic's health and what had happened. He didn't dwell on the state the fire had left the property in. He'd want to see for himself.

"Ah, well," he said, "I'll get suited up and go and see what's what. But don't you worry, Lizzie. Whatever there is to find, we'll find it and we'll nail these people. They're not getting away with it."

He stonked off to the back of the van and Dan saw him accept a set of overalls and start pulling them on.

"I've a good mind to call Joan out," he said. "These people are all up and about anyway. We can start questioning them now, while anything they saw or heard will be fresh in their minds."

"No," Lizzie said, "don't bother Joan now. There's nothing here that can't wait until the morning, by which time the CSIs and fire investigators might have some more useful information to work with."

Although Dan thought she was probably right, he half-wondered if she was being over-protective of Joan again. Around the time Dan had finally unmasked the Invisible Man, Joan Collins' partner, Charlie, had been going through her own ordeal, trapped underground in the dark, while Joan had suffered a serious head injury during Charlie's abduction.

For a while, both had struggled quite badly with post-traumatic stress and other after-effects, but Joan had been amazing, rarely missing work, knuckling down and doing her usual excellent work. Dan could only imagine the toll it must have taken on her, holding down a demanding full-on job whilst supporting her partner in an everyday struggle with demons Joan couldn't fight.

There had been moments when Charlie had contemplated abandoning her legal career because, every time she tried to get back to work, she broke down again. But in the end, these two phenomenally strong women had dragged each other through the darkness and back into the light. Lizzie was a caring boss, but Dan knew Joan thrived on work and hated the idea of being mollycoddled in any way.

Even so...

"Fair enough," he said. "I can write up notes for my report at home and we can start afresh tomorrow."

He looked at her. Her hair was untidy from bed, her facial scar visible, a rarity. It might have been the street lamps, but he thought she looked a bit haggard. Dominic looked worse, if anything. They'd had a scare, and coming down from the adrenalin rush was probably hitting them hard.

"Let me just talk to uniform," he said. "I want someone posted here until tomorrow. Tell me where your door keys are and I'll get CSI to pass me a set and to pack you a bag. Then I'm taking you both back to our place."

"No," Lizzie said. "You're not."

He laughed. "Well, you can forget sleeping at home tonight. Like Phil will let you trample over his crime scene. You're both done in and we've got a guest bedroom that's hardly ever used."

"Dan," she said, "you can be very sweet, but we can't come to you. This was aimed at me. Where I am, that's where they might strike again. I can't bring that risk to your door."

"Don't be silly—" he began.

"Don't you be silly," she retorted. "You've got Karen and Ellie to consider."

And, much as he hated admitting it, even to himself, he knew she had a point.

"Adam already invited us to hole up at his place," Lizzie said. Her brother lived in West London. "As soon as I told him about Cameron's visit. I stressed that his sister said he'd apologised, but that didn't stop him being pissed off. 'That bloody job again,' he said, but he was still concerned about us."

"I'm guessing you politely declined?"

"I did, and I'm doing the same to you. No way am I running away."

Dan knew when he was beaten

When Lizzie Archer had first turned up in Aylesbury Vale, it was fair to say that she and Dan hadn't exactly hit it off from the start. But working together, seeing through some tough cases and difficult personal and professional challenges together had built a close bond between them. Each could always trust the other to have their back.

The idea that he couldn't be completely there for her now hurt him but, at the same time, she was probably right. He couldn't allow her to bring danger to his door, not when he had his family's safety to consider.

"Fair enough," he said, surprised to find a lump in his throat. "Shall I at least look after Barney?"

"Would you mind?"

"Least I can do

"You're a star. So," she said. "A hotel, then. I'll get Phil to organise some packing."

"I'll need my laptop," said Dominic. "Then I'll make some calls. The Holiday Inn, the Travelodge…"

"Not the Travelodge," Lizzie said hastily. "It's where Rob was staying."

"I'll try the Holiday Inn first."

"We have a plan," Dan said. "I'll go and talk to uniform. You two speak to Phil."

"Okay." Her voice was uncharacteristically small. He suspected she was dead on her feet. He wasn't feeling perky himself.

"Look," he told her, "this won't take too long, if I have my way. Upmans, Connollys, whoever... I'm going to nail them fast." He knew it was just talk, but he meant it anyway. "The sooner we can put a stop to this and you can relax again, the better I'll like it."

10

When Lizzie had first arrived in the Vale, she had stayed at the Holiday Inn at Aston Clinton until something more permanent could be organised. So it was ironic that she now found herself right back where she'd started. Dominic had found someone on reception and impressed on them their desperate situation. Their room was ready and waiting when they arrived, carrying just a holdall each containing a few clothes and toiletries.

Dominic had been out for the count within moments of them crawling into bed. Despite her own exhaustion, she had lain awake turning scenarios and suspects over in her mind. She supposed she must have got some patchy sleep, but she still felt like an extra from *The Walking Dead* when they sat down to a hotel breakfast in the morning. She'd texted Superintendent Stowe, saying she'd be late in and explaining why. He'd texted back, urging her to take the day off, but she thought she'd go mad if she didn't keep busy.

The advantage of the Holiday Inn was that it was only about five minutes' drive from their home. With CSI and FSI vans, plus a marked police car, all bunched at the front of the property, they had to park a few doors away.

As they walked towards the house, Lizzie could see a couple of neighbours on their doorsteps, rubbernecking; one of them was the ever-watchful Margaret. She also saw a horribly familiar figure in earnest conversation with the uniformed officer who had been stationed on the edge of the drive to keep the public away.

"What the actual…" hissed Dominic.

They both quickened their pace. Rob turned away from the officer, smiling.

"Thank God you're both all right."

"Never mind that," stormed Lizzie. "What does it take for you to get the message? I warned you..."

"Whoa!" he held up his hands in surrender. "Look, this isn't what it seems."

"No?" Dominic was looking uncharacteristically aggressive. "What it *seems* is that a guy who's been hassling my wife, who turned up on our doorstep uninvited and unwelcome yesterday evening... a guy who was told in no uncertain terms to stay away from us... is here again." He scratched his head. "Why are you even here? If we hadn't had a problem last night, we'd both be at work by now."

Rob had taken a step back in the face of this onslaught. "Please," he protested. He brandished his envelope. "I wanted to apologise. For upsetting you."

"You did upset us," Lizzie said.

"Yeah," Dominic added. "The best apology you can make is to sod off."

"Dominic," Lizzie said mildly. She was too tired to be irritated, and the last thing she wanted was a scene in front of the neighbours, let alone a police officer.

He shrugged, continued to look daggers at Rob, but didn't continue his rant.

"Look," Rob said, mildly, "I'm sorry. I realise I've been out of line. To tell the truth, I've been pretty messed up lately. I've been way over the top, haven't I?"

"You can say that again," muttered Dominic.

"You can't behave like that," Lizzie said. "I did try to tell you."

He nodded miserably. "But this officer," he glanced at the uniformed officer, who had been looking unsure whether to intervene before things got out of hand, "says you had a fire last night."

"We did—" Lizzie began, but Dominic cut her off.

"Yes we did," he said, then, "since you mention it."

"We're both okay, fortunately," Lizzie said.

Dominic nodded. "Yes, but isn't it funny? Eh, Rob? You turn up in Lizzie's life like a bad smell, make a real nuisance of yourself, and we give you the bum's rush. Then, just a few hours later, someone's trying to burn the house down with us inside it."

"We don't know that for sure," Lizzie said, trying to play it down. Nothing had been released to the media or the public yet, and she was keen to keep it that way.

"I think *he* knows," Dominic persisted. "A fireman. Didn't you say you first met him when you were investigating a spate of arson attacks in London? So I'm thinking he knows something about setting light to houses."

"Now wait a minute," Rob protested, his own ire resurfacing. "What are you accusing me of?"

"Nothing, Rob," Lizzie said. "He's just upset."

"Just a bit," Dominic said. "You'd better jog on, mate, but don't be surprised if you find yourself being questioned about this."

"That'll do!" Lizzie snapped, her patience exhausted. "Look, Rob, apology accepted, but you're doing a lot more harm than good here."

Rob regarded Dominic with naked dislike. "And *this* is what you replaced me with?"

"Please go, Rob," she said.

He sighed. "Won't you at least hear me out? Maybe if you knew what's been going on in my life..."

"No, Rob," she said, "we had our little catch up the other night, when you said more than enough."

She frowned, her detective's brain still working in the background. Dominic had a point. Rob had been weird ever since he'd intercepted her in the police station car park. And he *did* know a thing or two about arson.

"Actually," she said, "before you go, you'd best give your contact details to this nice Police Constable. Dominic's right about one thing. Someone will probably want to question you about this."

He stared at her, his expression unfathomable. "Seriously?"

"Seriously. Now, we're going to speak to some of the guys who are investigating the fire. I really want you gone by the time we're done."

She didn't give him a chance to reply. The PC lifted the crime scene tape for her and Dominic to duck under. She could see three figures in white crime scene overalls working on the area just inside the door, but her husband halted halfway, taking hold of her arm.

"What?" she whispered.

He opened his mouth to reply, closed it, paused for a few beats, and then spoke quietly and calmly.

"Look, I'm sorry. Something about him just gets my goat. And how would you feel if some woman came and started making those sort of overtures to me in front of you?"

"I'd probably laugh."

"Would you though?"

"No," she admitted. "I might be a teensy bit tempted to deck her. Not a good idea to act on it though. Especially in front of a policeman. You'd be the one in the cells."

"I know. And I know he's wasting his time. I guess I should be sorry for him." He glanced over her shoulder. "He's gone, by the way. Do you think he's a suspect?"

"I think we have to treat him as one, yes, I do." She squeezed his arm. "Come on. Let's have a look at the damage in the cold light of day."

The doormat, which had been toast anyway, but also a section of her beloved tiled floor, had been removed. The man on his knees looked up.

"How are you doing, Lizzie?" Phil Gordon said.

"I've been better," she admitted. "How are you getting on? Just wondering when we can come home?"

He stood up carefully.

"Well, the good news is the fire was pretty localised, so I reckon we'll be done by early afternoon. Maybe sooner."

"Can you confirm it was accelerant? I'm leaving Dan to lead on this, but I'm still curious."

"Oh, yeah. I could tell straight away by the smell, although we'll get it tested at a lab anyway, in the hope we can get someone in court. I'd put a rush on it, but the powers that be would veto the cost for a relatively small fire."

"Not even for Lizzie?" Dominic pressed.

"Aye, well, that'd be nice. But, to be honest, with one of our own, we probably shouldn't have turned up at all, in case the Great British Public accuse us of favouring you."

"I don't think they can say that, Phil," Lizzie remarked, "the mess you've made. It looks a bloody sight worse than it did just after the fire."

He smiled. "Sorry about that. Like I said, if Dan can find a suspect or two, we need good forensic evidence – you know that. So we've taken some photographs, and taken a sample of the doormat and a piece of tile to identify the accelerant. Oh, and there was what was left of a rag that was most likely soaked with fuel, set light to and dropped through the letter box."

"Not a match?" Dominic asked.

"Ah, you'd never make an arsonist, lad. A match could go out before you even got it through the slot. No, a nice bit of burning rag is what you need. The pattern of the fire and the pattern of the burn pretty clearly show us that the liquid flowed through the letter box, and it's pretty clear the seat – the origin – of the fire is on this side of the door." He shook his head. "I know, I know. Nothing that wasn't bleeding obvious. The important thing is to pin down what the accelerant actually is."

"So if we find a likely suspect with traces of the same accelerant on their clothing, it's a point in our favour," Lizzie expanded.

"Of course," Phil said, "the bad news is that to get the accelerant analysis done could take weeks, or even months. The lab situation is a national nightmare at the moment."

"Wonderful," she said, even though she knew that already. "Oh, well. Maybe we'll get lucky with a witness or a camera." She looked at the door. "The door looks a mess. Will it still be secure until we can get a new one?"

One of the other investigators turned around.

"You're lucky there," she said, coming to join them. "Sorry, we haven't met. Sarah Steed, Fire Scene Investigator. Your door must be a fire door – FD30 or some similar composite, so it's stood up to the fire fairly well."

"It's what was there when we moved in," said Dominic.

"Well, I gather you put it out pretty quickly, which obviously helps. We haven't actually tried closing the door and locking it, but I think it'll be fine. It just doesn't look so pretty."

Lizzie nodded and turned to Phil again. "What about the approach to the house? Any footprints or whatever?"

"Not much," he said. "It was dry last night, of course, and your driveway is tarmac. No sign of anyone having obligingly stepped in a flower bed either."

"You're not going to turn much up, are you?"

He looked unhappy. "We'll keep working the scene, but it isn't looking great, no."

She sighed. "Okay, Phil. You can only do your best. I'll leave you to it and we'll get off to work."

11

Back in the day, before the coming of the monstrous blocks of flats, the Northfields estate had been smaller, consisting of two up/two down Victorian terraced houses. According to older locals, it had been a nice place to live, more like a village than part of the urban sprawl that Aylesbury had become.

Those flats had heralded the unwelcome changes that had led to the estate's notoriety. Local coppers joked that even the police dogs donned body armour and drew firearms before going there, and that they went in groups of four, just to be on the safe side.

There were times when it seemed not so much of an exaggeration. Council initiatives to sort it out had come and gone, but the reputation, and the behaviour that went with it, lived on. Some years ago, there had been calls to pull down the flats and replace them with nicer accommodation that didn't include hidden walkways, darkened stairwells and lifts that worked so rarely that they were more often used as toilets than means of travel. But doing so was easier talked about than done in cash-strapped times when public sector budgets were tight.

The Upmans, despite being a nightmare, didn't live in the block, but in one of the older properties. It was fair to say that 'house-proud' wasn't the first word one would associate with it, but it was a long way from some of the worst examples on the estate.

Gaynor Upman, tall, wide and blonde, rolled her eyes at the sight of the warrant cards, and became characteristically animated when told her home was about to be searched.

"You can't do that," she declared, filling the door frame with her formidable presence.

"We can if we've got one of these." DS Jason Bell showed her the search warrant. "I know you've seen one before."

Dan had decided to have Jason alongside him. Joan Collins was the better interviewer, but he half-suspected that Gaynor would try to intimidate a smaller woman. Joan was no pushover, but Dan wanted to keep focus. So, while he and Jason were here, Joan and DC Natalie Chen were leading enquiries among Lizzie's neighbours to see if anyone had seen or heard anything.

"I have," Gaynor sniffed. "Bloody perverts, going through my underwear. I swear some went missing last time."

"Really?" Jason raised an eyebrow. "You should have raised a complaint."

"Fat lot of good that'd do me. Think I don't know there's a conspiracy against us?"

"Gaynor," Dan said mildly, "the warrant says it's happening. So you can go on arguing the toss with us on the doorstep in front of the neighbours, or you can let us in and let us do our jobs."

She treated them to another eye roll and stonked inside, leaving them to follow her.

The air inside was pervaded by a slightly seedy, grubby smell that matched the state of the house. While the search team went about their work, Gaynor hovered, going from room to room, grumbling about the mess they were making.

The small living room was overstocked with flashy furniture. Gaynor announced their presence with grumpy protests about police harassment to her short, skinny husband, Carl, who sat slouched on the sofa alongside his middle son, Archie. Both were trying to feign disinterest. Dan assumed the youngest son was at school. Or off somewhere, playing truant.

He realised he had no idea how the family earned – or at least 'got' – their living, but he knew that pre-judging could be a mistake.

Long before every nook and cranny had been investigated, Dan had already decided they weren't going to find anything. If there had been any clothes reeking of accelerant, they'd either been washed and were drying on the clothes airer on the landing, or they'd been dumped somewhere. There was no sign of any container that might have contained the fuel, either. The tiny garden shed was a jumble of tools so rusty that they might never have been used.

Finally, Dan sent the bulk of the team back to base, remaining with Jason to ask some questions.

There were plenty of unoccupied seats in the living room, and not all of them were piled with unironed washing. Gaynor parked herself next to her husband, and Jason made to sit down on a bright green armchair.

"What do you think you're doing?" Gaynor jabbed a stubby finger his way. "You two can stand. You won't be stopping long."

He reddened slightly and straightened up. But he gave her a friendly smile. "My apologies."

"Just get on with it, will you?"

Dan deliberately made a meal of taking out his notebook and opening it at a blank page.

"First of all, thanks for inviting us in," he began.

She laughed scornfully. "Like I had a choice. So what are you trying to fit me up for now?"

"No one's trying to fit you up, Gaynor, but you were seen to make a threatening gesture towards a police officer outside Aylesbury Crown court a couple of days ago." He reminded her of the date and time.

"Never happened."

"DCI Archer says differently. Subsequently, her car was found vandalised—"

"Nothing to do with me. Who says it was me?"

"And last night there was a fire at her home."

"Yeah? Well, she needs to be more careful with her chip pan, don't she?"

He sighed. "It wasn't an accident, Gaynor."

"No? Shame. Did her house burn down? I call that karma, I do. Lying bitch. All coppers are liars. Look how you framed my Dougie."

"The jury didn't agree with you," Jason remarked.

But Dan didn't want to get into that. "We're not talking about that case. Where were you last night? Around 3am?"

She grinned. "In bed, of course. With me husband here. Sleeping like a baby. We had a nice shag before we went to sleep, if you want to know."

Carl had the decency to wince. Dan suppressed a shudder, trying to blot out the image. "I don't."

"Well, I always sleep well on a shag, that's all I'm saying. The boys were tucked up in their rooms, too. Apart from poor Dougie, in that awful prison."

"How do you know they were in their rooms, if you were asleep?" Jason asked.

"I know my boys. No way they'd be out, getting up to anything like starting fires. They like a laugh, but they're good lads."

"Their laughs seem to terrify the locals," said Dan. "Fireworks in bins, car vandalism – there's a coincidence. Threats of violence. Then there's the loud parties, the public drug abuse…"

"The locals are pussies. None of their complaints have ended up in court, have they? Besides, what's this got to do with a car or a fire? You found any actual proof that we had anything to do with it? Cos you planted it, if you have."

Carl Upman leaned forward casually, his face transforming as a crafty smile appeared. Whatever else he was, there was an intelligence behind his eyes.

"Have you, Inspector?" he said, his voice the wheezy rasp of a heavy smoker. "Have you got one shred of evidence?"

He hadn't, but he'd still wanted to see the family's reaction to being questioned.

"I can't comment on that," Dan said. "It's not unreasonable to speak to someone who has a grudge against the local police and establish their whereabouts."

"I suppose not," Carl said. "And you've got your answer, haven't you? Now, if we're not going to be talking about evidence, this interview is over. When you've got something more interesting to say, we can have another chat. In the meantime, you can see yourselves out."

"We're not nearly done."

"No? Arrest us then. Otherwise, piss off, the pair of you."

Gaynor, who was generally regarded as wearing the trousers in this household, was looking at him adoringly. There was evidently more to the relationship than met the eye. Archie was sniggering.

Dan heaved a conviction he didn't entirely feel into his voice. "Oh, we'll be talking again, Mr Upman."

"Missing you already." He was looking at his phone again, his thumbs busy.

"That went well," Jason said, back in Dan's car.

"Hardly surprising," said Dan. "I know we could have waited until we did have evidence to confront them with. But I wanted them to know we've got our eyes on them, in case they've got any other surprises in mind for Lizzie."

"You're liking them for the fire, as well as for the car, then?"

"They're my prime suspects, yes. Two attacks aimed at her inside forty eight hours, both with 'lowlife' written all over them? I know cops make enemies, but Gaynor's the one lowlife to have made a blatant threat, in precisely the same time period."

The other threat, made and apparently retracted, by Cameron Connolly, wasn't common knowledge within the team. Yet, even as he discounted it, Dan wondered. Cameron wasn't classic lowlife material, but there were plenty within the pyramid he and his family controlled who were. The Connollys had ears everywhere. What if word of Gaynor's cut-throat gesture and the vandalised car had reached them?

Neither Lizzie nor Dan had thought the fire had the Connollys' signature on it, but what if that was the whole point?

Lizzie's gut had told her Grace Connolly was sincere in her belief that Cameron had withdrawn his threat, but she didn't know the woman, and the conversation had happened over the phone, with no opportunity to study her facial expressions or body language.

Maybe it was time to pay Cameron Connolly a visit.

*

The door to door enquiries in Lizzie Archer's street were to take in as many neighbours as could be found at home. Joan Collins enjoyed being a team player, and would normally be as happy doing door to door as any other task. But she found herself feeling a little disappointed that it was Jason, and not her, who was accompanying Dan in his call on the Upman family.

She didn't begrudge Jason exactly. He was a good friend, and she'd been delighted when he'd been promoted to DS, and even happier that he'd been able to stay in the team at the Vale. She just couldn't help worrying that maybe Dan didn't think she was up to it any more. That he might feel she'd lost something of her edge following the traumatic events two years ago.

She knew she'd been very lucky to have made a full recovery from her own head injury, with no lasting damage, but recover she had. Charlie was something else, and it hurt Joan's heart to see her take one step back for every step forward. But Charlie was vocally determined that her own struggles weren't going to affect Joan's ability to do her job. On the very rare occasions Joan had wanted to take time out to support her, she'd practically pushed her out the door. If Dan had any difficulties with her performance, she wished he'd just come out and say so.

Or maybe she was overthinking, she thought. She'd been as shocked and upset as anyone about the fire at Lizzie's home, and acutely aware that the outcome could have been far worse than it had been. The whole team wanted to catch those responsible, and quickly, and if this was the part Dan wanted her to play, she would do it to the very best of her ability. And Joan had been asked to make sure she spoke to Margaret Pearson, directly opposite Lizzie's home, herself.

Dan had put the woman's age in her seventies, but Joan suspected she might be a little younger, albeit a little old-fashioned in her dress. She seemed disappointed that Joan wouldn't come in for a cup of tea and a chat. Perhaps loneliness explained why she apparently took such an interest in her neighbours. But Natalie Chen was working the street with her, and she didn't want her colleague to wonder where she had got to.

"My boss said you were one of the neighbours who came out after the fire," she said to her. "Even brought some tea over. That was kind of you."

"Well," Margaret said, "you've got to look out for your neighbours, haven't you? There's only me, since my husband died, so I'd hope they look out for me, too." She wrung her hands. "Poor Lizzie and Dominic. Are they all right?"

"They're okay. It wasn't nice for them, of course."

"It can't have been. What a shock! For all of us, really."

Joan nodded and cut to the chase. "But about last night. When did you become aware something had happened?"

"Only when the police cars turned up. It all got a bit noisy out there after that, and I'm a light sleeper at the best of times. I'd wake up if I heard a pin drop."

"Really?" Joan looked at her curiously. "What about before the police arrived? Around three in the morning? I don't suppose you heard anything unusual?"

She gave the thought consideration, and Joan waited patiently.

"Well," she said slowly. "I don't know you'd call it unusual. But now you mention it, I did hear someone walking down the street. The footsteps seemed to stop somewhere just opposite. I think I assumed someone was coming home. I remember looking at the time on my bedside clock, and it was... now, what time was it? Yes, I'm fairly sure it was five to three. Then I must have nodded off, but I soon woke up again."

"The police cars?"

"No, someone was running. I got up and looked out the window. There was someone running down the road."

"Which direction?"

But Margaret Pearson's hand was covering her mouth, her eyes stricken. "Oh, my God. You think someone *started* the fire." She pressed her knuckles to her temples. "Stupid. That could have been important, and I didn't give it another thought until now."

Joan patted her shoulder. "Don't worry about that now. But yes, it could be important, Margaret, so could you tell me exactly what you saw? What direction were they running?"

"Towards Walton Road." Margaret pointed off to her left, the opposite direction to where she had entered, or where Lizzie would normally enter on her way home from Aylesbury.

"Male or female?"

"Oh, a young lad, I think. He had one of those hoodie things up? Dark, maybe black or dark blue."

"No chance it could have been a girl?"

"I suppose it could have," she said doubtfully.

"But you think they were young. What gave you that impression?"

"I suppose I was just assuming again. I'm pretty useless as a witness, aren't I?" She looked upset. "Let me think. Well, they were slim, and they were quite athletic, I suppose. They didn't run like an older person, is the only way I can explain it."

Joan thought that could apply to anyone up to maybe forty, if they were fit. Gaynor Upman was somewhere around the upper end of that age scale, but no one was going to describe her as slim or athletic. One of her kids, though...

"Did they get in a car?"

"No. I watched them run to the end of the road and around the corner. Right, they turned, I remember that. Then I couldn't see them any more."

"Did you hear a car start up, or a motorbike?"

Margaret frowned. "I don't think so. But then, once I lost sight of them, I got back into bed. I might have drifted off."

"This is really helpful. I don't suppose you happened to look at your clock again?"

"Three minutes past three."

Joan made a note. "And was there anything else about them?"

She squeezed her eyes shut, as if willing an image to come. Opened them again. "He was carrying something. Like a briefcase."

"An attaché case?" Joan frowned, then looked at her. "It couldn't have been a jerry can, could it?"

"What?" Margaret's eyes widened. "You mean petrol? Oh, my God. But yes, it could have been. I knew it hadn't been a case, even as I was saying it."

"One last question. I don't suppose you have a CCTV camera that might have captured any of this?"

"Sorry, no. I wouldn't know how to work it."

"Okay," Joan said. "Can you do me a big favour, though? I'd love you to keep all this to yourself for now. We don't want people speculating, nor for people to think they remember something because they heard it second hand." She'd known it to happen.

"Mum's the word," Margaret said. "I know exactly what you mean. Some people do like to talk, don't they?"

12

When the Connollys' business had expanded into the Vale, and Cameron Connolly had moved into the area to take charge there, he'd made his home in one of the richest villages in Britain: Great Missenden. Of what estate agents probably described as 'generous proportions', the house stood in its own grounds on posh Martinsend Lane, at a comfortable distance from neighbouring properties.

Dan knew that Cameron had learned well from his father: a bit of generosity never went amiss if you were aiming for a nice thick veneer of respectability. Ask the locals, and they'd tell you how he invested a decent amount in raffle tickets at the village fete each year, donated prizes, paid a hefty – but not ostentatious – sum for his British Legion poppy, and generally put his hand in his pocket whenever money was needed, like donations to village restoration projects.

He also spent money locally, often spotted dropping in at the Nag's Head for a pint, or dining at La Petite Auberge in the High Street.

Unlike the late Murray Connolly, he didn't hang out with celebrities or court celebrity status himself. As a consequence, he was simply known as a nice guy not short of a bob or two.

The house had the security and privacy of its own gates and electronic security system. Cameron himself answered the intercom when Dan pressed the button on the gate, and cheerfully gave him directions to the brick-built so-called summer house that included his comfortable study. Not that Dan needed directions. He'd been here before.

The study hadn't changed much. Dan remembered the big desk, filing cabinets, comfy sofa and small meeting table. All tasteful and expensive-looking.

"I remember you," Cameron said to Dan as he showed them in. He jabbed a finger in Jason's direction. "Not you, though." He smiled. "I know the accent, though. I'm from Glasgow stock myself."

"Indeed," Jason said. Cameron looked as if he was hoping for more, but it wasn't forthcoming. Jason knew better than to share any personal stuff with him.

The two detectives settled on the proffered sofa. Or, at least, Dan settled as much as he ever would in this man's presence. The first time the Connollys had crossed his radar had very nearly been his last. He still bore the scar where the bullet had entered his body and, even though there was no organ damage, he'd lost enough blood that day for it to be touch and go.

Cameron Connolly hadn't pulled the trigger and hadn't been directly responsible for the shooting, but he and his family had surely been behind the chain of events that had led to it. As always, it just couldn't be proved. And now he stood by a fancy coffee machine, flashing a genial smile.

"Can I get you lads coffee? Tea?"

"We're good, thanks," Dan said.

Cameron sat behind his handsome desk. Dan noted that the ostentation even stretched to a very fancy paper knife, fashioned like a small sword with a jewelled hilt and sitting in a chunk of quartz or granite, like Excalibur, King Arthur's sword in the stone. Some sort of kingly allegory?

"So," Cameron said, "to what do I owe the pleasure?"

"Where were you last night, around 3am?"

He chuckled. "Direct. I like that. Of course, it's *Inspector* Baines now, isn't it?" As if noting Dan's attention to it, he reached out and withdrew the knife from its setting, turning it over in his hands. "Lizzie wasn't the only one to get a leg up after that shocking business with the body in the concrete, was she? Nice that it's all in the family. Give her my good wishes when you see her."

"I gather you didn't exactly offer her good wishes last time you saw her," Dan couldn't resist saying. *And you made threats against my little girl, you bastard.*

He held up his hands. "It's true. As you'd probably known, we'd just cremated my dad and my brother. I was a bit emotional. I wanted someone to lash out at. I was in the wrong."

"You followed her home."

"Guilty. It was a mistake."

"Still, you know where she lives now. And you didn't answer my question. Where were you last night?"

"Home in bed, like any normal person. Why?"

"What about your people?"

"My *people*?" He chuckled. "That makes me sound frightfully important. Do you mean my staff? Only I don't know what they do with their own time. You'd have to ask them."

"All right." Dan was prepared to play the game, up to a point. "Perhaps I could have a staff list then?"

"Sure. I take it data protection allows you to ask for that?"

"In connection with crime prevention and detection, yes."

"Good enough. Leave me a card, and I'll see it's emailed asap."

"For the record though," Jason said, "would any of them have been in Long Lees at the time we were asking about?"

"As, I said," Cameron began, "you'll need to..." He ground to a halt. "Long Lees? Has something happened to Lizzie? DCI Archer?"

His surprise seemed genuine enough, although Dan supposed he'd had plenty of practice in acting the innocent.

"All I can say," he replied, "is we're asking in connection with an incident in Long Lees in the early hours of this morning."

"And I just happen to have had a recent altercation with your DCI, on her doorstep, in that very village. I'm not stupid, DI Baines. What's happened? Because, I can assure you, it's nothing to do with me. But *is* she okay?"

"DCI Archer and her husband are fine. She'll be touched by your concern." He imagined Cameron would have ways of finding out, if he didn't know already.

"Well, that's good to hear. As I say, I was here all night, sleeping. My wife can vouch for me, not that it's much of an alibi, I know. But there'll be CCTV footage showing I didn't go anywhere. As for my 'people'..." He made quotes with his fingers. "...you'll be wanting to ask them for yourself. I'll get that list to you."

"Thank you."

"And I'll ask around myself. I'm not without contacts, purely professional, obviously, but I know people who have their ears to the ground."

Dan shook his head. "We can really do without people conducting unofficial investigations. However 'well meaning'." He took the opportunity to make air quotes of his own.

Cameron Connolly looked about to argue, then simply nodded. "Understood. Still, if I do happen to hear anything?"

"Let us know, obviously."

"Of course. So was there anything else?"

"We'll see ourselves out."

"One thing you should know, Inspector. I know my father had a bit of a reputation in Scotland, and it followed him down south, unfairly. And then my younger brother went off the rails a couple of times, and I understand how you guys took the opportunity to tar the whole family – apart from Grace, maybe – with that same dodgy brush. But we've never been charged with anything because there's nothing there. And, now Dad's gone, we're all determined that our image will be even more squeaky-clean. So, whatever you're investigating, it's nothing to do with us."

"Good to know."

"And, in the unlikely event that any of my employees is involved, I'll deal with it."

"I hope you mean you'll report back to us?"

He smiled, his eyes twinkling. "Why, of course."

*

"Impressions?" Dan asked Jason as he started the car.

"He's smooth, all right. I wouldn't trust him any farther than I could throw him. And I thought at times what he didn't say was much more interesting than what came out of his mouth. But I don't know, guv. I thought his surprise seemed genuine enough when we said there's been an incident in Long Lees. Although he was quick enough to make the connection with the boss."

"But then, if it was anything to do with him, he'd have been expecting us and had plenty of time to rehearse his lines. It'll be interesting to follow up those staff lists, when we get them."

"Unless he conveniently forgets to send them."

"He won't do that. He'll bend over backwards to be cooperative. Still, he remains on our suspects list, I reckon. We still need to speak to a guy called Rob Thomas."

"Who's he?"

Dan didn't feel entirely comfortable sharing the details, but the team needed to know what they were dealing with.

"He's actually Lizzie's ex from way back, before she came here."

"When she was in the Met?"

"Yep. He's suddenly turned up in our neck of the woods. It was him who sent those flowers that were delivered to the station. It sounds like he's practically stalking her. And he appeared at their house last night and this morning, when she and her husband were there. She says he claimed he'd gone round to apologise for his behaviour and then acted all concerned about the fire. Maybe he was, but it'll be interesting to know what his movements were last night."

"You think he might have started it?"

"It sounds like there's something going on with him. And he's recently quit the fire service."

Jason whistled. "So he should know a thing or two about arson."

"Exactly. Lizzie made him give some contact details to the uniform on the door. He's staying at the Travelodge, but it might be easier to give him a ring and ask him if he can come in."

"I could call him now, if you have the number handy."

He found it in his notebook and read it out. While Jason made the call, Dan drove up to the gates, waited for them to open, and drove out onto the road.

"Voicemail," Jason said. "Shall I try the hotel?"

"No, let's hang fire. We'll go back to the station and have a catch up meeting with the rest of the team. I'm itching to know what CCTV might have uncovered, and whether CSI found anything at the scene. This case could yet turn out to be an easy one to crack."

13

It felt strange to Dan to be having a briefing meeting without Lizzie's presence. She was usually Chief Investigating Officer for major cases, but she still tended to sit in on the ones where she wasn't, albeit adopting her predecessor's practice of sitting in the back. Dan and Lizzie's other DI, Lara Moseley, both appreciated the support.

He knew she was at a meeting with Lara at this very moment, catching up on a couple of her cases – one domestic violence and one indecent assault. Meanwhile, Superintendent Josh Stowe sat in the front row. When he'd first arrived, he would do so all the time, but his appearances had fallen off once he'd properly found his feet. That he was here for a relatively minor arson said much about how seriously he took an attack on one of his officers.

"As we suspected," Joan Collins kicked off her report on door to door enquiries, "almost all the neighbours were sound asleep when the fire started and only woke up when the excitement started with emergency services on the scene."

"Almost all?" Dan arched an eyebrow.

"The woman opposite, Margaret Pearson – the one you hoped might have seen or heard something? She's a light sleeper, and says she heard footsteps approach and then stop opposite, a little before 3am. Shortly after, she heard running. She looked out the window and saw what she described as a tall young man in a hoodie legging it up towards Walden Road."

"In a hoodie?"

"I know, I know. She admitted it could have been anyone. Fit and athletic, was all she was sure about. But get this. They were carrying what could easily be a jerry can. It has to be our arsonist."

"Will?" Dan turned to DC Will Tyler, who had been leading efforts with CCTV. "Any cameras that could have picked him up?"

"No, guv, not as such. Well, there might be private ones."

"None in Lizzie's road," Joan said, "but maybe some of the swanky houses in Walden Road have them."

"Trouble is, they'll almost certainly be motion detecting, so unlikely to help. However," Will went on, a smile stealing over his face, "Walden Road exits onto major roads at both ends, and we've been looking over ANPR within a radius of the boss's road. Traffic at that time was light, of course. I know we came across a handful of cars on the move in what sounds like the right place, right time. We'll run DVLA checks and see who the owners are."

"Top priority," Dan told him. He looked at Natalie Chen. "Natalie, can you give Will a hand with that, please? I mean, if a suspect's name pops up, it's bingo, but I want to know who these people are, anything we can dig up on them, and especially if they've got a record." His gaze swivelled back to Will. "Do we have a forensics report yet?"

"We do, although there's nothing new in it. I know you'll want to read it yourself, but it's confirmed that accelerant was poured through the letter box and a lit rag seems to have followed it in. No useable fingerprints, and it was dry last night, so no shoe prints either. Sorry. Phil Gordon wanted you to know he's been over everything three times, just to be sure he hasn't missed anything."

"I don't doubt it."

"Anyway, he said he was sorry."

Dan knew Phil liked Lizzie, so he didn't doubt that either.

"Nothing at the Upmans, either," he said. "If it was one of them that set the fire, then one lesson they might just have learned from the Mason Swain case is not to chuck incriminating evidence where it can easily be found. Like DCI Archer's neighbours, they say they were asleep in bed at the time in question. We spoke to Cameron Connolly" – he tapped the photograph on the incident board – "who she also has some history with, and he says the same. In his case, I believe him.

Even if he is behind the fire, he won't be the one who started it. More likely some young thug a fair way down the food chain."

"What did you make of Connolly?" Superintendent Stowe wanted to know. "I know the DCI doesn't think it's his style."

Dan shrugged. "Trouble is, sir, it's almost impossible to tell what's going on behind his eyes. For what it's worth, I don't think this is his usual signature either – not for a personal grudge – but he's clever enough to have opted for a method that we wouldn't expect or associate with him."

"He sent us a list of his 'staff'," Jason added. "It was pretty short. Just people officially on his payroll, I think. Apart from his so-called assistant, Cal Dougan, they're genuine gardeners, domestic cleaners, that sort of thing. I checked them out. Only Dougan's dodgy. I did phone him, and he was at home with his husband all night when the fire happened. Says they have CCTV that will confirm it."

"Lizzie mentioned a…" Stowe hesitated. "…an old acquaintance she's been having some problems with. Have you spoken to him yet?"

"Next on my list, sir. He wasn't answering his phone when we tried before. Of course, if the neighbour, Mrs Pearson's, guess that the figure she saw running is a *young* male is mistaken, then the man we're talking about – Rob Thomas – could easily fit the bill. Recently left the fire service, so he'll have kept in shape."

"A fireman turned arsonist?" Natalie Chen said. "There was a film on telly at the weekend where that happened. Robert de Niro was in it, I think."

"Maybe we should check de Niro's alibi," Will Tyler suggested. There were a few chuckles.

"At the moment, we've probably got as much on de Niro as anyone else," Dan said, "so maybe we should."

"So what's the story with this fireman, guv?" Natalie asked.

The newest member of Dan's team, Natalie had moved across from DI Lara Moseley's side to replace Jason Bell when he was promoted. The switch had been aimed at broadening her experience, and she fitted in well. One of the things Dan liked about her was her tenacity, and she clearly wasn't going to let the matter of Rob go.

He knew it was stupid, but he – and evidently the Super – felt awkward about sharing Lizzie's private business – although, with the kerfuffle in front of a PC this morning, practically on her doorstep, the word might already be spreading. And keeping information from the team was expecting them to work with one hand behind their backs.

"He's an ex-boyfriend, from years back," he said. "Apparently he showed up out of the blue a couple of days ago, saying they should never have split up, and he's been making a nuisance of himself ever since."

"He knows she's married?" Joan said, her face clouding.

"Dominic's met him, yes. He turned up outside her house this morning and was there last night, and I think it almost came to some argy-bargy."

"So he's stalking her?" Joan persisted.

"I doubt we could call it that yet," he told her, "but he certainly merits keeping an eye on."

"Bit odd, though," Jason mused. "Trying to burn her house down with her inside isn't the ideal way to rekindle her feelings for him."

"You'd think not," said Joan, "but he wouldn't be the first ex to decide that, if he can't have her, no one will."

She spoke from bitter experience.

"True enough," he conceded. "Jason, get hold of this guy as a priority. We really do need a chat with him. And Will, Natalie – put everything you have into running down those cars and who owns them."

He looked at his watch. The day was running away, and he had the sinking feeling that this case was going to spill over into the weekend, when he was supposed to be visiting his son in prison. It was something of huge importance to him, but so was making sure Lizzie was safe.

If he had to make a choice, he wasn't sure which way he'd go.

*

Lizzie's phone rang just as she was sitting down with a cup of coffee she'd made herself after her meeting with Lara Moseley. Dominic was back at the house.

"I owe Phil and his team a pint," he told her. "Not much they can do about the actual damage, but they've done their best to clean up and leave everything tidy. The insurance have made all the right noises too. They've emailed me a form to complete, so I'll try and do that at the back end of the day. Do you think you'll be late tonight?"

"Not too late, I hope. There's some stuff to catch up on after this morning's disruption, and I'd like to have a relaxing weekend for a change with a clear conscience."

"Good luck with that." He knew her too well. She could hear the smile in his voice. "The reason I asked is I might be out by the time you get home."

"Oh?"

"Yeah, I got a call from a potential client who found our website and might have a project for us. He's in Aylesbury today and suggested we meet in a pub this evening for a chat. The Five Birds."

"That dump?"

"I know. I wouldn't have agreed, but things are still picking up after lockdown, so you have to grab the opportunities."

"I get it. Any idea when you'll be home?"

"I'll have to play it by ear. Give you a call when I'm on my way."

"Okay, see you later. Love you."

"Love you too," he said, and was gone.

She raised her cup to her lips and a tap on her open door nearly made her spill the contents.

"Sorry," Dan said. "Didn't mean to make you jump."

"Come in," she said. "I've just made this. Want a cup?"

"No, you're all right. I just wanted to catch you up on the fire and where we are. Well…" He shrugged. "Where we're not, really."

He brought her up to date. No one, so far they could pin down, in the right place at the right time, but none of the possible suspects exactly had unshakeable alibis either.

"I agree with you about the cars," she said. "It would be rather good if we could put someone with links to the Upmans in the area. The Connollys, for that matter."

"Or Rob Thomas. He's not answering his phone and it seems he's not at the hotel either."

She made a face. "He's in the wind?"

"I'm not saying that. His stuff's still at the hotel, and his black VW Golf is in the car park. He can't be that far away. I'm sure we'll get hold of him soon."

"Well, he did say he was planning on settling here. If he's still clinging to that ridiculous idea, I suppose he could be out house hunting or interviewing for jobs. Wouldn't need the car if it's all in the town."

"His car's not on Will's list, but I suppose he could have dodged the cameras somehow last night. There are no Upman cars there, either, but they could have nicked one for the job."

She nodded, then looked at him. "How much have you told the team about Rob?"

"As much as they need to know to do their jobs. I didn't like it, but…"

"Dead right, though," she said, feeling some heat in her face. "This is just another case, and you need to crack it. And maybe I've been discounting him as a suspect just because I don't want to think it could be him. But I can't deny he's been weird. Even so, most of my money's still riding on Gaynor bloody Upman and her clan. So fingers crossed one of those vehicles is theirs."

"I was thinking of asking for overtime on this one," he said.

She put down her cup and gave him a sharp look.

"That's sweet, but you know better than that. We're already probably giving this more resource than a fairly small arson deserves."

She knew him well enough to know when he didn't like what he was hearing.

"Sheer luck it wasn't a bloody big arson," he pointed out. "Sheer luck this isn't a murder case."

As a victim, she felt exactly the same. She felt violated and threatened and was still trying not to think too much about what could all too easily have happened to her and Dominic. But this was her workplace, and she was determined to be professional here.

"I doubt the DPP would buy that," she said. "Okay, so Dougie Upman killed Mason Swain because he's a bloody idiot who most likely carried a knife to play the big man and didn't expect resistance to his mugging enterprise. It wasn't a planned, deliberate killing. And, although I certainly can see Gaynor setting the fire out of spite, would it have been in the hope that I'd die? Or more likely just blind maliciousness with no thought to the possible consequences?" She smiled. "Still, it was pretty reckless. It could be a lengthy jail term for somebody."

He nodded. "Whatever. I want to nail whoever did it sooner than later. We can debate the charges afterwards."

"And that's fine. But we both know we probably wouldn't have all hands to the pumps over the weekend if it was an ordinary member of the public's house. Besides, you've got your prison visit tomorrow."

"It won't take all day. I suppose I could reschedule, if it comes to that."

"No way. You're not missing that. You're going. How are you feeling about it?"

He frowned. "Honestly? Nervous. Maybe part of me is looking for an excuse to back out."

She couldn't imagine the turmoil he must be going through.

"And that cop from Scotland is coming down on Monday?"

"Yeah, DI Alec McGivering. I'll need to give him a fair bit of time, I think. Is that okay?"

"If it helps them clear up a number of murders, it absolutely has to be okay. And this is probably as good a time as any. You know this job. It won't stay quiet forever."

Her phone rang. Superintendent Stowe.

"I'd best take this," she said.

"Of course." He checked his watch. "I'd better see how Will and Natalie are getting on with those vehicles."

"Hi, Josh," she said as he headed for the door.

"Afternoon, Lizzie. It occurs to me that you still haven't given me an answer as to whether you want my job. I'm definitely going, by the way."

"Well, congratulations." She realised she'd still been hoping he wouldn't.

"Thank you. Look, I know after last night it's probably been the last thing on your mind but, if you're interested, I'm quite keen to get you recommended today, before the powers that be get wedded to some other candidate."

In fact, she'd given it a lot of thought today. She was still bereft at the idea of not being a detective, something she loved and was good at. But recent events suggested that a spell out of the front line might be no bad thing. And, although Josh had mentioned no other names, she could imagine a couple of other Chief Inspectors in Thames Valley who might be keen on succeeding him, and they weren't people she thought she would relish working under.

Of course, it could always be someone from another force, or another fast tracker parachuted in like Josh himself had. That had worked out well in the end, and she enjoyed the working relationship that had evolved. It didn't mean she'd get lucky a second time.

"Are you still there?"

"Yes, sorry. And the answer's yes." She took a deep breath. "I'd like to run for the job."

She'd said it.

"That's great." He did sound pleased. "I'm on that as soon as I get back to my office. Of course, there's no guarantee."

"I know that. I'm very grateful for your confidence in me."

"You've earned it. How are things with the house?"

"We're back in. Just a matter of claiming on our insurance and getting the damage fixed."

"I was at Dan's briefing. I wish we had someone in custody."

"Me too," she said. "But meanwhile, we've got plenty to do sorting out the mess they made. I'm in for a busy weekend."

14

With little he could do until either Rob Thomas was located or some of the team's other work yielded results, Dan found himself dwelling on the end of his conversation with Lizzie and thinking ahead – not for the first time – to tomorrow's prison visit. However many times he rehearsed what he might say in his mind, he continued to fear that he would make a complete mess of things and alienate his son before they could even attempt to build a relationship.

He kept coming back to the cases that were under review in Scotland and the North East, and the impending visit from McGivering. All his instincts told him to steer well clear of mentioning it tomorrow. To focus on establishing some sort of trust that could be built on, before getting onto more difficult ground.

The trouble was, if McGivering thought there was something there worth pursuing, he'd almost certainly want to interview Jack – *Peter*, he snarled at himself, *Peter* – and *Peter* would surely be convinced that Dan had known all about it and hadn't warned him.

He'd be damned whatever he did.

"Guv?" Will Tyler's voice cut into his thoughts. He realised he'd been miles away.

"Will," he said, reaching for some focus.

"We've run down all but one of those cars that were near the DCI's house last night, around the time the fire broke out. None of the owners looks likely to be our arsonist, on the face of it. Wrong ages, wrong locations. No criminal records. I mean, we ought to speak to them, to be sure, but…"

"Okay." He'd hoped for something more conclusive. "Let's do that."

"Joan and Jason are already on it. But—"

"Hang on." The penny dropped. "You said 'all but one'?"

"Yep. An old dark blue Vauxhall Astra. The owner's a Mrs..." He checked his notebook. "... Susan Bryson, aged sixty-four. She reported it stolen last night."

"Timing seems a bit coincidental."

"More than a bit." Will shifted his feet. "When I say it's not accounted for... it was found burned out in the Ivinghoe Beacon car park this morning."

The Beacon was a local landmark, with great views over the Chilterns on a clear day. The car park was the start of a footpath that led there, if you fancied the climb.

"I mean, whoever received the report, it was just another burned out car. Not what would normally get passed to our team."

"Quite." It didn't ease his frustration. "And are CSIs checking it out?"

"Well, it's been removed, but it's not high on their priority list."

"You mean it *wasn't*," Dan said. "It is now. It could always be an *actual* coincidence, of course but, if there's anything at all that connects to Lizzie's house fire, or any of our potential suspects, I want to know."

"A fire can hide a multitude of sins."

"We'd better hope we get lucky then."

Will smiled. "I guess there's a first time for everything."

"I'll give Phil Gordon a ring and try to get it shunted up the queue." He frowned. "By the way, I'm assuming there's still no sign of Rob Thomas."

"No. I'll keep trying though."

"Please. Can you also get someone to call the Travelodge if he still doesn't answer? There could be plenty of good reasons why we can't get hold of him, but it feels more than a bit suspicious, doesn't it?"

"On it, guv. Oh, and I'm also thinking it's a long walk back when you've just burned your transport. Whoever torched the car may have had an accomplice pick them up, but I've got someone ringing round the local taxi firms, just in case they did any pickups overnight from perhaps a two-mile radius of where the car was dumped."

"Good thinking, Will. If we get a hit, we can see what name was given – probably not the real name, although you never know if it was a dimwit Upman – and where they dropped them."

Dan could feel his early start beginning to catch up with him. Modern policing was all about 'best use of resources', and there were never enough resources to go around. Every now and then, a tragedy happened because something hadn't been judged important enough in the big scheme of things.

He really hoped this wasn't going to be one of those cases.

15

With the likelihood of Dominic being out for at least part of the evening, Lizzie hadn't exactly rushed home from the office, but she'd still got away relatively early by her standards. Dan had brought her up to date on all things potentially relating to the arson at her home. A burned out stolen car that might have been in the area but wouldn't be seriously checked out by CSI until next week. Still no definitive clues to the identity of the hooded figure Margaret Pearson had seen at the time of the fire. And no idea about where Rob was.

Rob. It wasn't clear how long he intended staying in the area. But the fact that his car and his stuff were still at the hotel suggested that he still wasn't taking the hint. He'd professed that he'd come here for her, and she really couldn't imagine him sticking around if he'd accepted that she wasn't interested.

Still, setting fire to her home with her inside would be a funny way of winning her back, especially if the fire had really taken hold, with fatal results. Unless he'd been playing out some mad scenario where he 'just happened to come along' and rescue her, earning her gratitude and more.

She couldn't really see it. It felt way too fanciful. Yet, she had to admit, the Rob who'd been haunting her the past few days was unrecognisable from the man she'd been in love with before she'd been disfigured. Something must have happened to effect such a change. She didn't buy that it was simply a realisation that he still loved her and had been wrong to dump her.

His mental health wasn't quite right, she acknowledged as she drove home, turning it over in her mind again. Something had tipped him into a fantasy world where Lizzie being happily married and not interested in him didn't fit the script. Had that made him not just a nuisance, but dangerous? He was erratic enough that she couldn't put her hand on her heart and say no to that.

As she approached her house, she was surprised to see Dominic's car in the drive. She hadn't expected him back so soon.

She let herself in and noted the low drone of the washing machine. A furry form came purring and seeking attention, seemingly none the worse for the trauma of the fire.

"Hiya," called Dominic from the kitchen.

"Hi." She surveyed the damage to her hallway. It was almost all too much, but she did her best to shake the feeling off. She slipped out of her coat, draped it over the bottom of the bannisters, and joined him. "You didn't go to your pub meeting then?"

He shrugged. "Yeah, but he never showed up. I tried calling him, but no reply. Bloody time waster." He waved a bottle of wine at her and she nodded. "Oh," he continued as he poured, "to cap it all, some stupid young guy blundered into me in the car park. Think he was on something, because I think he'd have gone down if he hadn't grabbed hold of me. Nearly had us both over. Anyhow, Christ knows what he'd been rolling in, but he got some muck all over my jacket."

"What sort of muck?"

"No idea. To be honest, I didn't even realise until I got indoors and switched the light on, and then I didn't really examine it too closely. Probably better not to know. I thought I'd wash it straight away and just hope it doesn't stain."

She rolled her eyes. "Marvellous." Sometimes shit just kept right on happening. "So that's what's in the machine?"

"Yeah. I added some of that stain remover powder." He handed her a glass.

She raised it in salute. "It's been as crap a week as they come, hasn't it?"

He sipped wine. "You could say that. I can't even be bothered cooking anything, can you?"

"At this time of night? Cheese on toast?"

His smile looked forced, but at least it was a smile. "Better idea. How about a takeaway?"

It sounded like the best idea she'd heard in ages.

*

Dan had changed out of his suit and was relaxing in the living room with a glass of wine before dinner when his phone rang and Phil Gordon's number came up on the screen.

"Phil? What can I do for you at this time on a Friday evening?"

"You can send me an IOU for a bottle of my favourite malt if you like my news."

He set his glass down. "What's the news?"

"Well," Phil began earnestly, "when you told me that burnt-out car might have been used in the attack on Lizzie's house, I thought the least I could do was take a team to have a look at it. Obviously, going over it properly will take time, and I'll make sure someone gets on that on Monday, but sometimes you get a lucky break straight off."

"And did you?" His pulse quickened.

"I'll let you be the judge, but we found the melted remains of a jerry can in the boot."

That got his attention.

"Did you now?"

"Oh, yes. I doubt it was used to torch the car. I mean, why put it in the boot if you're about to light it up? I'm suspecting there was a second can for that. But, wherever that one is, I reckon this can had probably been used earlier."

"As in starting a house fire in Long Lees?"

"Aye, that's my guess."

He nodded. "Mine too."

"I mean, who knows if we'll salvage any evidence worth a damn? Whoever set fire to that car made one hell of a mess of it, I'll give them that. But, come Monday, I'll get it crawled over. In the meantime, if you can find any other way of identifying the person who pinched it... I dunno, some CCTV that's been overlooked or whatever..."

"I'm not hopeful, but I'll get the weekend crew to keep looking. Assuming nothing else kicks off. You'll keep me posted on the forensic side?"

"Of course I will. Did you manage to pick up that ex-boyfriend of hers, by the way?"

"Last I heard, his phone kept going to voicemail and he hadn't returned to his hotel. As soon as he does, I'll know. Seeing as his car and his stuff's still there, I don't reckon he's done a runner or anything."

"Aye, well..." Phil hesitated for a beat. "I didn't like to embarrass Lizzie, but I couldn't help overhearing some of that row on their doorstep this morning."

"How heated was it?"

"Put it this way. I'd say Lizzie's hubby sounded more worked up than the ex was. I mean, you know him better than me, but I thought at one point he was going to lamp the feller. But then, I thought the ex was a bit too smooth-sounding, maybe protesting his innocence too much. And, let's face it, Lizzie and Dominic had a shock with the fire, their lovely house, all messed up. Only natural to be on a bit of a tight spring, especially if you think the threat's against your wife. I think my own sweet demeanour might have been tested."

Dan nodded, even though the person he was talking to was on the other end of a phone.

"Yeah, me too, I reckon. I just never realised Dominic could be riled so easily. It's a bit of a first."

They said their goodbyes and hung up. He sipped his wine reflectively, thinking about his own response when Lizzie told him Cameron Connolly had included his family in his threats. He'd said he'd kill him if he touched them, and he'd meant it at the time. He probably still did.

It sounded like Dominic hadn't been so rankled about Gaynor Upman. But then she hadn't talked about stealing Lizzie away from him.

He smiled to himself, knowing Dominic had no worries on that score. She'd confided to Dan more than once that her marriage was the best thing that had ever happened to her. He could still remember the person she'd been when she'd first walked into the office in Aylesbury: a bit spiky, a bit too quick to take offence. He'd realised later just how much her scarring and its aftermath had shattered her confidence. Even Dan had seen how the relationship had completed her.

Karen put her head around the door. "Dinner's about ready to dish up."

He stood up to take his wine through to join the woman who had made him whole again; her and Ellie, the child they'd toyed with naming Louise Elizabeth, after her aunt and her godmother. Somehow it hadn't felt quite right, so they'd turned the initials – L E – into a name that had felt perfect as soon as Karen suggested it.

Names. He had vowed to respect his son's wishes and call him Peter. He still had no idea of what sort of boy – *man* now, he amended – Peter McNeil was. He'd made another vow to himself though – not to dwell on what kind of man Jack Baines might have become, had the Invisible Man never come calling.

That way lay madness. Duncan McNeil had smashed his first family to bits, and almost taken Dan's sanity away with him. But those events had led him to the family he had today.

Tomorrow he would start to see how Peter might fit into that.

16

With a quiet, domestic weekend in prospect, and no particular plans, Lizzie and Dominic had decided to try and put their troubles to one side and have a decadent start to the day – no morning alarm, followed by breakfast in bed when they did surface.

As it turned out, the breakfast idea was delayed when Dominic had other ideas about how to start the day. Some time later, they were both ravenous and Lizzie had volunteered to go downstairs and arrange some cereal and toast.

While she made coffee and stacked a tray, she heard the odd car go by outside. None of them stopped, but she realised that each one brought with it a frisson of nervousness. If the arsonist could be identified and apprehended, she thought she would relax more. Rob had made a bit of a nuisance of himself, but he hadn't made any sort of contact since yesterday morning. She was still of the mind that questioning him in connection with the fire would be little more than a box-ticking exercise.

To her, it was pretty obvious that either Gaynor Upman or Cameron Connolly would prove to be behind the petrol attack – and that, whichever one it was, she probably had little to fear now from the other. Her instincts remained with Gaynor, but she knew she needed to keep an open mind and be vigilant. She'd told Dominic, Dan and Josh Stowe that she wasn't afraid. She'd told herself the same. Was she kidding everyone?

If she was so unconcerned, why had she slept so little last night? And why had the slightest sound outside had her getting up and going to the window?

She wondered if, subconsciously, she and Dominic were taking a quiet weekend as an opportunity to lie low. Inside their home they were not such easy targets, and nor was the house so vulnerable if it was occupied.

She shook such thoughts off as she carried their breakfast upstairs. Dominic was propped up in bed scrolling through the BBC news on his iPad.

"I don't know why I depress myself," he said. "Talk of another new strain of Covid, another boatload of migrants has overturned – twenty-odd dead this time – and more in-fighting in the government."

"If it's escapism you're looking for, we should subscribe to the Disney Channel," she said, putting the tray down between their respective sides of the bed and climbing back in.

"Not such a bad idea. Sometimes I think the world's being run by Disney characters anyway."

She was halfway through her breakfast when her phone rang. Cursing, she looked at the screen. Lara Moseley was the duty DI this morning, and her name had flashed up. Grimacing at Dominic, she accepted the call.

"What's up, Lara?"

"Morning, Lizzie. Look, I really hate to disturb you, but I thought you'd want a heads up. We've got a body on the Northfields estate. White male. Looks like a stabbing."

Gaynor Upman territory. Brilliant.

"Are you at the scene?"

"Yeah. I've got some uniforms securing the scene and CSI are on their way. I think it's going to be Phil, as he seems to get all the homicides. I dare say he'll be grumpy getting called out on a weekend."

"I'm sure. These buggers choose the worst times to kill each other. What about Dr Carlisle?" They needed a pathologist on the scene.

"I called her too. She's just back from a few days away, but she's coming. Otherwise, it would have been Alastair Fitzroy."

"Small mercies." Lizzie didn't like Fitzroy. He knew his work, but he always looked as if he should have retired years ago, and he acted like he was doing you a big favour turning out and considered everyone else to be stupid. She was always happier with Barbara Carlisle on the case.

"So shall I call Dan?" Lara asked. "Murders are his thing."

"Yeah. No, wait." His prison visit. Once he was sucked into the crucial early stages of a murder investigation, his day would be consumed by it, and he'd never be able to get away. "Second thoughts," she said, "I'll come myself."

"Really?"

"Yes, Dan's otherwise engaged today, and it's something important. I can take up some slack for now and pass the baton on to him later."

"If you're sure."

"Yeah. Let's have…" she ran through her options. "Let's have Joan there too, if you can get hold of her. Let me have the details."

When she looked at Dominic again, he was wearing a crooked smile. "So much for a bit of domestic bliss?"

"Afraid so. Strictly speaking, it's Dan's case, but with him visiting his son today…"

"Will you at least finish your breakfast?"

"I'll take my coffee in the bathroom and eat the toast in the car."

"I'll sort you out some clothes while you're showering."

Less than half an hour later, she was climbing out of her car in front of a depressing-looking, graffiti-ridden concrete block and watching where she was stepping as she made her way across a scrubby patch of grass, strewn with litter and worse to a corner where she could see the end of some blue and white crime scene tape fluttering in the breeze. It was drizzling, just to add to the misery of the situation. There was the inevitable crowd of spectators.

She walked around the corner and a uniformed constable lifted the tape so she could duck under. Lara stood talking to Joan Collins. Both were in white crime scene overalls, and they were a few yards away from a human-shaped lump on the ground. About a foot beyond the body stood a large, overflowing bin, as if whoever was responsible for the man's demise couldn't even be bothered to throw him away properly.

"Have you gone through the pockets?" Lizzie asked.

Lara shook her head. "Phil will apparently be here within minutes, so I thought it best not to disturb anything more than necessary."

Lizzie nodded. It made sense. "I'll go and get suited up. How bad is it?"

"Quite a lot of stab wounds, as far as I can see."

"I'd say it's what Dr Carlisle will describe as a frenzied attack," Joan added.

In these parts, that could mean anything from a falling out among gang members to a drugs deal gone wrong, to someone looking at someone else's girlfriend the wrong way. Before a young man left home in these parts, he checked his pockets for keys, phone, wallet and knife.

"How old?" she asked.

"Not your usual Northfields casualty," Joan said. "Maybe mid-forties?"

"Really?" Organised crime maybe, making some sort of point. It wouldn't be the first time.

She went back to her car, retrieved her own overalls from the boot, and pulled them on. Fortunately, anyone who was out and about was rubbernecking the scene over by the flats, or she'd probably have a group of teenagers ogling her, sniggering, and making lewd comments.

She returned to join her colleagues, depressed that the quiet spell in the Vale had ended in the worst possible way for some poor devil.

"Okay," she said. "Let me have a look at him."

The three walked over to the body, which lay on its back, the arms and legs in unnatural positions, making it look like a marionette tossed into a corner. Her gaze lingered first on the considerable amount of blood that stained his dark jacket, before moving up to the face.

The ground seemed to tilt beneath her feet. The world turned monochrome.

She heard someone gasp, realised it was her, and recoiled before she could stop herself. Her blood was pounding in her ears as she forced herself to look again.

"No," she moaned. "No, no, no, no, no."

A mass of conflicting emotions were twisting her guts. Shock. Sorrow. A kind of grief. Maybe even a certain guilt.

"What's up?" Lara asked. "Are you okay?" Her gaze flicked to the body then back to Lizzie. "Do you know him?"

"Yes," she said. "I know him very well." Her mind raced. "Shit. I can't be here."

"Boss?" said Joan. "Lizzie? What's going on? Who is it?"

She stepped away. "His name's Rob – Robert Thomas."

Joan frowned. "The one we wanted to talk to about the fire?" She studied the face. "Christ, you're right." She looked at Lizzie. "But… he was your ex, wasn't he?"

"Yeah." She still couldn't quite believe it. "Yes, he was. It was a long time ago, as you know, but since he showed up he's been making a nuisance of himself, and we've had a couple of altercations with him. Including yesterday morning at the house."

"So you feel a bit conflicted?" Lara said.

They all knew that was an understatement.

"Rather more than that," she said. "You know and I know that I – and Dominic, I guess – have to be treated as potential suspects, at least for now. Until we've been eliminated."

It was so obvious that neither of them bothered arguing. On one level, she knew she had nothing to fear. Yet, if this had been her investigation, she and her husband would have been the first people she'd have questioned.

She chewed her lip. "I don't even know if you two should be here."

"Someone has to be," said Lara.

"I know. But I was tight with my old team, Dan's team. I regard them as friends. You too, Lara. If there's even a suggestion of bias, then none of us should be in a position where we could be accused later of tampering with evidence. Even though we all know that's not going to happen."

"But…" Lara trailed off. Perhaps she was reluctant to accept it, but she was experienced enough to see the situation for what it was.

"What do we do, then?" Joan was glancing over at the onlookers now, as if she half-expected them to start hurling accusations of corruption.

"We keep our distance here. Make sure the scene's secured. Wait for Dr Carlisle and Phil's team. Meanwhile, I'll speak to the Super. He's going to have to get a team from outside the Vale – possibly outside Thames Valley – to run with this. Oh, bugger, what if even Phil and Barbara are compromised?" Her head was spinning with implications.

Lara moved closer. "Look, Lizzie, I don't know the ins and outs of your relationship with the man, either when you were together or lately, and I see we need to be beyond reproach. But someone's got to process the scene, take a look at the body in situ. We have to weigh the risk that anyone we know could be accused of evidence tampering against the real risk of evidence being lost or degraded while we wait for the B Team to arrive from God knows where." She glanced down at the body. "I mean, we can't just leave him there while someone rustles up a so-called neutral team, can we?"

Lizzie saw her point but was still in an agony of indecision. Into her jumble of thoughts about the handling of the case, memories of Rob, happier memories, kept intruding. Whatever else there was between them, there was no getting away from the fact that she'd loved him once, and had thought he'd loved her. Most recently, he'd insisted that he still did.

The old Rob she'd known had been fearless, and not only when it came to the things he'd done in his job. She'd always felt safe with him. Had that fearlessness, or perhaps some reckless determination to intervene on someone's behalf in a dangerous situation led to his death? Or was it just a simple case of a mugging gone horribly wrong?

Whatever had been wrong with him – and she'd decided something had gone very wrong – he hadn't deserved to die a horrible, violent death and wind up here. It made her sad and it made her angry.

She finally nodded. "Yeah, you're right, Lara. I'll speak to the Super and see how he wants to play it, but so long as CSI bag and record everything, and there's a proper evidence chain, that's got to be a good start." She took her phone out of her bag. "I'm afraid things are going to get pretty messy though."

17

There had been some form of prison in Aylesbury since 1810, and the current version had been constructed as a county gaol in 1847, close to the workhouse, a hospital and a number of other public buildings. In 1890, it had become an adult women's prison, changing again to a girls' borstal in the 1930s. Later still it had become an adult male prison and then a male Young Offenders Institute. Since 1989, it had held only long-term male prisoners aged between eighteen and twenty-one, although there were rumours that might change again.

Its early Victorian design, modelled on Reading County Gaol, featured a surprisingly elegant façade, its red brick walls softened by bright white paintwork around the doors and windows and on the corners. It didn't for a moment make Dan forget that within those walls were troubled and violent young men, some of them murderers. He knew the prison took rehabilitation seriously, with full and part-time education programmes, PE and vocational courses. There were even opportunities to take on award-based courses like the Duke of Edinburgh's Award.

Dan had no idea how many, if any of these opportunities his son might be taking advantage of, nor whether he was making the most of them. He'd decided that a major part of his icebreaking strategy would be about finding out as much as he could about Jack's life here.

Jack.

Even now, despite his avowed intention to go along with his son's wishes and think of him only as Peter, he was finding it almost impossible to do so in practice. He was terrified that the name Jack would pop out of his mouth early in his visit. That their meeting would be over before it started, never to be repeated.

He'd visited prisons a few times before, so he knew the procedures well enough: the ID requirements; the dress code; the strict controls on what you could take in with you. Dan checked his phone and other prohibited items into a locker, using a refundable one pound coin.

Prison visitors' rooms had always struck him as bittersweet places. People were being reunited with their loved ones, but under strict supervision, with no privacy – hugs were only permitted at the beginning and end of the visit. And there was always a parting, with the prisoner returning to a cell and the visitor returning home without them.

Dan was a strong believer in prison, as a punishment, a deterrent, and a form of protection for the public. And, if it was done well, he thought it could play a part in rehabilitating criminals who really wanted to turn their lives around. But he also recognised that it was hard on the human beings whose lives it touched. Plus, it wasn't exactly a haven for angels. Some individuals were there because they were dangerous. It must be terrifying for many of the inmates to be constantly rubbing shoulders with such people.

On his way here, he'd found himself thinking about the late, largely unlamented, Desmond Connolly. Stabbed repeatedly with a sharpened toothbrush handle. The word was that there were no clues as to the killer's identity, and no one was talking.

Desmond had been a cocky little shit, convinced that his family connections were all it took to make him a big, hard man. His ham-fisted off-piste attempts to prove himself had led to several deaths and landed him a life sentence. But Dan had been prepared to bet that he'd imagined those same connections would make him untouchable on the inside. How had he felt when he'd discovered how mistaken he'd been? And that his mistake was about to cost him his life?

Dan wondered, not for the first time how *Peter* was coping, and how safe he felt.

He spotted his son as soon as he entered the visitors' room. He sat alone at a table in the middle of a room that contained several tables, many of which were already occupied by prisoners and their visitors.

Peter raised a casual hand as Dan approached, and he stood up. When Dan reached him, he realised the one thing he hadn't really thought through was what to do at this point. A hug, in all the circumstances, seemed ridiculously over-familiar, and most likely wouldn't be welcomed. A handshake felt way too cold. If there was some sort of happy medium, Dan was damned if he knew what that might be. By the time he'd decided to hold his hand out, Peter was sitting down again, his expression unfathomable.

Dan sat opposite him. "Well…" He hadn't thought through what his first words should be, either. "Here we are," he said.

Lame! How lame is that?

"Aye," Peter said, "we are."

"I'm glad you decided to see me."

"Well, one thing this place gives you is plenty of time to think. Like I said in my letter, one of the things I needed to think about was you. How I felt. What I thought. But you know what?"

"No."

"All that thinking, and I was no wiser. I can't say I had some sort of revelation and came up with a good reason to meet you. I just couldn't think of a good reason not to, either. So in the end, I thought, you know, sod it. Let's do it and see what happens."

"So… how are they treating you?"

"It's nae so bad." The Scots accent wasn't so strong, but the phrasing was unmistakeable. "I'm doing courses. A level English, barista training—"

"Barista? I didn't know you could do that."

"Nor me. I just thought, when I get out of here, I'll need a job, and I seemed to remember the cafés were always hiring, up in Scotland. I'm learning guitar, too. I can play the intro to that Led Zeppelin song, 'Stairway to Heaven', pretty well."

Dan smiled. "That's something we have in common, then. Well," he amended, "I'm not sure you'd say *I* play it especially well." He paused for a beat. "What about the neighbours in here? Any trouble?"

Peter shook his head. "No. No one picks on me, if that's what you mean. It seems having a serial killer for a father, and there being rumours of me helping him, has a bit of kudos attached to it. Weird, right?"

"I'd have thought it might make you a target for some people."

"What, wanting to show everyone how hard they are? Well, it hasn't. Maybe they don't fancy their chances. My dad always reckoned the world was divided into sheep and wolves."

Dan ignored the reference to 'my dad'. "And you're a wolf?"

A shrug. "I'm not a sheep."

Peter offered no further comment. In the lull, Dan studied him, properly studied him, in the flesh for the first time.

The eyes, he thought, were pure Louise, his mother. Pure Karen, come to that. The other features? He'd looked at them in photographs. Sometimes he thought he favoured his father, sometimes his mother. The tight waves in his hair surely came from Dan.

"Well, then," Peter said. "That's us all caught up. Oh, wait. Your wife was pregnant. She must have had it by now."

Dan nodded. "A girl. Ellie."

"And it all, you know, went okay?"

"Yeah. All good, thanks." He hated how much this was like a chat at the bus stop between two vague acquaintances.

"I'm glad. Really." Peter sighed. "But we're not actually here to talk about courses and prison life, and your new kid, are we?"

"Aren't we?"

A headshake. "No. There's a damn great elephant in this room, Dan, and that's all you want to talk about, right? My dad. Me being his son, whatever the DNA might say. What I knew. What I *did*. So we've broken the ice. I suppose *I'm* curious, too."

"Curious about what?"

"About why you'd even *want* me in your life. I mean me as I am, not the little kid you probably dreamed about for nigh on twenty years. The me who tried to kill your wife and unborn child. And, I suppose, I'm curious about whether I'd want *you*. In *my* life. And in what way."

Two things struck Dan. The first was that, for some reason, he hadn't expected his son to be quite so articulate. And secondly, whatever Dan had tried to prepare for, he'd never expected the conversation to get so blunt, so quickly. He also realised that any amount of planning and preparation would have been fruitless. Because there were two people in this meeting, and neither of them was controlling the agenda.

Still, he sensed that giving bluntness, and honesty, back would be appreciated.

"Okay," he said. "So, first things first. I do want you in my life, in whatever way is going to work. Karen feels the same, by the way."

"Really?" Peter looked sceptical. "I find that hard to believe, after what I did to her. Nearly did."

"Oh, don't get me wrong. She still has nightmares about that. But you did stop yourself. That's important to us both. And..." He paused. "I need to be careful what I say here. I know Mac – Duncan – brought you up. He was the only father you ever knew for most of your life. I'm not going to ask you about that life – not for now, not unless and until you're ready to talk about it." He hesitated again. "Look, all I mean is, maybe it wasn't a normal upbringing—"

Peter burst out laughing. "Normal? You think there even is such a thing? And *you're* not exactly well placed to talk about normal, are you, Dan? I mean, Christ, you obviously think my life with Duncan was fucked up." He frowned. "And, yeah, obviously it was. But just look at *you*. Married to your dead wife's sister. My *mum's* sister. Her *twin* sister. My aunt. And, I suppose, my stepmum, too. Oh, yeah, and little Ellie. My sister and my cousin at the same time, and here's me old enough to be her dad."

He shook his head again. "Jesus, Dan. Now *that* is what I call fucked up. I mean, fair play, none of you has killed a load of women and children, or anyone else. That's sick, I know it is. But sick takes a lot of forms. I mean, when you fuck Karen, do you imagine you're fucking my mum?"

Dan held up a hand, desperately trying to quell the irritation, the resentment welling in him. "Whoa. Where's this coming from?"

"Did you hope Ellie would be a boy? Just like me?"

Dan breathed deeply.

"You're right," he said finally. "None of this is normal. And I never set out to fall in love with Karen. I suppose loss and grief drew us together, but I've never seen her as a substitute for your mother. And wanting a child together had nothing to do with you. Not replacing you, nor anything like that."

"If you say so. Well, my *upbringing* was a lot more normal than you might think. I went to school. We went out – cinema, the odd musical, even a couple of gigs. Oh, sure, Dad drummed it into me to keep our home life private, and maybe that's why I never really made close friends. None in here, either, if you're wondering. Could be I'm naturally not very social. This conversation might be the longest I've had in my entire life."

Dan tried to imagine the young man in front of him as a strange, lonely little boy. It wasn't so hard.

"But you still haven't asked me, have you?" said Peter.

"About what?"

"Come on, Dan. Neither of us is stupid. That night at your place, when you turned up like a one-man cavalry and saved Karen, Dad hinted that there'd been more killings since he stopped being the Invisible Man, and that maybe I'd had a part in them. You must want to know. I bet it's been eating away at you."

What was it someone had said? No plan survives first contact with the enemy? Dan's plan had been to steer clear of any of this stuff for their first meeting, but his son had brought it up anyway. Because he was feeling a guilt that he wanted to assuage?

There was a cold feeling in his gut.

"Okay," he said. "I'm asking."

Peter made a face, as if he'd tasted something bitter. "What do *you* think?"

"I..." What could he say? He'd asked himself the same question over and over. "We don't exactly know each other well, do we?"

"You're a cop. A detective. You must question suspects you don't know from Adam. What's your detective gut feeling telling you?"

"It can't be like that. Not with you. I want you not to be a killer. I've told myself over and again that you're not."

Peter smiled, but there was a weary sadness in his voice. "But that's not an answer, is it? I mean, you saw me try to kill Karen."

"And you stopped."

"Sort of."

"There were two of you. You and Mac. Only one of me. You could have killed us both, but it was you who stopped it. I think, deep down, you know what's right and what's wrong."

"Do I?" Another shrug. "People are so complicated, aren't they? I mean, you said you find it harder to go with your gut about me than with total strangers. But maybe I did choose not to kill my birth father and my mother's sister, when it came to it. Maybe, yeah, maybe I *did* think that felt wrong. But so what? Doesn't follow that I'd have had the same worries about a stranger, if my dad wanted me to do something to them."

"If Mac wanted...?" Dan looked him in the eye. "He'd groomed you. Brainwashed you. Was controlling you."

Peter laughed without humour. "Yeah, that'd be convenient. And that was quite revealing, too, Dan. I think you just as good as said you *did* think me capable of murder. Good to know."

That irritation rose again, and his attempt to smother it was only half-hearted this time. "I just don't know what we're doing here, Peter. You agree to see me, after two years, and all we're doing is playing games. Is it important to you to know I don't think you've killed anyone?" He shook his head. "How can I possibly say that, and still be completely honest with you? I only remember a two-year-old toddler. You spent nigh on twenty years being brought up by a psychopath who killed women and children for the fun of it. Who, whatever else happened, brought you to my house, intending for you to kill Karen and our unborn daughter. I…"

He realised he was crying, tears rolling down his cheeks. He swiped at them.

"How can I…? I… Everything in me wants that to have been the only time, and you didn't even go through with that."

Peter raised an eyebrow. "Maybe that *was* the only time. Maybe Dad was just messing with your mind."

Except Police Scotland and Northumberland Police were looking at eleven cases and seriously wondering if they were the Invisible Man's handiwork.

And Peter? What was going on here?

Maybe Mac hadn't been the only one playing mind games.

"Okay, just tell me," he pleaded, ashamed of his desperation, but unable to help it. "Please. Tell me you haven't hurt anyone and I'll believe it."

"Really? I don't think it can be as simple as that, unless you're a moron. And I don't think you're a moron. You don't come over as one, and morons don't get to be police inspectors. Do they?"

Peter yawned, not in a mocking way. He looked a little grey-faced. "I'm tired now. Like I said, this must have been my longest conversation ever. And pretty stressful. For both of us, I'm guessing."

Dan stared at him, incredulous. He was being dismissed? "You want me to go?"

"We'll talk again, I promise, and maybe I'll feel able to tell you more. I'll have a think, okay? And I want to know more about *you*, too. As we stand, you're just some copper who happens to be my real dad. In fact, before you go, why not tell me one thing about yourself. Something that, I dunno, makes you real. If you know what I mean."

And he did. Of course he did. But what to say? As suddenly as his resentment had kicked it, so it was gone again.

"Okay," he said. "Okay. I'm a football fan. I used to go before you were born, but I got out the habit. I still look for their results."

"What team?"

"Queens Park Rangers."

The ghost of a smile. "QPR. They're shit these days, aren't they?"

Dan laughed for the first time since he'd arrived. "You're not wrong. They keep looking like they might do something, but then it all falls apart. We're as likely to get out of the Championship going down as up."

"My team, Aberdeen, aren't much better. The Old Firm have the top two places sewn up, mind, so I guess anywhere in the top six isn't bad in the Scottish Premiership."

"You used to go?"

"Nah. Armchair supporter. Look, I really am tired now. Sorry." He almost sounded like he meant it. "But come again, yeah?"

"Yeah." It was a clear dismissal this time, but Dan rose without rancour. This was going to take time. And, whether Peter had committed crimes or not, his true father would stand by him.

"Bring photos next time?" Peter suggested. "I'd like to see what... *our* family look like."

It was a small thing, but Dan smiled. "Yes. I can do that."

18

As soon as Lizzie had spoken to her boss about the body on the Northfields estate, she hadn't even had to tell him why she felt the need to distance, not only herself, but the whole Aylesbury Vale team, from the investigation.

"I agree," he'd said. "You need to go home. I'll speak to the ACC, and recommend that someone from outside Thames Valley comes in. Could be Hertfordshire, Bedfordshire, maybe even the Met. Obviously, you and Dominic will need to be questioned."

"We've nothing to hide."

"Of course not. At least you get the weekend off after all."

"I don't think I'm in the mood to enjoy it."

"No," he'd accepted. "I can see that. You've had a shock. So take a break and I'll see you on Monday."

Dominic was just stepping out of the shower when she finally got home.

"I didn't expect you home so soon."

"Don't tell me you've only just got up."

He grinned. "Bloody cheek. I decided, with you buggering off, I'd get straight up, get a few jobs done in the garden, rather than shower and then get dirty. But I thought you had a body? I thought you'd be there for the day."

"Yeah, well…" She decided it could keep until he was dressed. "I'll go and make some coffee and I'll tell you all about it when you come down."

At the kitchen table, his expression changed from mild interest to horror as she shared her news.

"Jesus. Poor Rob. I mean, I know we didn't exactly hit it off, but I wouldn't wish that on him. And we're *suspects*?"

She put her hand on his. "Not really. Well, potential suspects, I suppose, but it'll be routine. Whoever gets to do the investigation has to question us, especially as I've admitted we've had trouble with him."

"Are you sure?" Barney sprang up onto his lap, and he stroked the ginger fur. "I mean, do we need alibis? Lawyers?"

"I really think lawyers is a bit premature," she said. "As for alibis, I guess so, inasmuch as we'll be asked what we were doing at key times. But I've no more idea than you have as to what those times are. I don't even know the time of death yet, and no one's going to share much information with me until we're in the clear."

"Well," he said, "*you're* okay up to the evening – you've got God knows how many police officers who can alibi you. I was here on my own with only Barney to vouch for me, and the last time I had a conversation with him, he wasn't speaking any known language."

"We know he was alive yesterday morning when we spoke with him—"

"Rowed with him."

"Rowed with him then – here. He was dead by this morning."

He shrugged, then sipped his coffee thoughtfully. "Of course, I did go out on that wild goose chase last night."

"True. If that's relevant, it'll probably help if that clown who wasted your time can confirm that he's the reason why you went out."

"Then I'll ring him after I finish my coffee."

"No real rush. It's not like you went anywhere near the Northfields. I really wouldn't worry."

"Okay." He seemed to relax a little. "Are *you* all right, though?"

She closed her eyes. "Am I all right? I don't know, really. He was a big part of my life once, so I'm definitely sad. Sorry I wasn't kinder to him too. I don't think *he* was all right, Dominic, although I've no clue as to what was wrong with him. And I suppose I'm upset that, in these last days, there was all the aggro between us, and that he was only here at all because of some delusion that I'd just fall back into his arms."

"Yeah," Dominic acknowledged with a wince. "Poor sod. Talk about wrong place, wrong time. And you've no idea at all what happened?"

"None. I made myself scarce and got Joan and Lara to do the same. Forensic and post mortem will answer some of the questions, but I dare say there'll be a lot more to do. I just hope there's a quick result."

"But you can still go to work on Monday?"

"Yeah, yeah. I just can't have anything to do with the case. Chances are none of the evidence that's collected will even be stored at the station."

"But once you're eliminated? Will you and your lot take over?"

"Doubt it. Depends." She took a sip of coffee. "Anyhow, it all means I've got the weekend off after all. So how about you show me what you did in the garden?"

*

Dan was surprised how tired he felt by the time he got home from the prison.

Karen was bagging leaves in the garden, while Ellie toddled around getting in her way.

"How was it?" she asked. Too casually?

He gestured vaguely, totally unable to offer a more coherent response for the moment.

If he'd gone in there with a whole bag of conflicting emotions, he had a whole matching luggage set full of them now. He hadn't expected to really get to know his son in just one visit, but he was amazed at how little of a handle he'd been able to get on the young man his boy had become.

Peter had been all over the place, it was fair to say. There had been some spite there, some defence of the monster who'd raised him. There had been curiosity about Dan and his new family, but even that had felt somewhat detached.

Dan interviewed suspects for a living, and he considered himself good at it. Yet even he was floundering to see what exactly the visit had accomplished.

His mind went back to the last few minutes of their time together. Peter had said he was tired and, in all fairness, he had looked it. Maybe he'd found the build-up to their meeting as stressful and worrisome as Dan had.

But then they'd talked football and Peter had asked to see some family photos next time.

Karen's anxious eyes were searching his face. "That bad?"

He sighed. "I just don't know at all. I can't work out if he's a mess and doesn't know it, a mess and he does know it, or – worst of all – not a mess, as far as he's concerned. He called our set-up – you and me – sick, but I don't know if that was just lashing out in defence of his own past. But there's to be a next time. That's good, right?"

She shrugged. "I suppose so. It could take you months or years to build some sort of relationship with him, if that's even possible."

She came over and hugged him. "You've got to give it time. As much time as it takes. We all have."

"Thank you," he said, suddenly humbled.

"For what?"

"Supporting me on this. I know it must be hard—"

"It is. But I love you. And I loved little Jack. We have to try and find him again and go forward."

"I love you too," he said. "You're amazing."

She grinned. "So I've been told."

She turned to watch Ellie, picking up fistfuls of fallen leaves and throwing them up in the air like confetti. God knew what game she was playing in her head.

"I'm half-surprised you came home," she said.

"Oh?"

"You haven't heard the news?"

"Nope. Radiohead in the car all the way home. What did I miss?"

"There's been a body found in Aylesbury. A murder investigation's being launched. And what with you being the murder detective…"

He groaned. "It's the first I've heard of it. What's the betting Lizzie's keeping it away from me today because of where I've been? I mean, it's good of her, I suppose…"

"Yes it is," Karen said tartly. "I'd think they can muddle through without you for one day."

"Yeah. Of course. Still, I'd better ring her."

"Or wait until she rings you?"

He dithered. "I could do that. Ah, but like you said, it's my team that usually does the homicides."

Karen giggled suddenly.

"What?"

"Our daughter. I reckon her developing vocabulary's going to be littered with words like 'murder', and 'homicide', and 'blood splatter'. She's either going to be a cop or a serial killer when she grows up."

"Not funny."

Her face clouded. "No," she agreed, "it's really not." She flapped a hand at him. "Oh, go on and call Lizzie. You'll only be twitching for the rest of the day, and I can't put up with that. I'm getting a cup of tea. Want one?"

He kissed her once more. "I'm a lucky man."

"Don't you forget it."

Ten minutes later, he'd spoken to Lizzie and they were drinking tea in the kitchen.

"Wow," Karen said. "Who saw that coming?"

"Not me," he admitted.

"And you said Lizzie seemed upset?"

"Well, yeah. Whatever else has happened, Rob meant a lot to her once. In the last few days, he's popped up out of the blue causing trouble and then got himself brutally murdered." He shook his head. "At least now I know why I haven't heard a peep about this case. Because it's not going to be my case, not with what's been going on with Lizzie and Dominic and the victim."

"But they'll be discounted, right? And then the case'll come back to you?"

"Maybe." He shrugged. "They'll follow the evidence and might get an arrest by dinner time – whoever 'they' turn out to be. Or they might get so into it that it makes sense for them to run with it. The whole thing sounds odd, though. Apparently, apart from making unwelcome overtures to Lizzie, he was looking for property and a job. He's not going to find a proper job or a des res on the Northfields, is he?"

"I'd imagine not. Are you thinking he was dumped there?"

"Dumped, lured… Or maybe he was just wandering around and found himself there at the wrong time. Saw something he shouldn't and that was that." He picked up his mug, didn't drink from it, put it down again. "One thing I know. We at least *know* that estate, and getting anyone to talk is like getting blood out of a stone, even for us. Good luck to a team from outside."

19

It was late afternoon when Lizzie's phone rang and her boss's number came up.

"We've got a team to handle the investigation," he said. "They're en route even as we speak."

"From where?"

"Bedford."

Something prickled at the back of her neck. "Do we have a name?"

"A DI Nancy Fleetwood."

"Uh huh. And who's her DCI?"

Wait for it...

"Name of Bill Smith."

She found herself nodding at the inevitability of it. "Oh, well, that's just great. The icing on the bloody cake."

"You know him, then?"

"Oh, yeah. This is turning into National Blasts from the Past Week."

"You don't sound pleased." He sounded concerned. "I take it you two have some history?"

"I'm not sure 'history' is quite how I'd characterise it. He was at the Met when I was, and our paths crossed a fair few times. He's maybe five years older, but I got my DS and then my DI ahead of him, and I got all the unreconstructed bullshit. Well, you can imagine. I must have slept with the right people. Or they had quotas to fill. Anything but merit."

"Really? Good grief."

"I know. Smith was what they used to call old school, even though old school was supposed to be over. But you know as well as I do, it still goes on now. He used to take the piss out of anything he saw as progressive, so naturally we fell out over that too."

"But he transferred to Bedfordshire?"

"The year before I had my injury. Which suited me fine. Oh, I never got to the bottom of why he left, not that I tried that hard. All I cared about was, he was gone. Until now."

"Is this going to be a problem?"

"I hope not. Like I say, I'd not call it a 'history' as such. We just didn't like each other, and we didn't get on. But who knows? Maybe he's mellowed. After all, he's got a woman DI now, so maybe that's something. Maybe he won't set foot in the Vale himself."

"Ah," was all Josh said in response.

"Oh," she said. "Marvellous."

"I think he's just coming as a courtesy thing. He knows there's an officer with a possible conflict of interest, but he doesn't know who yet."

"Oh, he'll know. The Met's a smaller place than you'd think, and you never completely leave. I still speak to old colleagues there, I'd bet Bill does the same, and then the old colleagues will talk together. I'm sure he knows I'm here. How long did he think about taking the case on?"

"Not long."

"I bet he didn't. He knows, all right. I'm thinking, as soon as he knew the case was here, nothing would have kept him away. Even if he didn't know I was the officer with the conflict, he'd still love to swoop in and solve a murder on my patch. Wait until he hears I'm a possible suspect."

"Look," Josh said, "I'm worried now."

"Don't be. I never liked him, but he was an okay copper in his way. Don't get me wrong – if he can see me squirming a bit, he'll delight in it, but he really isn't the type to fit someone up. Especially a fellow officer, however much he dislikes her. With any luck, he'll interview me – we are equal rank, after all – make it as uncomfortable as he can, then bugger off back to Bedford and leave DI Fleetwood to do the heavy lifting."

"If you're sure. Only it wouldn't look good if I started trying to pick and choose who comes in."

"It's fine," she said. "I'm not about to try and dictate who questions me. As I think I said before, I've nothing to hide."

124

"Okay." There was still a concerned edge to his voice. "And how are you holding up? These last few days have been a nightmare for you."

"I was hoping for a peaceful weekend to shake it off, but that's probably not going to happen now, is it? I'll live."

"Anything untoward, you let me know, okay?"

"Thanks, boss, but I'd like to fight my own battles if I can. If I go crying to my male boss, that'll just show I'm a useless girlie who doesn't deserve anything. If I get your job when you go, he'll probably think I earned that on my back, too."

"Yes? Well, he'd better not say as much. Or rather, it had better not get back to me if he does. One of the reasons I've joined the force is to help change things." He chuckled, "There's still too few senior officers who look like me." He paused. "Is my ethnicity going to be a problem for him?"

"I doubt it." In fairness, Smith had never displayed any racist tendencies. "It was women he thought were outshining him he had issues with. If you brush up on beer and rugby before you meet him, I'm sure you'll get on like a house on fire." She burst out laughing. "Whoops. Unfortunate turn of phrase."

"Call me if you need anything?"

"Sure." She checked her watch. "I reckon it's wine o'clock now. Have a good evening."

"You too."

She hung up and sighed. Bill Smith. Mr Misogyny himself. This really was the week that kept on giving. She remembered him trying it on when their paths first crossed on a training course. He was all smarm and sweat and seemed to take the brush off as merely playing hard to get, in the face of his imagined irresistible charm.

She could still see the ugliness that twisted his face when she insisted she was *seriously* not interested. He'd decided there and then that, while he didn't care who he shagged, she'd only put out for men who could further her career. It couldn't possibly be that he simply wasn't her type.

She'd heard the occasional whisper and rumour afterwards that she wasn't the only one he'd tried to get into bed.

Sometimes he succeeded. Apparently, getting married hadn't caused him to call a halt.

Nowadays, a fair few police scandals seemed to revolve around WhatsApp groups sharing unpleasant and offensive messages. She wouldn't be surprised to find that Bill Smith was in his element in such forums.

And now she and Dominic were to be questioned by his team. She'd meant what she said when she'd told Josh she didn't think he'd try to stitch her up. But she thought she'd better curb her hostility and practise smiling and playing nice before he arrived.

*

Conversation between Dan and Karen inevitably kept returning to his prison visit as the day went on. He still couldn't quite fathom why she showed so little sign of being angry at, or afraid of, the young man who'd tried to kill her, but her support brought him a comfort he wasn't sure he deserved. Each time they talked about it, emotions flooded back to him, until he felt as if he'd run back to back marathons.

It was Karen who pointed out that, for a first meeting he'd been so nervous about, they'd actually packed in quite a lot.

"We know a bit about his upbringing, and he's showed at least some interest in our family. I take that as encouraging."

"I suppose it is," he acknowledged. "The other stuff about further murders Mac may or may not have committed, and whether Peter had any part in them... well, that's trickier ground."

"It has to be. He has to be able to trust you and believe that you trust him. You were never going to manage that in one visit."

He knew she was right, but it still gnawed at him. The crazy thing was, he thought, he wanted to know the truth only if it was a truth he could live with. DI Alec McGivering from Police Scotland was descending on him on Monday, seeking his help with maybe getting closer to that truth. What if the worst emerged, and his son, who he'd hoped for so long was alive, turned out to be a killer like the man who'd raised him – maybe not by nature, but certainly nurtured?

What then?

He wasn't sure he could live with that. Or rather, he thought a part of him that had been only half-alive all these long years would finally die, and he had no idea what kind of a man would remain.

"There's one thing you haven't said anything about," she said. "Something we've hardly talked about since Peter's arrest."

"I don't know what you mean."

"No?"

Of course he knew, even though it was a subject that made him feel queasy. He didn't respond and she just sat looking at him. She was using a trick he'd used often enough when interviewing suspects. Now the woman he loved was using it against him, and he knew he had to be the one to break that silence.

"The dreams?" he said finally.

"And the visions."

Several years ago now, he'd started to be haunted by dreams of a boy he knew to be his son, even though that boy had been ten years old – not the toddler who'd been abducted and whose fate was then unknown. It was as if the figure in his dreams had been ageing in real time.

It hadn't stopped at dreams, either. For a while, he'd even seemed to have vivid waking visions of the youngster. He'd been prepared to put most of it down to some sort of breakdown he'd seemed to be headed for. Until Lizzie had forced him to receive some counselling.

For a while, the dreams and visions subsided, but then he'd started to have a new, recurring dream, at first just unremembered snatches, but they'd become clearer over time. He was on a beach, looking up at a house on a cliff, from which a pale-faced figure looked down. His counsellor had told him these things stemmed from suppressing his grief for Louise and for his son. But, the night Karen had nearly died, it turned out to be much stranger than that.

"I was there that night, remember?" Karen said. "When, not only did you recognise Peter, but he recognised you. Because he'd shared your dream. It was something so insane, we've never been able to explain it satisfactorily, and you eventually made into a taboo subject. I'm betting you didn't mention *that* to him. Did you?"

"No," he agreed. "I didn't mention that."

"Why not? Maybe he'd have understood."

"Why?" He put his hands to his head. "Because everyone has to draw a line somewhere. We covered some difficult enough stuff as it was. I don't think either of us wanted to get into the loony tunes stuff."

"And yet…" she persisted. "Loony tunes? Well, maybe. But you *did* have a recurring dream. A house overlooking a beach. A face at a window who you instinctively knew was your son. The house where Mac and Peter were living; you found it on an online satellite view, using Mac's postcode, after you started to suspect him. And, without any prompting from you, Peter said he'd had a dream where he was in that same house, looking down on the beach and he saw you."

"Yes," he said shakily.

"Yes." She took his hands in hers. "Maybe we'll never know how that happened, but it still happened. I mean, we did some research, didn't we, before you declared the subject closed? We found lots of stuff about shared dreaming. The idea of telepathy, or some sort of mass collective consciousness. Or, more plausibly, some sort of bond between the people who share the dream."

"And yet, you and Lou had the strongest bond I've ever known. You seemed to know things about each other, like how you were feeling. But you said you'd never shared a dream."

"We're not talking about me and Lou," she said with a sad smile. "I'd be really interested to know if that dream he had of you on the beach was a one-off, or whether he remembers any of the other stuff, even those visions."

"I think that was something else. For a start, he always had a Queen's Park Rangers shirt on when I 'saw' him, and now I know he followed Aberdeen."

"So maybe part of what you saw was blanks being filled in by your subconscious." She squeezed his hands. "Look, I'm not saying go diving in with this heavy stuff. But sooner or later, you do need to talk to him about it. Who knows? It could be the key to unlocking your relationship."

And with that, Ellie started crying, demanding to be fed, and the debate was over for the time being.

20

Lizzie was beginning to worry that she was turning into an insomniac. But then, she had a lot on her mind right now, enough to keep anyone awake nights. The few snatches of sleep she'd managed had been beset by bad dreams.

She knew she needed to snap out of her current mood, beset by tiredness and worry. One thing on top of another had brought her close to a very bad place, a place she'd found herself in towards the end of her time at the Met, when her life had seemed to be in ruins.

She was determined not to go there again, if she could help it. Yet here she was, drifting listlessly through Sunday morning while Dominic was out on the drive washing cars that she hadn't thought were especially dirty. She suspected he was keeping busy because he was more worried than he was letting on. He'd suggested they go for a walk later, and maybe it was just what she needed to clear her head.

It might lighten her mood if the burned-out vehicle in Ivinghoe could be positively connected to her house fire, especially if Phil Gordon and his team found something that might lead to a suspect.

Phil had been at pains to remind her that, contrary to what most people imagined, fire didn't always destroy all DNA and fingerprints – although, the way her luck had been running, she wasn't allowing herself to hope too hard on that score. All the same, she wished resources and overtime budgets could stretch to giving a bit more priority to car theft and criminal damage. Those days were long gone, though. She knew the cost couldn't be justified, so Phil's wizardry would have to wait until Monday.

Not for the first time, she turned the three likely suspects over in her mind.

The fact that Rob had been murdered didn't automatically rule him out as the arsonist, of course, although she still struggled to see him as a serious suspect.

She couldn't get him, nor the sight of his dead body, out of her mind. Ever since that first shock at the crime scene, she'd been racked with sadness and guilt. In all those years since he'd abruptly ended their relationship, she'd seen it only from her point of view, dismissing whatever he might have been feeling as secondary to the physical and mental consequences her injury had wrought upon her. So she'd blamed him – hated him sometimes – for deserting her when she needed him most.

Too late, she finally accepted that Rob had also had a right to be affected by what had happened. She knew about survivor guilt. The man had had his own demons to battle and she'd dismissed his feelings as selfishness. She'd been hostile when he'd shown up like a bad penny the other day and, yes, his crass attempts to pick up the relationship as if nothing much had changed, hadn't helped.

Nor had it been normal.

Too late again, she saw the extent to which his behaviour had been all wrong, not normal for Rob, not normal for anyone. He'd been a human being, and he probably really had needed professional help. If only she'd been more sympathetic, maybe tried to steer him towards that help, then maybe whatever had led to that grim discovery at Northfields would never have happened.

What could have wrought such an alarming change in him? Could it have led to his terrible death? And was it possible that the two, and perhaps the fire as well, were in some way connected?

Maybe Rob's family and erstwhile colleagues could shed some light. No doubt someone from Bill Smith's team would be talking to them, trying to build a picture of the victim.

She hoped they were as thorough as she would be herself. She wanted justice for Rob, and would love to be the one who achieved it for him. But she doubted in her heart that it would happen. Even after she'd been eliminated from enquiries, she knew she was too personally invested and involved with the victim to be sure she could remain detached and objective.

She turned her thoughts towards Cameron Connolly and Gaynor Upton's brood. Her instincts still told her that responsibility for the fire was more likely to reside in one of those camps. Both twistedly vengeful towards Lizzie for the consequences of their family members' crimes.

If the Connollys were behind the fire, then – even if Phil got lucky with some evidence – tracing anything back to Cameron wouldn't be easy. It would be so much less complicated if the Upmans could be implicated.

Whoever was responsible, every day they were at large carried the threat that they might come back and try something again. One more reason why she wasn't sleeping. One ear was permanently open for suspicious sounds.

And now she had the added joy, in the shape of Bill Smith, to look forward to. She very much doubted if he'd changed his spots. If he could make her uncomfortable, chances were he'd make the most of it.

Unless she was wrong. People *did* change, she reminded herself. Whatever bad blood had been between them had been a long time ago. Maybe he was an altogether different proposition now.

She had a feeling she'd find out soon enough.

*

As it turned out, she didn't have long to wait. She'd just made some coffee and was about to take a cup out to Dominic when she heard the front door open. She stepped into the hall.

"Good timing," she began, and then she saw that Dominic was not alone. He was followed inside by a balding man in a quilted jacket and an auburn-haired woman in an emerald-green coat. She didn't recognise the latter, but the man was all too familiar, right down to the thin-lipped smile that always managed to look sarcastic.

"Lizzie," DCI Bill Smith said. "You've hardly changed a bit."

"Nor have you," she lied. The years, far from being kind, had made him all the seedier.

"Oh," he said, "and this is DI Nancy Fleetwood."

The women shook hands.

"And this is—" Lizzie began, indicating Dominic.

"Oh, we've done the introductions. You got married."

"Couple of years ago. And how's Lucy?"

"Ah," he said. "She's the *former* Mrs Smith now."

Lizzie didn't find that hard to believe. Lucy had always been too good for him. "Sorry to hear that," she said.

He shrugged. "It happens. We wanted different things. And I still get to see my kid every other weekend, when I'm not working. Luckily this wasn't my weekend to have him."

She nodded, wondering what sort of a role model Bill Smith might be.

"So you're running with the Rob Thomas case?" She made it a question, even though she knew the answer.

"I am. I gather you and he have some ancient and – more importantly – modern history and you've recused yourself and your division."

"It was the right thing to do."

"Indeed. Well, you'll be pleased to hear I'm keeping this one hermetically sealed, so to speak, so everything's above board. My own team, CSIs from Bedford, even a pathologist from my neck of the woods."

It was text book stuff. She approved and said so. "Although once I'm in the clear, maybe we can think about my team taking it back?"

He shrugged again. "We'll see."

"Want some tea? Coffee? I just made some."

"Coffee sounds great," he said, "but I think we won't be here that long."

"No?" She relaxed a little. This was sounding even more of a mere formality than she'd dared hope.

"No. Because we've had a bit of luck, actually. My CSIs were processing the body and they found two phones in his pockets. A smartphone and an unregistered pay as you go."

"Unregistered?"

"Weird, eh? I mean, he's got a perfectly good smartphone. So we're thinking the other one was for getting up to no good. You know, like a burner?"

She grappled with the idea. The man who'd come to Aylesbury to find her was so altogether changed that maybe she probably shouldn't be surprised.

"Have you got into them?" She hesitated. "Sorry, I shouldn't be asking. It's not my case."

"No, it's not." He smiled. "But for the record, yes we have got into them. And that pay as you go really is a strange one. No prints on it, and all the calls are between Friday night and this morning. A single number – one outgoing and several incoming."

"And have you been able to identify whose number that is?" If so, why were they wasting their time here?

"Oh, yeah."

There was no mistaking the glint in his eye this time. She sensed something was coming and that she wouldn't like it, but she fought down the churning in her stomach.

"So forgive me," she said. "That sounds like a big lead, calls to and from a dodgy phone on the night Rob died. Why are you here, instead of identifying and arresting the caller?"

He smiled again. "You're right, of course. But, well, we did need to see you to tick the box – and, as it happens, we've got the phone with us. So, since it's a murder case on your patch, I thought we might call that number while we were with you. You know, give you a piece of the action?"

She stared at him. "What? But... he could run, if he realises you're on to him. This isn't the way..."

He waved a hand dismissively. "He can't run. We have uniforms outside his house. I know this is a bit theatrical, but..." He actually winked at her as he held his hand out to Fleetwood. "Nance?"

She opened her bag, rummaged around, and produced a clear evidence bag containing a basic Nokia. She handed it to Smith.

"Here we go," he said. "Let's see if anyone picks up."

He jabbed a few keys through the plastic, pressed the call button, and put the phone on speaker.

The ringback tone commenced. Seconds later, Dominic's familiar ring tone shrilled from his pocket.

Smith smiled at him.

"Go ahead," he told him. "Answer it."

"It'll keep," Dominic said.

"Answer it," Fleetwood said. It was, Lizzie realised, the first time she'd spoken. She had some sort of Midlands accent, and there was a flintiness in her tone. Suddenly, Lizzie had a sinking feeling in her stomach.

Dominic shrugged and pulled the phone from his pocket. Thumbed a key to accept the call.

"Dominic Newman."

With hideous inevitability, his voice echoed from the Nokia's speaker. Smith's grin was shark-like.

"Well, well," he said. "Mr Newman." He chuckled as he met Lizzie's eyes. "Gotcha."

A wave of nausea washed over Lizzie, but she beat it down, knowing she had to recover fast. To take as much charge of the situation as she could.

"Right," she told Smith. "I've no idea what's going on here, but neither of us will be saying another word without a solicitor present."

She was still trying to process what was happening, but she'd been a cop long enough to recognise the inevitability of her husband being arrested. At least she'd be able to organise the best legal representation possible. Indeed, one name had instantly entered her head.

Smith raised an eyebrow, then shrugged. "That's your right, of course. Well, I'm arresting both of you on suspicion of murder." He nodded to Fleetwood. "Caution them, Nance."

Fleetwood started to advise them of their rights.

"Whoa," Lizzie protested. "*Both* of us?" she'd said.

Dominic looked as if she'd slapped him.

"I didn't mean it like that," she began.

"Stop talking now, please," Smith said. "You can talk all you like at the station. You'll go in separate cars, of course."

"Adina Walker," she said to Dominic. "Tell them you want Adina Walker. A solicitor. Say nothing else."

"I won't tell you again," said Smith.

"I'm done," she said. She held her hands out in front of her. "Are you cuffing us?"

"That won't be necessary, will it?" Fleetwood eyed her boss.

"I don't think so," he agreed. "Get some uniforms to escort them to the cars."

To be fair to him, any glee he had felt about arresting her and Dominic was concealed behind a veneer of professionalism, albeit a thin one. Even so, he couldn't resist a smirk as he produced a search warrant with a flourish.

"Don't worry," he told her, "I won't be going through your knicker drawer personally. The PolSA team and CSI can deal with all that."

She bit back the smart retort that came to mind and just looked at him, stony-faced. A search was the least of her worries. She was still trying to understand why Rob had called Dominic. Why her husband had called back, more than once.

She was confident he had a good explanation. But why on earth hadn't he told her?

21

With no progress on Lizzie's house fire likely before Monday, and a local murder that was off limits, Dan was finding a weekend off a mixed blessing. Try as he may, he couldn't settle. His visit to Aylesbury prison and the meeting with his son had left him hurt, confused, angry and hopeful – a jumble of feelings that he couldn't stop trying to untangle.

Anyhow, now he had a free Sunday, and he was doing the best he could to put all these things to the back of his mind. They were going out this afternoon, taking Ellie to enjoy some of the play equipment on the village green. Meanwhile, while Karen did some baking, he was doing what she called 'waving a vacuum cleaner about' – his latest attempt to shoulder some of the domestic chores.

He felt his phone vibrate in his pocket and switched off the machine. Superintendent Stowe's name was on the screen.

He accepted the call. "Yes, sir."

"Dan. Sorry to interrupt your Sunday."

"How can I help?"

"I'm not sure you can, really, but I thought you ought to know. It's DCI Archer."

He felt himself tensing, a world of possibilities swirling in his head. She'd had threats…

"Is she okay?"

"She's not hurt, if that's what you mean. But it's not good, Dan. She and her husband have been arrested."

"What?"

The Superintendent had a dry sense of humour, but wind-ups weren't at all his style. Dan's mind reeled.

"I know," Stowe was saying. "I can't believe it myself."

"The Rob Thomas case?"

He'd known the investigation was going elsewhere – at least for now – so that she and Dominic could be ruled out as suspects before Lizzie, or anyone who might have a loyalty to her, could be allowed anywhere near the case. He hadn't for a moment imagined it would be anything more than a formality.

"Suspicion of murder," Stowe said. "Both of them."

"Christ. I mean, in his shoes, I'd have certainly wanted to speak to both of them. You know about Lizzie's past with Rob?"

"And the more recent issues. I know Dominic has made some unfortunate accusations about Mr Thomas."

"Unwise, perhaps, sir, but uncharacteristic too. In any case, to go from there to serious suspicion of what sounds like a pretty savage murder seems quite a leap."

"You might as well know," Stowe said. "Lizzie wasn't thrilled about the DCI from Bedford who's heading up the investigation. Some previous bad blood. But she insisted she could be professional about it."

"Why wouldn't she? After all, sir, I can't believe for a moment they're involved in this. She said that, whoever was in charge of the case, they could no more conjure a case out of thin air than anyone else could. And I agreed."

Now he had a very bad feeling about this. "Maybe I spoke too soon."

*

Lizzie sat in a cell in Luton police station, still trying to process the nightmare that seemed to be the culmination of the past few days' events.

On arrival at the station, she'd been booked in by the custody sergeant and had handed in her property. She'd been asked if she wanted a solicitor. "Adina Walker," she'd said.

Smith had stared at her. She'd told Dominic to ask for the same solicitor, and she knew as well as Smith did that the same solicitor representing multiple suspects in the same case wasn't always a great idea.

It was feeling as if strokes of luck were few and far between lately, but Walker had been available and had expected to arrive within less than an hour. Which meant she would be here any minute now.

Meanwhile, Lizzie had had nothing better to do than to worry about what sort of case Bill Smith thought he was building, and how much water he thought it would hold. And, trying to step back and view the case with her detective's eye, she found there were some matters that she had a bad feeling about.

Her train of thought was interrupted by the cell door swinging open.

"Your lawyer's here." said the uniformed officer outside. "We've arranged a room where you can consult with her."

Lizzie and Adina Walker had crossed swords countless times on opposite sides of an interview. Walker, tall, black and elegant, had an accent that reminded Lizzie of old-fashioned BBC English, crisp and crystal clear. She was often the duty solicitor representing Lizzie's suspects, and the slightest weakness in the police case would be mercilessly exposed. Occasionally, Lizzie found her irritatingly pedantic – no matter how right or wrong she was. But she had always admired her as a professional, and she could think of no one she'd rather have representing them.

"Well, this is a surprise," Walker said after the door to the interview room closed, leaving them alone. "I never expected us to be on the same side."

"And we might not be now," Lizzie said. "That's your call, I suppose."

"Quite. You and your husband have both asked for me to represent you, and we've both seen where that can lead. Two or more defendants in the same case, and suddenly they're trying to throw each other under the bus to save their own skins. And then you have a conflict. You know that, so why—?"

"Yes, I know that, of course I do. But there's no conflict, Ms Walker, I promise you."

"Adina, please. I never expected to be having a conversation like this with you, but we can get back to formalities next time we're on opposite sides. For now, let's make it Adina and Lizzie, agreed?"

"Agreed," she said readily, and was rewarded with a rare Adina Walker smile. "Look, I know you've probably heard this before, and no doubt it sometimes ends in tears, but I know *I'm* not guilty, and I can't believe Dominic is. I know him too well."

"I've heard that one before, too."

"I'm sure you have. But I'm not some airheaded, love-blinded woman, Adina. Even if Dominic has done something wrong, there's no way he'd try to pin it on me."

Adina smiled again. "I hope for your sake you're right. Even if you're both innocent and singing from the same hymn sheet, you know better than most how the police can try to play one suspect off against the other. But okay, I'm happy enough to represent you both for now. However, if I see a conflict developing..."

"I get it."

"There's other stipulations. You can't use me to pass information to each other, and I won't share any legal advice I give you with your husband. Nor vice versa."

"That's fine. I want this by the book."

"So tell me the story so far."

22

The décor and furniture were a little different, but the interview rooms at Luton police station were otherwise much the same as those at Aylesbury, or in London in her Met days, or any other police station that Lizzie had been in before. But this was the first time she'd been on the wrong side of the table.

No matter how often she told herself she knew the score when it came to police interviews, she still found herself dry-mouthed and nervous as a cocky, chubby DS called Chris Woodger started the recording. Smith introduced himself and made a slightly pompous speech about DCI Archer's right to be questioned by someone of at least equal rank. Others in the room, including DI Nancy Fleetwood, identified themselves, ending with Adina Walker.

"So," Smith kicked off, "tell us about your relationship with the victim."

"Rob and I didn't have a relationship. Well, not recently."

"But you had one before, right? And you'd had, shall we say, interactions more recently, am I right? That's why you did the 'decent' thing," he made quotes with his fingers, "and asked to be kept off the case. So how about you start at the very beginning? When you first met him?"

Her stomach churned. So that was his intention. Some sort of emotional strip tease. She glanced at Fleetwood, hoping to see some sisterly support there, but the DI had eyes only for her boss, like an apprentice watching their master at work. It crossed her mind that he was probably screwing her, and then she immediately reproached herself for making assumptions.

She willed herself to relax.

"Okay," she said, "so I met Rob in 2009..."

She tried to keep it brief and only surrendered details when asked for them. She was able to gloss over the whole business of Rob's unwillingness or inability to make love to her after her scarring, wrapping it up as guilt that he hadn't got involved when she'd put herself in harm's way.

"And that was it until a few days ago," she continued. "He'd found out where I was working, through a mutual friend, and he waited for me outside the station and asked if we could go for a drink."

"Did that alarm you?" Smith interjected.

"Not at the time, no," she said. "Well, not immediately. I mean, I thought it was all a bit weird, but I agreed. I wish I hadn't. In no time at all, he was talking about what a mistake he'd made letting me go and how he wanted to start again. Me being married didn't seem to be an obstacle. He sent me flowers, turned up at my house..."

"He was stalking you?" Fleetwood suggested.

"I suppose you could say that, although I thought it was at the low end of the spectrum. I was more annoyed than scared."

"So he turned up at your house," Smith played back to her. "To what purpose?"

"It was quite bonkers. He made it pretty clear that he hadn't given up. He thought I just needed time to see we were meant for each other."

"And your husband?" Nancy Fleetwood interjected. "Did he hear any of that?"

"He was the one who answered the door, so he was right there. Rob didn't seem to care about that. And no, Dominic didn't like it."

"Things got heated?"

"Only a little."

"Heated in what way though?"

She thought the truth was the best policy, as she couldn't know for sure what he thought he knew. "Well, he got a bit macho in fact, which isn't normally his style."

"No?" Smith grinned. "A *bit* macho? We hear Dominic subsequently more or less accused him of starting the fire."

"Hear from whom?"

"Did he accuse him or not?"

She hoped he was just trying to wind her up.

"I wouldn't say he accused him. He pointed out that Rob knew all about fire and, yes, he implied he could be a suspect. Which I didn't disagree with. I still don't, even though I'm not sure I believe he'd have done it."

"Quite aggressive again, by all accounts. We've spoken to the officer who witnessed the whole exchange."

"It was mainly posturing. How would you feel if a guy kept turning up and hitting on your wife in front of you?"

Smith shrugged. "We're not talking about me, though, are we? And there's quite a pattern here, isn't there? What with Mr Newman's history of violent behaviour."

The last sentence caught her off guard.

"What... what on earth are you talking about? What history?"

"His caution for assault." Smith smiled again. This time there was something wolfish about it. "Oh. Hasn't he told you? I mean, it was a long time ago, but still..."

She knew something nasty was coming. Had no idea what it might be. But, "Oh, that," she said, trying to sound casual. "So what do you think you know?"

"You tell me, as you know all about it."

"I want to hear it from you," she insisted.

"I don't think that's unreasonable, Chief Inspector," Adina said.

Smith smirked. He was obviously having fun now.

"All right. I think you're kidding a kidder, but I'll humour you." He leaned back in his chair, as if he was about to tell a fireside tale. "He was in his twenties. A guy in a bar in Harrow chatted up his girlfriend, then followed her outside when she went to the toilet. What happened next... well, recollections vary, as they say. The upshot was that the man you claim is a lover, not a fighter, decked him. The guy suffered a head injury and spent twenty-four hours under observation in hospital."

Why was she only hearing this now, and from this twat?

"Depending on who you believe," Smith continued, "either Mr Newman got concerned and went out to find the other man molesting his girlfriend, or she'd agreed to meet the guy outside for a quickie up against the wall and Mr Newman caught them at it."

"You obviously know what the girlfriend said?" Her tone was light, but she felt sick.

"Oh, she said it was the molestation. It was really all a bit 'he said, she said' in the end. They didn't think putting the bloke in hospital could just be let go, but they decided a caution was sufficient, rather than trying to make more of it. The point is, he accepted it."

She floundered for a beat, and then Adina came to her rescue.

"So what, Chief Inspector? He was young, in trouble with the police, probably scared. Most likely, accepting a caution was just about making it all go away."

"Ah, but we all know accepting a caution is an admission of guilt."

"Even so," Adina persisted, "the caution will have expired. It wouldn't show up on criminal record checks."

"Course not. Fortunately for us though, it still lies on the file. As, again, you know." He gave another of those maddening shrugs.

Lizzie found her voice. "Caution or no, he was just attempting to protect his girlfriend. That's a bit different to what happened to Rob."

"You think?" He shrugged again. "I'd say it's a pattern. It's exactly what he does whenever someone moves in on his territory. Gets mad. Gets violent. Even in front of a uniformed constable."

"He didn't get violent with Rob. Just a bit of verbal pushback."

"Not then, perhaps. But later..." He paused for a beat. "Did you know Robert Thomas wasn't well?"

She processed the question, sensing there was more behind this too than met the eye.

"Not as such," she said finally, "although it wouldn't surprise me, the way he was behaving."

"Well, he wasn't well," said Fleetwood. "Poor guy. We spoke to a couple of his former colleagues. It's really sad. It all started a few years ago, when he attended a fire in Cricklewood. Six kids dead, and pretty horrific by all accounts. In the emergency services, we expect to see all sorts, but we're only human. He didn't cope well with that one."

Lizzie felt that twinge of guilt again. She'd thought he wanted to open up about something, and she hadn't wanted to know. Was this it? Would it have made a difference?

"Not coping how?" she heard herself ask.

"Stress," Fleetwood said. "Depression. He split with his girlfriend."

"You mean his wife?"

"Oh, he's never been married."

"That's not what he told me."

"I understand he'd told colleagues he was going to propose before the fire with the kiddies, but he didn't, and then he got erratic. He was put on medication, but sounds like he didn't much like the side effects and didn't stick with it. The relationship didn't survive."

"But..." Lizzie shook her head. "He *told* me he'd been married. Divorced."

"He often got confused, we're told. And he was never the same again at work. Often signed off with stress, anxiety. In the end he was medically retired."

"He said he quit."

"Did he? Well, like I say, he got confused. Couldn't tell reality from fantasy. I'd imagine that was what you saw in the last few days. He needed your help, right?"

It hurt like a slap to the face. She glared at Fleetwood.

"I didn't know any of that. How could I?" *You didn't ask. Didn't listen.* "And I didn't owe him anything. And what does any of this have to do with anything anyway? I haven't denied there were a couple of verbal altercations. Are you seriously trying to turn that into a murder case?"

Adina Walker leaned in and whispered, "Calm down. You're doing fine."

"No," she said, heat rising inside her. "I mean, apart from a couple of rows and those phone calls, have you got any actual evidence?"

145

Fleetwood opened her mouth, but Smith silenced her with a gesture and leaned forward. "Well," he said, "since you ask. DS Woodger, would you like to do the honours?"

Woodger pushed some photographs across the table to her, quoting its exhibit number, and explaining for the record that they showed a man's jacket, black.

Lizzie's mouth was suddenly very dry, her heart pounding. This was what had caused her the most unease when, back in her cell, she'd played back the events of the last couple of days. This was what she'd feared. For an instant, the world seemed to spin.

"This," Smith said, "is an item that was recovered from an ironing basket in your utility room in the course of our search. Still ever so slightly damp. Can you say whose jacket it is?"

"It looks like my husband's. Dominic's jacket."

"Did you wash it for him?"

"No, he washed it himself, the night before last. We don't go in for gender stereotyping," she added, knowing it was an unnecessary thing to say.

"All right. And you can see the brownish spots on the surface?"

She could, only too well. There was a faint ringing in her ears. "Yes."

He nodded encouragingly, as if he was a tutor and she was his star pupil. She felt condescension coming off him like waves.

"And what are they? Any idea?"

Yes, of course. But that wasn't what Dominic told me.

The frenzied attack on Rob. The killer must have been covered in blood.

She tried to keep the tremble out of her voice. "He said someone had fallen against him in a car park and they must have had mucky hands."

"Mucky?" A raised eyebrow. "That's a word for it, I suppose. It looks like blood to me. Surely that's what you thought, when you first saw it?"

"When I got home, the jacket was already in the washing machine. Dominic washed it himself, took it out of the machine himself."

"And why did he wash it?"

"I told you. He told me someone had bumped into him in a car park in the dark. They must have had messy hands. He didn't know what the mess was. He'd just tried to get it out quickly."

"Erasing evidence?"

"That's not at all what my client said," Adina interjected.

"He feared the stain might set," she elaborated. "He decided to act quickly."

"And you believed this?"

"Why wouldn't I?"

Smith raised an eyebrow. "Seriously?" He leaned back in his chair. "You're an experienced police detective. Doesn't this all seem mighty convenient to you? I mean," he chuckled nastily, "he spins you some cock and bull story about going out on spec to meet a potential client in a pub. A client who doesn't show up. And then he has a tussle with this mucky person."

"Not a tussle."

"A struggle?" Fleetwood suggested.

"A collision."

Smith raised his eyebrows. "If that's what you say he said. But even if that didn't set alarm bells ringing at the time, surely you'd have put two and two together once Rob Thomas's body was found. A body I gather you were first to identify. I mean, you recused yourself from the case, not only because you had a previous relationship with the victim, but you and your husband had had a couple of run-ins with him. You must have wondered what that mysterious mess on the jacket was."

Should she have? No, it had never crossed her mind. Not even when Smith had produced his search warrant. Not until she'd been in the cell, mulling over those phone calls, thinking about the search. Then she'd seen it in a different light.

"I had no reason to doubt what he'd told me," she said. "I still don't. Whatever those marks are."

"Well, DCI Archer, here's the problem. You know that, whoever washed it, they didn't do much of a job, because those brownish spots remained. And we had them sprayed with Luminol. You know what Luminol is, am I right?"

He was dragging it out and – she thought – enjoying it.

"Obviously," was all she said.

"Well. For the benefit of the recording and Ms Walker, Luminol is a water-based solution that's capable of detecting blood, even if it's been diluted as much as – how much, DS Woodger?"

"Ten thousand times."

"Ten thousand times. Once it comes in contact with blood, it causes the blood to glow blue. As you know. So can you guess what happened when we sprayed that jacket?"

"You tell me." She was getting fed up now. But also scared. Very scared.

"It lit up," he said. "Like a Christmas tree. So your husband's got blood all over him and yet he doesn't recognise it for what it is? Even if it's remotely likely that this mysterious clumsy person was in fact plastered with blood."

He had a point. Dominic may not be a cop, but everyone saw a fair bit of blood in their lifetime. How easy was it to see it and not realise what it was? But then, he'd had a lot on his mind. Rob's behaviour. The house fire.

"He told me he didn't scrutinise it that closely. It's a dark fabric, it was dark out, and he just wanted to try and get whatever it was out and save it staining. Knowing him, he'd have used the setting recommended on the label. And," she added, "he'd know as well as I would that too hot a wash can set a stain."

"If you say so. Or how about this for a scenario? He gets a call from Rob Thomas asking to meet. Maybe Rob wants to apologise for his behaviour, maybe he wants to tell Dominic he's not giving up on getting you back. Who knows? But Dominic, he knows if it gets ugly that he won't stand a chance against a former firefighter, so he takes a knife along, just in case."

"My husband?" she scoffed. "Going out tooled up? No way. I bet if I check the knives at home, none are missing. Come to think of it, you evidently didn't find a likely murder weapon at the house, or you'd be gloating over that, too."

"No one's gloating," he said, shaking his head. "And for all we know, he bought a knife somewhere on his way to the meeting. A meeting he didn't tell you about, by the sound of it. How well do you really know him?"

"How well do any of us know anyone?" added Fleetwood. "Whoever the call was from, they never turned up."

"Let's say it was Rob, though. Humour me. Maybe Rob did ask Dominic to meet him. A clear the air thing. And Dominic, knowing the stress you were under, agreed, hoping he could persuade his rival to desist and go back to London? He lies to you about why he's going out – precisely because he doesn't want you stressing about that too. They meet – we don't know where yet."

"You're getting CCTV from that pub car park?"

"Of course. But we know the body had been moved from where he was killed."

"The post mortem's been done already?"

He grinned. "We don't mess about. We know quite a lot about the murder weapon, and we *will* find it. But livor mortis" – the pooling of blood in the body after death – "tells us he didn't die where he was found. So, anyway, Rob and Dominic meet, the conversation gets heated, it gets physical, and Dominic winds up using the knife."

"Rather a lot of times, as a matter of fact," Fleetwood added. The double act was beginning to grate.

"*Very* heated," said Smith. "Whoever brought the knife to the meeting, this wasn't some sort of 'got stabbed in a struggle' incident.

"Pure speculation." But, however much she still had faith in Dominic, she found herself praying that Adina Walker was as good as Lizzie thought she was. "Just as a matter of interest, will you be testing Dominic's car for traces of Rob?"

"Count on it. Yours too. Interesting that he was washing them when we came to call. Sunday chore, or getting rid of evidence?"

"You know it's not that simple."

"Yeah, well. If we find nothing, it's hardly conclusive, is it? The body could have been wrapped in something you've since disposed of."

"Whereas, if the blood on the jacket *is* Rob's..." Fleetwood said.

"Well, exactly. Unless you seriously think some random person with Rob Thomas's blood all over him just happened to bump into your husband, of all people. And, you won't be surprised to hear, a sample of that blood is being tested even as we speak. On priority. If it *is* Rob's – and I'd have a flutter on *that* horse – well..." He turned his palms upwards. "That leaves one question, doesn't it?"

"Oh," she said, "I think it leaves rather a lot of questions. Which particular one do you have in mind?"

"Well, it's one of two things will have happened. Either you believed your husband's preposterous fairy tale."

"Or?"

"Or he told you the truth when he got home. Something much like I just suggested. He confesses, and you take control. You wash the jacket for him in an attempt to cover his tracks."

She stared at him and then burst out laughing. "Really, Bill? And that's the best you can do? You said yourself, I'm an experienced murder detective. I'm too forensically aware for a rookie error like that. If I knew, or thought, it was blood, I'd have called the police. Or, if I really wanted to cover it up, then I'd have got rid of the jacket altogether. Like you say we'd have got rid of whatever we wrapped Rob's body in. Burned it, binned it somewhere. At the very least washed it on the highest temperature. And I'd have certainly checked it for residual spotting afterwards." She shook her head. "Do me a favour."

He nodded patronisingly. "I know, I know. Thing is though, people can forget themselves under stress, or in panic. Or..." she was certain his pause was for effect. "Or maybe neither of you thought this murder would come back to haunt you. After all, it's a nice jacket. Expensive-looking. Washing instructions recommend thirty degrees."

"You really think I'm that stupid," she snapped.

Adina laid a restraining hand on her arm. But Smith was visibly enjoying himself, grinning broadly, his teeth bared, a predator scenting blood.

"What's a few blemishes?" he said. "If a constant reminder of killing a man isn't a problem for you. Hell," he chuckled, "maybe it's a badge of honour: he stood up for his wife and dealt with the scumbag who was pestering her. Maybe every time you see those dots of blood, it'll remind you."

"Detective Chief Inspector," Adina interjected. "It seems to me that you're accusing my client of complicity in a murder before we even know whose blood is on the jacket."

Smith looked on the brink of a rejoinder, then leaned back in his chair.

"You're right, of course. We mustn't get ahead of ourselves. I'm just trying to get at the truth here. Which I will. I wonder what Mr Newman will say. Whether he'll confess. Whether he'll say what part you played in all this, DCI Archer. Because that's what you really have to worry about now. Ms Walker makes a fair point, but we all know that blood will turn out to be Rob Thomas's, and then it's game over for your husband. It's just a matter of whether he takes you down with him. Aiding an offender, perverting the course of justice... take your pick."

"DCI Smith," Adina said, "whatever my client's husband may or may not say, the fact remains that she arrived home on Friday night to find that jacket already in the wash. Even if you are able to connect Mr Newman to Robert Thomas's death – and it sounds like you have a long way to go with that – my client knows nothing of that. Instead of putting all your focus on my client and her husband, I'm a little surprised you're not looking for other leads."

"Yes? And what leads might they be? Who else had a motive for killing Rob Thomas?"

And Lizzie knew that, whatever her personal view, however much she loathed Bill Smith, were she in his shoes, she'd have had Dominic down as a prime suspect too.

She'd known that, even before this interview started. But she'd thought beyond what Smith apparently thought was obvious.

"Open your eyes, Bill," Lizzie said, reaching for calm. "I know you don't like me, but you know as well as I do that coppers make enemies. I know I have. There have been threats in the past week that I've reported to my Divisional Commander. What better way for them to hurt me than to frame my husband for murder? If I'm suspected of any complicity, so much the better."

"Very convenient. Or very fanciful." Smith stretched. "Let's all take a break. If Mr Newman's story matches yours, and maybe says the blood on the jacket is where he cut himself shaving – and the lab backs it up – maybe I'll think about what you said. But I really wouldn't hold my breath, if I were you."

23

The Chief Constable's office had inevitably been briefed on the arrest of one of its own officers, and had considered it imperative to issue a statement to the media. The one saving grace was that no names were being released at this time. The line given to the press team was simply that a man and a woman had been arrested and were currently being questioned, and that one of them was a serving police officer.

Superintendent Stowe had still been furious when he broke the news to Dan and Lara Moseley, who'd initially been asked to keep Lizzie's arrest to himself until the facts were clearer.

"I just can't imagine why anyone would think it was a good idea," he'd stormed, the nearest thing to a crack in his normally calm exterior that Dan had ever witnessed. "You know me – I'm passionate about transparency, but that's not the same thing as rushing to release half-baked information. Now the arrest of a police officer will be the story, and the media will be gagging for a name."

"They'll get one, too," Dan had said. "Local media have their ears close to the ground, and some cops have big mouths."

"Exactly," Lara had agreed. "And, once Lizzie's identity is known, she'll be hung out to dry."

"Well, there had better not be any leaks from inside this division," Stowe had said grimly. "I think it's time for you both to put your teams in the picture, but make it clear that God help them if anything that appears in the media gets traced back to them. I'll have them wishing they were only on traffic duty."

So Dan had gathered his own team in the briefing room and had made sure the door was firmly closed before telling them what had happened to their DCI. For several seconds, a stunned silence followed. He wasn't surprised. He was still reeling himself.

Joan Collins was the first to break it.

"It's just ridiculous," she declared, her expression a mixture of shock and anger. "And DCI Smith from Bedford arrested her personally? I suppose you know there's bad blood between them?"

"I don't know you'd call it bad blood," he said. "She admitted when we spoke last night that she doesn't like him."

"That's a bit of an understatement. He came up in conversation down the pub one time. I'd not long come out as gay, and we were talking about prejudice in all its forms. Sounds like the guy's more than a bit of a misogynist, who resented her getting promotions quicker than him. Made some nasty insinuations about how she came by them."

"That's more or less what she told me, and she certainly wasn't looking forward to seeing him again. I don't think she was going so far as to say they were sworn enemies though."

"All the same. If she had a conflict of interest over the murder case, surely he has one too, given his history with Lizzie. She should have complained at the outset."

"I'm sure she would have," he said, "if she'd thought it was necessary, but she reckoned objecting would look more suspicious than going with the flow. She thought the best thing was to grit her teeth and just get through it."

"In fairness, guv, he must think he's got some sort of evidence," Jason Bell said. "He can't have arrested her or Dominic just because they had a bit of a row with Rob."

"But what evidence can they have?" Joan looked mystified. "We all know what we'd be looking for – murder weapon, DNA, fingerprints, trace transfer."

"And motive, means and opportunity," Dan pointed out. "Dominic getting shirty with Rob in front of one of the uniforms outside the house – hardly his usual discreet self? That could be seen as a motive of sorts."

"Yeah, some guy who's been hitting on your wife and maybe being involved in your house being set on fire tends to be a bit annoying. But even if that counts as motive – and you might say they had the opportunity too, if they don't have a checkable alibi – what about the means? What about the murder weapon?"

"Your guess is as good as mine. If they have, and it's been wiped clean of fingerprints, then Lizzie and Dominic are neither ruled in nor out. And even the Super doesn't have much in the way of details. Just that they're both under arrest on suspicion of murder."

"So the clock's ticking?"

"You know how it goes. They can hold them for as much as ninety-six hours, seeing that it's murder, before they have to charge them or release them. Hopefully it'll be the latter. At least they've got a good lawyer, the Super got that much out of DCI Smith. They're both using Adina Walker for now."

"Wow," Natalie Chen said. "She's the best. But both?"

It had surprised him too. "I know, but I'm sure she knows what she's doing, and I can't imagine there'll be any conflict, since I can't believe either of them is guilty."

"Me neither," Joan concurred. She looked at Dan. "So what are we going to do about it?"

"Us?" He frowned. "It's not our case. That's kind of the point of DCI Smith."

She rolled her eyes. "Seriously, guv? He's stitching her up."

"We don't know that."

"Well, I for one am not sitting around waiting for them to be charged."

"Nor me," said Jason. "We all know how this works. Once the CPS decide there's a case to answer, it gets harder every day to claw your way back from that."

"And if it gets to trial," Will Tyler added, "much as I like to think the justice system is fair, it's not like the police have a great reputation right now, with the negative stuff that's been hitting the press lately: cops guilty of sex assaults, even murder, all the racism and misogyny…"

"I know," said Dan. "I know. That sort of muck can stick to the whole force."

"And could colour a jury's outlook on this," Natalie added.

"And if she's remanded in custody," Joan said, "that's a total nightmare. We all know how cops fare in prisons."

"It wouldn't be a picnic for Dominic either," said Jason.

"No," Dan agreed. "The cons have a habit of sniffing out people's secrets and, once the word gets out that he's a copper's husband, he'll be a target by association."

"And not much chance either of them would get bail," Natalie said. "Not in a murder case."

He sighed. "It all stinks but, much as we all want to help, I ask again: what do you think we can do?"

Joan blinked. "Guv, we stop it getting that far, that's what. First off, we need to find out what evidence the Bedford mob think they have against Lizzie and Dominic and test their case to destruction. And we have to find out who really killed Rob Thomas."

Her chin jutted, her expression pugnacious. He took in the rest of the team, nodding, equally animated. Pride swept over him and he felt a grin tugging at the corners of his mouth.

"Oh," he said dryly. "Well, if that's all…" He rocked back in his chair. "Even if we had any sort of insight into the case, you're talking about meddling in an ongoing investigation. Mounting a private investigation. Breaking every rule in the book, and a few laws, to boot."

She grinned. "Yes, I am. You know as well as I do that Lizzie's had all our backs, one way and another, since the day she arrived." She sobered. "She saved Charlie…"

And Dan knew she'd saved him, too, more than once.

"And she's fronted up when senior people in this very building were guilty of wrongdoing," Jason said. "Now she's the one in trouble. I'm with Joan. We can't just sit on our hands and let the system take her down." He looked at Will, then Natalie. "You two don't have to risk getting in trouble. You can forget you heard this."

"No way," Will said.

"I'm in," said Natalie.

"So what's it to be, Dan?" Joan said. "Because, whether you're with us or not, you're going to have to stop us."

He looked from one expectant face to another, his mind flooding with memories of all the times Lizzie had been there for him, through some of the darkest times of his life.

"Obviously I'm in," he said. "But we can't just go crashing around with our size nines. This is career-limiting stuff we're talking about. You should all be aware of that."

Joan flapped a dismissive hand. "Message received. Scary, right? So what are we gonna do?"

He turned it over in his mind before replying. "It's all about the case DCI Smith thinks he's building. He must have more – probably a lot more – than Dominic and Rob having a row."

"Agreed," Joan said. "He's got to have evidence. We need to know what it is. Because either they're reading it wrong or…"

"…or someone's trying to stitch them up," Jason said. "If not Smith, maybe someone else."

"Exactly." Dan furrowed his brow. "Right, so I know I said we're supposed to stay away from the actual evidence, but there has to be a way of finding out what it is."

"So we need an in to the Bedfordshire force. I bet they're talking about it around the water coolers."

He made a big show of scratching his head. "If only we knew someone with contacts all over the place."

"Yeah," Joan said, smirking, "if only."

"So leave that to me," he said. "But this isn't going to be easy, trying to conduct an unofficial murder enquiry in secret. We can't do it here, either. We'd best start meeting in the evenings at my place."

"Karen won't mind?"

"I'd be surprised. She'll probably bake cakes."

He said it knowing that this could derail his career, with consequences for the family finances. But he knew Karen better than she knew herself. She knew what they owed to Lizzie.

"So, six of us, with Karen," Jason said.

"Seven," Joan said, "with Charlie. She'll want to help, and a trained lawyer could be useful."

"How are we going to communicate?" asked Will, ever the practical one. "I could set up a WhatsApp group."

"And can we set up a board or something?" Joan asked. "Like we use in here?"

"Good idea," Dan agreed. "Actually, we've got a whiteboard Karen bought for work projects. It's gathering dust in the room we use as an office. In fact, we'll set that room up as our HQ."

"All that and Karen's famous cakes?" Joan grinned. "The case is as good as solved."

24

Adina Walker didn't look at her svelte best when she came into the station at 6.30 am on Monday morning to be present at another interview between Smith and Lizzie. He and DI Fleetwood sat across the table. DS Woodger wasn't present this time. Fleetwood did the honours with the recorder.

"This won't take long," Smith said. "We've decided to release you. For now. You're not completely off the hook yet…"

"What about Dominic?" Hope and fear mingled. She could hardly breathe.

He shook his head, and fear won. This was real. This was happening.

"No chance," he said. "Sorry." She wondered if he was. "It's a cop's husband we're talking about. Since it could all get nasty in the media, I've done my best to pull some favours on getting DNA tests on those blood stains quickly. Even so, we're not likely to get any results this side of tomorrow. Maybe Wednesday. Either way, we'll have them well within the thirty-six hours we can hold him for. If they're Rob Thomas's – and I'm still betting they are… well…" He shrugged. "I don't need to draw you a picture, do I?"

"If they're Rob's blood, then that person collided with Dominic on purpose. Did you look at the CCTV from the pub, by the way?"

"We did. And we've spoken to the bar staff. They confirm your husband was there for a while, nursing a soft drink and fiddling with his phone. And, before you ask, yeah, his phone definitely received and made the calls to the burner found on Rob."

"So Rob phoned him to set up the meeting?"

"We still don't know the order of events, nor where they really met, but it wasn't the Five Birds. The staff can't swear how long Dominic was there, but no one joined him. As for someone bumping into him outside, the camera did capture that, but you know what I think? He deliberately went to the pub for a while to try and establish an alibi, just in case. The collision in the car park was pure accident, but he remembered it when you asked why the jacket was in the wash, and it was a convenient excuse."

"But you're going to find that person, right?"

"Oh, yes. That mysterious person." He gave her his very best condescending smirk. "I really wish I could, but it's dark, he's got his hood up – can't blame him with the weather so crap. It could be anyone. If he gets in a car and drives away, it's outside the camera's field of vision. If you want to believe it was the real killer, you hang onto that. But also thank your stars your husband is as insistent as you are that it was him who put the jacket in the washing machine, before you got home. On balance, I think I just about believe him, at least for now. If that changes, you'll be back before your feet touch the ground."

"If you've quite finished, DCI Smith," Adina said, "you said you were releasing my client, so this meeting is at an end."

Outside the station, it was almost light. Lizzie's mood was dark.

"I'd run you home," Adina said, "but they'll be resuming questioning Dominic shortly." She checked her watch.

"I'll be fine. Getting Dominic out is all I need you to do."

Adina's look was not unsympathetic. "I don't think I can pull that off until those DNA results come back, and I have to say it's not looking good. If that blood's Rob Thomas's—"

"Oh," Lizzie sighed dejectedly, "we both know it will be. Case closed as far as Smith's concerned. And then, yeah, I wouldn't rate our chances at trial either."

"Even if they can't produce a murder weapon and connect Dominic to it, we know only too well that jurors watch cop shows, and they do set an awful lot of store by DNA. Even if the blood's all they have, it could be enough."

"I know you'll do all you can for him. I can't ask more."

Adina briefly squeezed her arm. "I promise I will. So what are your plans now?"

"Blag a lift home. Get a shower. Then think about how I can find out who really killed Rob."

*

Dan was already up and moving about when Lizzie called to say she'd been released from Luton nick, and would he mind picking her up.

"I'd find a taxi," she'd told him, "but I could do with a friend just now."

He knew she'd be the first person he'd call, if he was in her situation.

"On my way," he said with no hesitation. "It might take me a while."

"That's okay. I'll find a café and text you where it is."

He found her in a corner of a small café just around the corner from the police station, a cup cradled in her hands, a half-eaten pastry sat on a plate in front of her. She looked hunched and small and didn't seem to notice him walking in. She only stirred when he sat down beside her.

He studied her face. She was the strongest woman he knew, and he'd never seen her looking so vulnerable. Eyes red from crying. Lower lip trembling. Her hair, usually immaculate, so askew that the crescent scar on her cheek – that she usually made so much effort to conceal – was peeping through.

He pulled her into a hug, and she sobbed into his shoulder.

"It's okay," he said. "I'm here. I've got you."

She nodded wordlessly, then pulled away. "I'm sorry." She gave him a half-smile, half-grimace. "What a pussy, eh?"

"Let's just get you home and you can tell me what's happened."

She stared ahead, her voice flat. "I already told you all that matters. They're still holding Dominic. And it looks bad."

"How bad is bad though?"

A twitch of the shoulders. "Really bad. Look, can we get out of here? I feel like I'm going to lose it, and I'd rather not do that this close to the station. For all I know, Bill bloody Smith gets his coffee in here. He'd love to see me like this. Bastard," she added savagely.

In the car, she squinted at Dan's dashboard clock.

"Shit, you'll be late for work. And I bet you had no breakfast, either."

He glanced in the rear-view mirror, signalled and pulled away from the kerb.

"I let Joan know I'd be a bit late. She was going to tell the Super. I'm sure he'll understand but, if he doesn't, tough. So long as I'm there for the Police Scotland guy."

"Shit, I'd forgotten that."

"I've plenty of time. So come on. Spill."

She started to talk, and then the words tumbled out of her. He listened, not interrupting once.

"Wow," he said when she'd run out of words. "You're right. It's bad."

She looked at him, then barked a laugh that was probably just the right side of hysterical.

"Shit," she said. "I hoped you'd say we had nothing to worry about."

"Yeah, well. Much as I'd love to lie to you…" He made eye contact. "I hate to ask you this…"

"But is there any possibility he *did* do it?" she said flatly.

He nodded and braced himself for hostility. She simply sighed, rubbing at her puffy eyes.

"I can't blame you for asking, I suppose. If it was anyone else, and I had the case Smith's building, maybe I'd be pretty sure he did. I mean, with my sceptical copper's hat on, I can't deny there's things that would bother me."

"Such as?" A few had occurred to him, but he wanted to hear from her.

"Well, like the blood, the blood on the jacket. How the hell could he not see it was blood? I mean, if he didn't, he didn't, but…"

"Yes, but sometimes, things really are as mind-numbingly stupid as they sound. He told you it was dark and he just wanted to try and stop it staining. He had a lot on his mind. He was probably pretty distracted, and this was just one more piece of rubbish in an exceptionally lousy week. Maybe he really didn't want to investigate too closely. Maybe he feared that the other guy had been rolling in dog shit and he'd rather not know."

"Then, there's that caution back in the day for violence."

Dan shrugged. "Yeah, well. It sounds to me like he was protecting his girlfriend and the guy attacking her came off worse. I don't even know why he was cautioned, given that the woman backed his story."

"Nor me, really. Maybe the other bloke had connections. But what really bugs me, Dan, is this. He marries a police officer, but never, ever, thinks to mention it to me."

Dan had initially thought the same, but now he examined the question again.

"These things are seldom black and white. Maybe he was scared you'd be put off him. Or embarrassed about it. There's any number of reasons he never told you. Or he didn't tell you at the outset, when you were just friends, and then, I dunno, maybe once you grew closer, it felt harder to bring it up."

"Maybe. He still should have told me."

"Maybe he thought you knew. That, as a cop, you'd have checked him out. When you speak to him, you can ask him. But we both know people are complicated, Lizzie. Yes, he should have told you. Just because he didn't, that doesn't make him a thug under the skin. Or a killer. Point is, take that and the blood away, and I think your theory that someone's framing him actually carries quite a lot of weight."

"You honestly do?" She sounded relieved. "Because, to tell the truth, I'm struggling to think straight. I'd got to the point where I half-thought I was doing a fair bit of straw-clutching."

"I'm not surprised."

"I even wondered if Rob himself had made an enemy who had reason to kill him. But, like everything else in this case, that doesn't make a whole lot of sense. They'd have to somehow stumble on the bust-up with Dominic, know or find out the background, and decide on an elaborate frame-up, presumably to cover their own tracks. I just don't see it."

"Nor me. But look, why would Rob even use a burner phone to call Dominic? Something funny about that too. It all seems so unnecessary. Why not use his own phone?"

"If he meant Dominic harm, he might not."

"He might not, but you're right. There's just too much about this case that doesn't add up, isn't there? I mean, you'd have to believe that Rob either pulled off posing as a potential client, or he lured him to a meeting anyway. Then you swallow the notion that it all goes wrong for Rob, he ends up dead, and Dominic – rather than tell you, or go to the police – coolly wraps his body in something, moves it to the Northfields for some unfathomable reason, and dumps it there, Then he disposes of the murder weapon and the wrapping, goes home and just as coolly tries to wash the blood out of his jacket."

"Smith would say he tried to cover it up in a panic."

"A panic that turned him into the kind of blithering idiot that, despite being married to a cop – and I bet you've bored him a few times on forensics…"

She cracked some sort of smile. "Might have."

"Despite that, he washes the jacket on a low temperature. He doesn't get rid of it, like he apparently thought to dump the knife and this mysterious wrapping he just happened to have handy." He rolled his eyes. "Come on, Lizzie. It's bollocks."

"You really think so?" Her eyes were moist, but there was hope in them.

"Honestly. Look, I know Dominic well enough to know that, even if things had played out something like that, he's not going to unravel the whole thing with such a rookie error. Much more likely someone else used that phone to make the call, then planted it on Rob's body. Same person probably deliberately got Rob's blood on him, intercepted Dominic and made sure he transferred some to him."

She inclined her head, a little more like the Lizzie he knew now. "Well, it's a theory. A good one. But it's only a theory. Smith still has the arguments, the calls, the blood on the jacket. If I go to him with this, he'll pooh-pooh it. I've already decided it's down to me to try and find out what really happened. Not that I have a clue where to start."

He smiled. "Good thing you're not alone then."

"What do you mean?"

"How little you know your team. The Super said I could brief them, and they're all guns blazing to find the real killer. Charlie and Karen are on board, too."

"That's so lovely," she said, "but I can't allow it. I'll probably be putting my career in the toilet, meddling with someone else's case for personal reasons. I can't take you lot with me. You've all got too much to lose."

"Our choice. None of us are kids, you know. Yep, we could all get disciplined for this. Maybe. But you can hardly turn us in for helping you without turning yourself in. I mean, look at Natalie. She's been on my team the shortest time, but she didn't hesitate. And she's as driven and ambitious as they come. She still chose to get involved. Because she cares about you. We all do."

Tears spilled down her face again. "Now look what you've done. And I suppose you've worked out how to do this covert investigation without anyone noticing?"

"Not entirely, no. We need to find out what's going on in that investigation. If we can. That's why we need someone with the right contacts. We're going to need some help."

She stared at him. "As in *outside* help? No. No, no, no. This'll only stand a chance of working if we keep it between us."

"Yeah, well." If she didn't like the idea, she was going to hate the reality.

"You said contacts. What sort of contacts?" She groaned. "Christ, no."

"If there's a weak, leaky link in your DCI Smith's team—"

"He's not *my* DCI Smith."

"We need someone connected. A networker."

"*Ashby?* You're talking about involving *Steve Ashby* in this mad conspiracy? Aren't you?" She shook her head vehemently. "No. Not happening."

"Ah."

She slammed her fist on the top of the dashboard. "Fuck, Dan."

He'd known there were a million and one reasons why she'd think it a terrible idea. They could both remember when Steve Ashby had been a lazy, time-serving, self-centred sexist. When he'd moved on a few years ago, it had been under a cloud – demoted from DI to DS, thanks to an old transgression, uncovered by Lizzie, and probably lucky not to be dismissed.

Yet, once he'd got over the ignominy, the word was that he'd knuckled down and could well be headed for DI again. And, to be fair, he'd improved as a human being and was in a steady relationship with DS Amy Petrescu, whom he'd transferred to Oxford to join.

More to the point, when Joan's partner, Charlie, had been kidnapped, he'd been eager to help the team out in trying to find her.

Lizzie had admitted herself that he'd changed for the better. But Dan knew she didn't entirely trust him. On the surface, the leopard might seem to have changed its spots – but it was hard to shake the notion that you didn't have to scratch that surface too much to still find a loose cannon.

He held up his hands placatingly. "Lizzie, you'd both been arrested. None of us was prepared to sit around and watch you get charged and packed off to prison on remand."

"So you've already spoken to him." It wasn't a question.

"On the phone last night."

"Fuck!" she said for a second time, this time with more emphasis.

"He didn't hesitate. He knows a couple of people who are now in Bedfordshire and, as luck would have it, he knows a DS on your man Smith's team."

"Stop calling him my man." But she looked a little curious now. "This DS. Does he or she have a name?"

"Not yet. But Indiscreet is his middle name, according to Ashby. You know the type: some cases, they can't resist showing off that they're in the know. So our networking expert is going to see what he can get out of him. Subtly, of course."

"Does Steve Ashby even *do* subtle?"

"We'll see, won't we?"

She clutched at her head. "I can't believe I'm agreeing to this. Okay, one stipulation. The Super can't know. He can't be seen to countenance it. I still don't think you should be doing it. Getting Dominic exonerated is my job."

"And I still say the clock's ticking, Lizzie. Dominic's either going to walk out of that station with no charges, or he'll be charged, with the whole runaway train of remand, a prosecution and a trial picking up speed. I've got to be honest: my money's on the latter. So we're doing this, whether you like it or not. And no, of course we won't be confiding in the Super."

"Well, thanks. I can never repay any of you, whatever happens." She frowned. "*Ashby*, though? Not a hint of a gloat?"

"Oh, the irony that he's helping someone who got him reduced in the ranks isn't lost on him. In a way, he's got the most to lose, too. With his dodgy background, it might not just be his promotion chances that are scuppered. Maybe his entire career. Yet he's helping you," he said.

She blinked. "I don't get it."

"Would you believe, he reckons you actually did him a favour. Seems he'd been carrying guilt around like a ton weight, and it was eating him up, day after day before we found out about his past. He knows the outcome could have been worse, and at least everything was out in the open. In a funny way, I think he feels he owes you one."

She'd been looking thoroughly miserable. Now she squared her shoulders.

"Okay," she said. "So if our favourite theory is that Dominic's being framed to hurt me, who's behind it? There are two obvious candidates..."

"The Upmans and Cameron Connolly?"

"They're the first names that come to mind, yes. Although it all feels a bit too clever for Gaynor and her brood, doesn't it?"

"Maybe. You can see Gaynor torching a house for revenge. This does seem a bit elaborate for her, but don't underestimate Carl. He might not exactly be Brain of Britain, but he's probably the wits of the family. But what about Cameron?"

"It sounds more his style, doesn't it? He threatened not only me, but the people I love too. Plus he's got eyes and ears everywhere. He saw me with Rob that first day, and you can bet he's found out all about him. And when Rob came round after the fire – I'd be surprised if what happened there hadn't got back to Cameron too, somehow. He could easily have kept his hands clean while orchestrating Rob's death, the call to Dominic, even the smearing of blood onto him. He's got plenty of minions who'd find it well worth their while to do his dirty work, and good for their health to keep schtum afterwards."

"I know his sister was adamant he'd recanted his threats," Dan said. "He even looked me in the eye and said as much. But so what? He's more than capable of lying to us, and to his sister I dare say." He stifled a yawn. "If I was running an official investigation, I'd question him *and* the Upmans. I guess I can still do that, in connection with the fire, and try to bring the murder into it…"

"Be careful not to let them know Dominic and I have been arrested, though. It's not in the media yet, and I'd like to keep it that way."

"Hmm. I can probably pull it off with the Upmans. Cameron Connolly, though… No flies on him. Even if he doesn't already know what's going on, he'd make it his business to find out."

She fell silent for a few moments, then a half-smile stole over her face.

"Tell you what," she said. "You find an excuse to talk to the Upmans. Leave the Connollys to me."

"To you? You're going to confront Cameron?"

"I'm thinking something more subtle. I hope his sister's still in the area. I just might fancy a bit of art shopping."

25

Josh Stowe had told Lizzie, quite kindly, to stay home, at least until Dominic's situation was resolved, which was exactly what she wanted.

She had half-expected Grace Connolly to have returned to Scotland by now. But her luck was in. When she'd called her mid-morning, it emerged that Grace intended sticking around at least until next weekend.

"Fraser and I are still staying with Cam," she explained. "There's a lot we still need to sort out as a family. But you're the last person I expected to hear from."

"You're the last person I expected to be phoning. Even now, I'm not sure I should be doing this."

"Okay…" A note of edgy caution already.

"Look," she said, "I'll come to the point. I'm betting you already know, through your brother, that we've had a house fire."

There was a pause on the line. "Cameron had nothing to do with that. You do know the police questioned him?"

"Only vaguely. Since I'm the victim, I'm keeping out of the investigation."

"Well, it's not his style, even if he were prone to violence."

"Which, of course, he isn't."

"Of course," Grace repeated. "But you and your husband?" Her tone softened a little. "You're both okay?"

"We're fine. Thanks for asking. It could have been a whole lot worse, for us and for the house."

"That's good."

The line fell awkwardly silent, and Lizzie realised this was going to be even harder than she'd imagined. In their previous dealings, she'd felt Grace was a very different character to Cameron. But she also recognised that, just because Grace appeared to be the respectable one, that didn't make it so. Even if she was, Lizzie was prepared to bet she would always put family first. She was bound to be as naturally suspicious of an approach from the police as Lizzie had been when Grace first got in touch with her.

She hoped what she had in mind would help. Now it came to it, it felt like a pretty flimsy pretext. Could she carry it off?

"Anyway," she plunged in, "this is not an official call, and only indirectly to do with the fire. Here's the thing. Our hall got a bit damaged, and I'm thinking it'd be a perfect excuse for a makeover. And I've been thinking for some time about a nice piece of art to go there. Something to catch the eye when people first walk in."

"Makes sense. What's that to do with me, though?"

"Well, I looked at your website after we talked before. To be honest, it was a bit of a know thy enemy thing at first."

"I'm not your enemy, DCI Archer."

"Well anyway, I do like your work, but I don't know a great deal about art." She reached for a note of diffidence. "I don't suppose it'd be appropriate to meet up for a chat about some of the options I've been looking at?"

A moment's hesitation. Then, "I can't see a problem. Unless you're trying to trick me into saying something to incriminate my brother."

"No tricks. Just about the art. Any chance you'd be free for a coffee this morning?"

Another pause. "Actually, I could be. Where and when?"

They met at Rumsey's in Wendover, the same place Lizzie had once been stupid enough to meet with Cameron a few years ago. It was her favourite café in the whole of the Chilterns, and she thought she deserved a treat if she was going to do this.

She got there early and watched Grace striding purposefully across the road, tall in the same dark coat she'd had on the other day, when Cameron had followed Lizzie home and started issuing wild threats. They went inside, found a table, and made small talk until their orders were taken. Lizzie ordered pavlova and a honeycomb milkshake, and Grace went for the salted caramel cheesecake with a blackcurrant shake. Judging by her slim frame, Lizzie guessed it must be a rare indulgence.

"So…" Lizzie said as the waitress walked away.

"So… I'm still thinking there's an agenda here, and this so-called interest in one of my works is just a ruse to pump me for information."

"So why did you come?"

"I suppose I'm shallow. Easily flattered." It was said without obvious guile.

"I honestly do like them," she admitted. "I love the way the figures in them look so natural, as if caught off guard."

"Thank you." She looked pleased. "So is there one you especially like?"

"I could only really afford a print, I'm afraid. I'd have to think long and hard about the prices for the originals, or even the special editions. But how about we look at the ones I fancy, I show you some photos of the hall where I'd most likely hang it, and you can help me choose? Then I'd have to talk it over with my husband."

She watched the other woman's eyes as she said this, looking for a reaction. If Cameron had any part in framing Dominic, mention of him didn't seem to register.

She got out her phone and showed Grace a couple of the paintings she especially liked and then showed her a couple of photographs she'd taken of her damaged hall. While they were talking artwork, they both relaxed somewhat. The food and drink arrived. In the end, it came down to the one she'd liked best all along: a middle-aged woman who reminded her a bit of her mother. She was staring into the distance with a vivid sunset behind her that somehow captured all the colours of the rainbow without looking in any way artificial.

"It really would be a great choice," Grace said. "Tell you what – why don't I gift you a print?"

"No," she said firmly. "Not only wouldn't I hear of it, but… the truth is, my accepting anything from your family could be misconstrued. No offence," she added.

Grace's eyes widened. "You think I'm *bribing* you? With a sixty quid print? You came to me, remember."

Lizzie shook her head vehemently. "No, no, it's a nice gesture, but that's the rules, I'm afraid. And it's not just you. It really doesn't matter who I accept things from. We have to be so careful. It's all a matter of perception."

The other woman seemed to relax a little again. "All right. If you do decide to buy it, full price it is."

They ate in silence for a few moments.

"So have you always painted?" Lizzie ventured.

"Always. I mean, I dabbled in some other arts too: dance, acting, bit of poetry. I always came back to brushes and canvass. How about you? Always a copper?"

"As was my dad. But I'm surprised Cameron hasn't winkled that out and mentioned it."

"Seeing as he 'knows things'?"

"Well... yeah."

Grace Connolly smiled and shrugged. "Okay. Busted. Cam's told me all about you. You've shown an interest in him, and he's returned the favour."

"Does he know you're here?"

"I thought it best he didn't know. There would only have been an argument."

Lizzie managed a smile. "Well, speaking of him keeping his eyes open, you were with him when he saw me going for a drink with my ex, the day of your family funeral?"

"He was your ex?"

"Cam didn't bother finding *that* out?"

Grace shook her head. "If he did, he didn't tell me. Maybe, after Fraser and I talked some sense into him, he decided to let sleeping dogs lie."

"So you didn't know my ex had been murdered?"

Grace had moved on to her milkshake. She almost choked on her straw. *"What?"*

"Friday night, apparently. Stabbed to death somewhere and dumped on a notorious estate."

Grace's eyes widened again. "Oh, but wait... that was on the news..." She stared at Lizzie. "They arrested someone. A police officer? God, not someone you know? Not *you*?"

She sipped her own drink. "It's been a bit awkward. He turned up out of the blue after ten years or more and started making a bit of a nuisance of himself. You know, wanting me back. Pissing off my husband. There was a bit of a public row actually, so I've had to take myself and my team off that case, too."

"So you *were* the one under arrest?"

Lizzie made a show of looking awkward. "I've probably said too much already. Like I said, someone else is looking into it."

"But you're in the clear now?"

"Not quite. I shouldn't say this, but I bet Cameron does know already, even if he hasn't said. My husband was part of the public row."

"He's not a suspect, surely?"

If she was aware that one suspect had been released and one remained in custody, she was hiding it well.

"I'm sure it'll all be fine," Lizzie lied. "I can't pretend I'm completely unworried though. I mean..." She paused for effect. "I'm sure if they thought they had some sort of evidence..."

"What sort of evidence, though?"

"I don't know. Unless something had been..." she shook her head. "No, that's ridiculous."

Grace stared at her. "You mean, like... planted? By who? Oh," she said, "I see..."

"No, you don't," Lizzie said quickly. "Honestly, Cameron's by no means the only one I've fallen out with lately."

"Yeah, but... killing a man to try and get you into trouble..." She looked sharply at Lizzie. "This whole meetup has felt weird from the start. You must take me for a fool. Being friendly, pretending to like my work, and all the while hoping I'll accidentally shop my brother..."

"It honestly is mostly about the art." Lizzie hoped her poker face was good enough. "I mean, okay, I did wonder what he might have seen or heard..."

"Or done, right? Look, whatever you think of Cameron, two things I'll say for him. He's direct, and he does things with finesse. Does that sound like the person you're looking for?"

Lizzie thought a crude killing and an attempt to frame Dominic – maybe her too – was actually pretty clever, and right up Cameron's street. Way too clever for the Upmans.

But, "You're likely right," she said with an exaggerated sigh. "It's not like I've only just started making enemies. And I'm probably worrying unnecessarily anyway. They'll find some lowlife who was off his head on drugs, most like."

"Look," Grace said, "if Cam hears anything useful, and he tells me, I'll be sure to pass it on."

"That'd be brilliant. The guy was being a pest, but he didn't deserve that. We had something once, after all."

"It must have been a shock."

"Yeah."

She was already wondering how much better off this meeting had left her. It had seemed like a good idea when she'd conceived it. But trying to worm something out of Grace, without seeming to be probing, was always going to be a difficult trick to pull off.

Assuming there was even anything to worm out in the first place.

She couldn't quite shake the notion that, having seen Lizzie and Rob together on Wednesday, Cameron would have made it his business to find out who he was. She had little doubt that his research on her would have unearthed her injury 'in the line of duty'. It had been made much of in the media at the time, and at least one picture of her and Rob together – supplied by Rob's mother without asking either of them if they minded – had been splashed over the tabloids.

Rob would have been recognisable as the same man Lizzie had been to the pub with. And then he'd been named as a murder victim, his picture published. He'd changed, but not that much. How likely was it that Cameron would miss something like that, in his own back yard? Had he really not said anything to his sister? And, even if not, did that necessarily signify anything?

Even if Grace was truly not part of the 'family business', it was unlikely that she'd betray anything her brother had said or done that even hinted at involvement in Rob's death. But, Lizzie admitted to herself, there were none of the tell-tale signs she often saw in a liar or someone with something to hide.

Unless Grace Connolly was a very good liar indeed.

"Are you all right?" Grace touched her elbow.

"I'm sorry. I'm fine. It's just talking about Rob – my ex. A bit upsetting, you know?" She shrugged. "But enough about me. I haven't asked you how *you're* coping. Two close family members lost on the same day. It must be hard on you all."

"Not easy. And Cam and Fraser are being dicks about how they carve up Dad's business empire. I'll be glad when I get back to Scotland and leave them to it."

"He didn't leave a will?"

"Oh, yeah. It's clear enough who gets what, but it's not just about ownership. It's who takes the really big decisions, and the will is maddeningly silent on that. Neither of them is a big compromiser." She smiled thinly. "Now *I've* probably said too much."

The conversation moved onto more mundane ground, and she was struck again by how different Grace was from Cameron. They had a coffee before they left.

Lizzie insisted they each paid for their own orders, and it turned out Grace had already mentally totted up the two amounts, to the penny.

"I'm a Scot," she grinned.

"This has actually been nice," Grace said outside. "A little weird, but nice. I know you know Cam's not a fan of yours, but you're really nothing like I expected."

She watched her walk away, a trim, upright figure, taking long, brisk strides. She was no further forward in finding out who had really killed Rob. But mentioning that she'd been making enemies for years made her think. She wondered again if she was obsessing too much about recent threats?

Maybe she should dredge her memory banks for some other suspects.

26

As Dan sat down in a meeting room with DI Alec McGivering from Police Scotland, he tried to ignore the nagging feeling that he'd rather be anywhere but here right now.

He'd like to be pressing Phil Gordon for something, anything, from that burned out car. He'd like to be rattling the Upmans' cages and seeing if they were stupid enough to betray a complicity in the Rob Thomas murder.

Most of all, though, he'd like not to be assisting an enquiry into possible new Invisible Man murders.

He actually hoped that he wouldn't be able to help McGivering see a connection between his various cold cases, nor a link to Duncan McNeil's two-month killing spree here in the Vale. It would make it so much easier to believe that Mac's hints – that there had indeed been further killings with young Peter playing a part – were mere piss and wind.

Anything pointing to the contrary would keep alive the possibility that his son was at least accessory to murder. It might even lead to proving it.

He'd told himself a thousand times that this would be better than not knowing. Now he wasn't so sure. He'd thought he could look at it through a professional lens. He found he really couldn't.

Not that he had anything against McGivering. He'd come across as a decent man and a good copper in their previous communication and, in the flesh, he was someone Dan could warm to.

"So how do you want to play this?" he said, once drinks had been organised and small talk had been shared.

"Well, look. I know you must be busy…"

"It's an awkward time, as it turns out. My boss is unexpectedly away…"

"And you're having to stretch yourself a little further. I understand. I'm down until tomorrow evening, and pretty much at your disposal. I've got some files here – not the full case files for all eleven victims, but what I think are key to our purposes. Crime scene photos, a few stills of the victims when they were alive. Forensic reports. I'm assuming you don't want post-mortem reports? There are copies of the conclusions."

"I never understand half of the detailed stuff anyway."

"Oh, nor me. Anyhow, I thought I'd have a quick skim through with you, you can ask me any questions you have off the bat. Then I'll leave them with you. Do you reckon you'll have time to look at them today?"

"I'll make time." He half-smiled. "You do appreciate that, after he moved back to Scotland, McNeil was assisting your lot as a consultant on cold cases?"

McGivering didn't smile back. "The irony's not been lost on me. At least he didn't work any of these. Anyhow, once I've acquainted you with the cases, I thought maybe I'd have a drive around. See where the Invisible Man plied his trade back then. I picked up a hire car from the airport. Give me a shout when you've had a chance to look at the files and I'll come back for a chat. "

He nodded. "I think I know what I'm supposed to be looking for, but tell me anyway."

McGivering sighed. "Look, Dan, I'm not a fool. I can only imagine how difficult all this must be for you, what with your lad and all – for a hundred different reasons. I feel bad asking you to do it. But, as to what to look for, no agenda from me. Just anything that you think might resemble Duncan McNeil's signature, or any other insights. If you think one case, or all of them, are not his handiwork, say so."

"I've got a couple of cases in particular that need some attention, but I should be able to make some time and head space for this around mid-afternoon. Is that okay? I know I'm being a shit host, but—"

McGivering literally waved the apology away. "It's fine, honestly. I haven't come here to be nursemaided." He hesitated. "I know we're only doing this at all because McNeil as good as told you he'd done more killings. And he implicated your son. You must sometimes wish he'd never said it."

"All the time," Dan said with feeling.

"I'd be the same. But, you know, there are eleven people who are dead, and whose loved ones have no answers and no justice. If I can get closure for just one of those families, I'll be glad he did say it."

"Yeah, well, what can I say? I spent the best part of twenty years wanting answers of my own. Whether my boy was, by some miracle, still alive. There's still so much I don't know, and part of me doesn't really want to know. But I know what I owe to those families. If anything jumps out at me, trust me, I'll say so."

"I know you will, and I'm grateful." He drank the last of his coffee. "So let's have a quick canter over these folders."

McGivering had talked him through five of the cases when Dan's phone rang. He glanced at the display. Phil Gordon.

"Sorry, Alec," he said. "I really need to take this."

"Of course."

He took the phone out into the corridor.

"Hi, Phil."

"Morning, Dan. I thought you'd like to know. We might have something. You know, that burned out car."

He felt a small jolt of excitement. "Tell me."

"Too soon to know if it's helpful, but we may have got lucky. As I think I said, people often assume that fire ruins all DNA and fingerprints, but it's not always the case. For example, the flames can sometimes what we call 'set' a mark into the paintwork and preserve it. But we can also get something that's happened here. The fire has caused the plastic lining inside the roof to melt and fall off, and it's sort of encased the seats or other areas with a protective layer."

"Right."

"Imagine you've got, I don't know, say a lump of lead, and you pour molten plastic over it. The plastic cools and you've got your lead inside it."

"Okay," Dan said. "Got it."

"So here's the thing. That layer can withstand heat up to nine hundred degrees or so."

"Nine hundred? You're joking."

"Never more serious. So we were thinking we might find something tasty inside the melted plastic and, sure enough, there's a second plastic jerry can on the passenger seat. It has to be the one used to set fire to the car. So I'm having it analysed, and pulling in some favours to speed it up, seeing as it's to do with one of our own. But don't tell anyone about that."

"Our secret. When might you know more?"

"I'll keep you posted."

"Today would be excellent." Some evidence linking the Upmans to Lizzie's house fire would be an excellent reason to drag them to the station and shake them to see if anything about the Rob Thomas murder fell out.

"I'll do what I can," Phil said.

Dan's detective's nose was practically twitching. He hoped Steve Ashby was getting somewhere with an inside lane on the Thomas investigation. Something he could use to put the Upmans even more on the back foot and hope everything unravelled. He still thought Carl Upman might just be smart enough to have devised the frame-up.

"Thanks," he said.

They ended the call. He'd been tempted to rope Phil into his unofficial investigation, but he'd decided to keep it just within the team. The fewer people knew about it, the easier it was to keep it quiet, and the fewer people would be in trouble if the shit hit the fan.

He was already determined to bear the brunt and protect his people as much as he could if it came to it. He'd pressed Karen on whether she was really okay with it. With a young child and a mortgage, and a tricky economic climate, this wasn't the ideal time to be risking a demotion or worse.

"Yeah, well," she'd said with a straight face. "You might have to go into the sex trade to make ends meet. You could be a niche market for the grannies."

Meanwhile, he'd wait on Phil before having another go at Gaynor Upman and her brood. It would give him a bit more time to focus on Alec McGivering's cases.

Maybe the gods didn't want him to put it off.

*

Two hours later, he pushed aside another of the Police Scotland folders. He'd opted to remain in the meeting room while he worked, to avoid anyone passing or visiting his desk seeing them and asking questions. The concentration had been tiring, but he'd worked through six of the eleven cases up to now Nothing had struck any chords with him so far. The part of him that wanted nothing more than for these to be eleven unrelated cold cases seemed to be winning.

He checked his watch. Ten past one. He knew he should take a break, but he thought he'd crack on to half past. One more.

He pulled another file to him and began to turn the pages.

One thing all the cases did have in common was that they made grim reading. For some reason, it was the unremarkable ordinariness of the victims that got to him. This folder was a case from Duns, in the Borders. Sixty-three-year-old widower Andrew Storey had been struck on the head from behind: a blow heavy enough to knock him unconscious, the post mortem had concluded, but he would probably have suffered concussion at the worst. His hands had been tied behind his back with one string of a striped chef's apron, and he had been strangled with the other string.

Andrew had evidently been a keen cook, delighting family and friends with his creations and winning awards in the odd local cookery competition. He'd been killed in his own kitchen, the crime scene photos a stark contrast to a picture of him in earlier times, standing smiling in the same kitchen in the very apron that had been used to snuff out his life.

Dan almost missed it. He had turned several pages before he returned to those photographs for a second look. And there it was.

Or rather it wasn't.

It was a long way from conclusive – it was only one case out of eleven, and there could be several numerous explanations for what he thought he might have seen. But it was more than enough to persuade him to go back to the beginning and focus in on the photographs with a fresh eye.

Half an hour later, he was more than halfway to convinced.

27

Lizzie had come home, but Dominic's absence, and the lack of distraction, made it all too easy to succumb to misery and worry. Barney was a comfort. Dominic's lap was his preference when both were home, but typical cat fickleness made him as happy to snuggle up to her.

When her mind was occupied, she was able to fool herself that she or Dan's team would turn something up that would help to exonerate Dominic, bringing an end to this nightmare. Without a focus, she could only imagine the worst that could happen.

She'd bought a bottle of red wine, some cheese and some biscuits on her way home, and she sat at the breakfast bar, thinking and running searches on the Internet. She'd crossed plenty of people during her career: here in the Vale, and previously at the Met. Of those she could recall, by no means all had uttered dark threats or shown any enmity towards her. Some were still in prison. Tony Noakes, the arsonist in the case on which Lizzie had met Rob, might bear a grudge against both for his life sentence, but he'd died earlier this year.

She'd made a list of people she'd helped put away who might have it in for her. Five of them were now at large, although none had been released especially recently. If one of those really wanted revenge against her, surely they'd have acted some time ago. So why now?

Maybe something had changed for the worse in someone's life and they blamed Lizzie.

She mulled over the bloodstains on Dominic's jacket, the result of, she now suspected, a not-so-accidental collision with a young man. None of her old enemies fitted the bill, so if one of those were behind this, they must have had help. A family member? Someone who'd been paid?

She ran down those five names, looking them up on the Internet.

*

The best part of an hour later, her brain felt like mush, but she also thought she had taken this particular exercise as far as she could. Of the five possible grudge holders, two had died since their releases. A third, John Mitchell, seemed to have turned his life around in prison and now helped run courses for a charity working with young offenders.

That left Anne Bright, who'd put a love rival in hospital with life-changing injuries and – mercifully – no memory of the attack; and Tyrone Barron, drug dealer, pimp and all-round charmer. For good or ill, neither showed up on the Internet after the initial publicity surrounding their releases. Some deeper digging was required.

The team were meeting at Dan's tonight. Will Tyler would be better at this than she was, so maybe she'd get him to do some discreet follow up if she thought there were any strong candidates. She was making a note for Will when her phone rang.

Her brother's name was on the screen.

"Hi, Adam."

"Hi?" he echoed. *"Hi?* What the hell, sis?"

Not quite the greeting she was expecting. "What's the problem?"

"When were you going to tell us you and Dominic had been arrested?"

She'd deliberately not told them, telling herself it could wait until, with any luck, Dominic had been released without charge. Even when it had become apparent that this might well not happen, she'd kept it from them. She wasn't sure why.

"How do you know that?"

"Seriously? I just heard it on the news, Liz."

"What?"

"They said you'd been released, and that was about all that was good. In connection with a *murder*? Rob's?"

Her head spun. Surely if, for whatever reason, a decision had been taken to tell the media about the arrests, then common courtesy would have dictated that she be notified. If Dominic had actually been charged, they'd be bound to make that public – but surely Adina Walker would have been in touch to tell her so.

"Look," she said, hearing lame defensiveness in her voice, "it isn't what it sounds like."

"Liz, I've no idea what it sounds like. Funny thing is, I heard Rob's name on the news the other day and never made the connection. I mean, 'Rob' and 'Thomas'? I didn't imagine for a moment it was *our* Rob. What's going on? And why haven't you been *talking* to us?"

"You're right," she acknowledged, guilt and downright foolishness racking her. "I'm sorry. I-I can't explain. Maybe I didn't want to worry you."

"Oh, right." He oozed bitterness. "Like you didn't want to worry me when you told me one of the biggest gangsters in the country had threatened you and your family? *Us*, in other words? Is this murder to do with it? I mean, I take it you and Dominic *didn't* kill Rob?"

"Of course not."

"Oh, good." More sarcasm. Maybe she deserved it. "Well, I couldn't see it. It's obviously all a stupid mistake."

His faith brought a lump to her throat. "Thank you."

"Yeah, well. But bloody hell, Liz. The Police. That bloody job. It killed Dad, and it's got a lot to answer for with you, too, one way and another. And now my sister's all over the news."

"There must have been a leak."

She couldn't believe Bill Smith would be behind it, not personally – he was professional, if nothing else – but maybe one of his team had too big a mouth or wasn't above selling titbits to the press. Steve Ashby had as good as told Dan that there was a loudmouth close to Smith who loved showing off, so that was where her money was for now. One thing was for sure. She wouldn't tolerate it.

"I'm sorry you found out that way," she said.

"Look, are you all right? Do you need anything? Has Dominic got a decent lawyer?"

"The best."

"And you can afford him?"

"Her. And we'll have to."

"Let me know if it's a problem."

She blinked away sudden tears of gratitude, too emotional to trust herself to speak. These days, there was always something for her to cry about.

"We're family," he said. "I know we've had ups and downs in the past, but it's behind us now. You need to tell me about stuff like this."

"I will," she promised. A hideous thought hit her like a thunderbolt. "Oh, Christ."

"What?"

"If it's in the media, chances are they'll be camped outside my door any time now."

He didn't miss a beat. "Well, get out of there. Chuck some things in a bag and come to us."

Lizzie's brother had never moved far from the corner of West London where he and Lizzie had grown up. These days his family lived in a substantial Edwardian terraced property in Dollis Hill. The décor, and some of the less subtle architectural tweaks, shrieked Nic, Adam's loud and flamboyant wife, and really wasn't to Lizzie's taste, but she thought she could live with it, and Nic's shrillness, in exchange for being hidden away from the media.

Being around her niece, Ruby, and nephew, Luke, would be no hardship either.

But, "I can't," she said. "There are things I can try and do to help Dominic, and I need to stay local. But thank you so much for offering. I love you for it."

"You're sure?"

"No. But I don't think I have a choice."

"Well, if there's anything we can do – anything at all – just call, any time, night or day. We're here for you."

By the time they ended the call – and Lizzie's initial shock had run through a gamut of emotions, before settling on rage –

the only question was whether to ring her boss or get straight onto Bill Smith herself and be done with it.

Before she could decide, the choice was made for her as her phone rang again and Smith's number showed up on her screen.

"You've got a nerve ringing me," she began, her fury hot.

"Lizzie, listen," he jumped in. "Look, you've obviously heard the news, and I'm really sorry. I have no idea how the press got hold of the story. It wasn't from me, and I'm sure it wasn't from my team."

"No? Sounds like you're captain of a leaky ship from where I'm sitting."

If she'd struck a nerve, there was no sign of it in his voice. "I trust my team. All of them."

"Well, someone's been talking, either because there's something in it for them, or to get at me. My *name*, Bill, for Christ's sake."

"And if I can get to the bottom of it, I will. But what you just said – that was the other reason I called – to warn you, in case you didn't know. Have you got somewhere else you can stay? You don't need the media hoopla."

"Thanks for your concern." Her tone was acid, even to her own ears. "I'm staying here."

He audibly sighed. "Look, I know we've never got on. I'll even admit I might have smirked just a bit when I heard you might be in trouble, although I never seriously thought you were a killer. You're too straight up for that. But I'm a professional. If I do find this leak comes back to my team, the person responsible will be on a gross misconduct charge before they know it. That's a promise."

"Whoa, rewind," she said. "So you actually don't think Rob's death is anything to do with me?"

"Not really, no."

"And Dominic?"

"I did think for a while you might have been trying to help him cover it up—"

"So you do still seriously suspect him?"

"Ah," he said. There was a pause on the line. "Okay, then. I probably shouldn't be telling you this, but I have to say I think we've got a solid case against him. That blood on his jacket was confirmed as Rob Thomas's about an hour ago. We'll be charging him."

The words were like a hammer blow. *"No,"* she whispered.

"You'd do the same, with the evidence we have. You know you would. For what it's worth, you've got him a bloody good lawyer."

"But you still won't countenance the possibility of a fit-up?"

"We both know that's just wishful thinking."

"Are you bailing him?" She knew the answer, but she had to ask.

"You know we can't. I suppose he can make his case for bail when he appears in the magistrates' court for the formal stuff."

"Where will he go?"

"Newlands, I should think."

Over Bletchley way. The very prison where Desmond Connolly had met his end.

The doorbell rang twice, intruding on the chaotic jumble of thoughts threatening to overwhelm her. By the time she moved over to the window, it was ringing repeatedly, accompanied by hammering on the door. There were a couple of reporters outside with cameras and microphones.

"Oh, God," she said. "It's started." She moved away from the window before she was spotted and caught on camera.

"DCI Archer?" a male voice bawled through the letter box. "Can we have a word about Robert Thomas? Your side of the story?"

"What's started?" Smith asked.

"The circus has come to town. Naturally they want a statement."

"Take my advice. Tell them nothing and get out of there."

"What's the point? They'll only follow me." There was supposed to be a team meeting at Dan's tonight. She didn't want to bring the press to his door. Maybe she could join by video call. The one useful legacy of lockdown.

"So what are you going to do?" he demanded. "Nothing stupid, I hope."

"Never you mind," she told him. "You should be worried about how stupid *you're* going to look when your so-called solid case collapses around your ears."

"What do you—" he began, but she cut him off.

"DCI Archer!" The voice persisted.

She ignored him, slipped into the hall and went upstairs, moving into the back bedroom and shutting the door to reduce the noise. She sat down on the bed and stuffed her fist in her mouth to keep herself from howling.

A week ago, she couldn't have been happier. She was married to the best man she knew, and everything had been going her way.

How quickly her life had fallen apart.

28

"Okay," Dan said. Alec McGivering had rejoined him. "So this might be a load of old bollocks. Or it might be something. Here's what started me wondering."

Before phoning the Scot, he'd photocopied the pages from the files he thought were interesting.

"Andrew Storey," he said. "Altogether, I've found three photographs on different files taken when the victim was alive in the same room as their body was found. So let's start with this one."

McGivering peered at the side by side images. "What am I looking at?"

"It's more a case of what you're not looking at." He saw the other man frown. "Here's the thing. The nickname 'Invisible Man' was coined by Duncan McNeil himself. He fed it to one of our more talkative officers, who used it in earshot of a journalist, just as Mac had hoped. As soon as the name hit the headlines, Mac started playing up to it. He started leaving doodles at his murder scenes. A pair of glasses and a smoking cigarette. The disembodied glasses and fag were old fashioned special effects in a 1950s *Invisible Man* TV series. He was taunting us."

"As far as I know, nothing like that was found at these scenes."

"No. That would be too obvious. But see here. The picture of Mr Storey in his kitchen. See that on the window ledge behind him?"

McGivering squinted. "Isn't it one of those, oh, what were they? The adverts?"

"It's a Homepride flour grader," Dan said. "Plastic figure. Black suit, black bowler. My mum had one for a while, only a bit bigger than that one."

"Okay."

"So look at the crime scene. You can see the same window ledge."

"No flour grader." McGivering shrugged. "So what? Maybe he got bored with it. Put it somewhere else."

"Possible," he conceded. "So let's look at these other two pairs. Again, you're seeing an earlier image of the crime scene."

Alec McGivering studied the pairs of photographs in turn. He took his time, then looked at Dan.

"I see it," he said. "Or rather, like you said, I don't. With Andrew Storey, the flour grader man has gone. Fergus Jackson – a small photo of a man on the wall. Jean McKinnon – an Elton John poster." He looked at Dan. "You're saying this is the opposite of the cases in your area."

"More or less. If I'm right, instead of leaving an Invisible Man doodle at the scene, he's taken some sort of representation of a man away. I bet you'll find those items weren't anywhere in the houses after the killings."

"You're saying he made the man invisible?" McGivering nodded thoughtfully. "Maybe."

"If I were you, I'd do two things. One – speak to those victims' families and friends. See if those items really went missing or, as you suggested, they'd just been removed between when those photos were taken and the murders. And two—"

"Try and find out if anything like it happened at the other scenes."

"Yeah. I'm not suggesting you'll find it at all eleven scenes, and I don't say it's definitely not a connected case where there isn't anything you can see…"

"No," McGivering said, "no, I get it. That's a good thought and something to dig into. Anything else?"

"If there are other missing 'man' items, you could see if anyone has pictures with them in."

"After he went to prison, Duncan McNeil's had his house sold complete with contents. It's a long shot, but maybe the new owners kept some things that were taken from victims' houses. So, lots to do." The Scot frowned. "I don't suppose you've managed to come up with something linking at least these three victims?"

"Nothing calls out to me. Maybe there is no link."

"These people all lived alone, Dan. How did he know?"

"You've got me. I suppose if you did get pictures of those items, I could show them to Peter – my son – and see if he remembers seeing them."

"You could – although you reckon McNeil implied he'd been a participant in some murders since the Invisible Man."

"I know. And it's something I haven't really wanted to ask but – now I *do* think Mac could have killed at least some of these people…" He grimaced. "Is there any evidence that more than one person was involved in their deaths?"

"Inconclusive, I'm afraid. And, of course, you can't prove a negative."

"I know. Just because you found no sign of Peter, doesn't mean he wasn't there."

"I'll go away and make some calls," McGivering said. "Let you know what I find out."

He left Dan musing, trying not to think the unthinkable. His theory would probably turn out to be a load of old bollocks, just as he'd said it might be. Without it, there was nothing. He should be glad, because – although it didn't rule Peter out – it was nowhere near ruling him in either.

He just didn't know what it was he hoped for.

He headed back to the team office to find an almost palpably tense atmosphere. Joan Collins saw him coming, intercepted him, and steered him back into the corridor.

"Whoa," he protested mildly, "what's going on?"

"I thought it best you don't hear this in front of the team," she said. "In case you go ballistic."

"I never go ballistic."

Joan simply raised her eyebrows. "Course not. Anyhow, it's all been happening while you've been away from your desk. I didn't want to disturb, but now you're here…"

"You're worrying me, Joan. Spit it out."

She nodded. "Okay then. The media has got hold of Lizzie's arrest. And it's just been confirmed that Dominic's been charged with murder."

He stared at her. "Damn." He shook his head. "Well, if that blood was Rob's, it was pretty obvious that would be the outcome. It doesn't stop us seeing if we can find out who the real killer is." The whole of her message sank in, and his blood began to boil. "But how come the media has *Lizzie's* name? Don't tell me the bastards have rushed it out there."

"I've never seen the Super so angry. He was going to take it up with his opposite number in Beds, although it seems their DCI has already called Lizzie and denied it came from him and his team."

"Really?" He wasn't convinced. "Steve Ashby thought there was at least one big mouth there, and I bet he can find out what really happened. But bloody hell – poor Lizzie. How long before the gutter press get hold of her address and she's under siege?"

"She already is."

"Then we need to get her out of there."

"I called and offered her to stay at ours. Apparently her brother's offered too. She's staying put. She doesn't want to bring the media to anyone else's door."

"This is a nightmare."

"She says she'll do a video call to the meeting tonight. She'll have some stuff we can follow up. She still feels guilty about mixing us up in all this. I told her not to be stupid."

"Good. Because I for one am going to turn over every rock in the Vale if need be, to find the bastard who did this to her."

29

"I'm telling you, Dan," said DS Steve Ashby, "the minute I heard the news I phoned my mate Woodger, on DCI Smith's team. I've been making out that Lizzie and I have had some run-ins – actually true – and that I've broken out the popcorn, ever since she and her hubby were nicked – not true. He said he was as sure as he could be that the press never got it from there."

"But he would say that, wouldn't he? You said yourself he liked to talk."

"Yeah, but in fairness, I've only known him to be loose-lipped around other cops. And he's a terrible liar. I reckon if he was the source, or he thought one of his team was, he wouldn't fool me, not even down the phone. Look, maybe there was no leak. They released Dominic's name once they'd charged him. These media types are clever. How hard can it be to connect him to Lizzie?"

"But the names were out there before he was charged. And anyway, she still goes by Archer at work. They deliberately didn't put their wedding in the papers or anything. *Someone*'s thrown them that particular bone and started the feeding frenzy."

"I still think you can track someone down online if you've a mind. There are websites dedicated to finding people and addresses, and it's pretty hard not to have some sort of online footprint. But they *did* find her, so it's academic in any case, isn't it?" said Ashby. "And it's the least of Lizzie's worries now. Once he's in Newlands on remand... hopefully he won't be anywhere near the real hard cases for now, but it could still be shit if they find out who he is and who he's married to."

"And whoever tipped off the media has made sure of that, haven't they?"

"I take it you haven't spoken to her yet?"

"My next call," said Dan. "I'm desperately trying to find a crumb of comfort to offer her. There's nothing. I mean, we're all agreed that the best thing we can do is to make a better job of solving the case than those guys have up to now."

"Assuming they *have* made a bad job of it."

"Oh, come on, Steve. They've grabbed at the easy answer and not looked anywhere else."

"The easy answer is often the right one."

"What, you think Dominic might be guilty?"

There was a long pause. "Well, I don't know he isn't," Ashby said. "But then I'm not bosom buddies with them like you are. Don't get me wrong," he continued hastily, "I'll do whatever I can. I know you know Lizzie. But how well do you really know Dominic? Take away your personal interest and you can't really blame Smith, can you?"

Dan knew he was right. Hell, even *he* couldn't say he harboured no doubts at all about Dominic. He wouldn't be the first decent, upstanding citizen pushed too far.

"No," he admitted. "Not really. Doesn't mean he's got it right though. The real trouble is, we're doing this alternate investigation with one hand behind our backs. We can't see evidence, we can't question suspects…"

"Actually," Ashby said, "we might not be able to see evidence, but Woodger did let slip a couple of snippets from the post mortem, for what they're worth. Time of death was around the time Dominic told Lizzie he was waiting for a 'client' who never turned up."

"So it's possible Rob was murdered quite close to where Dominic was waiting. Maybe there was one killer, maybe more than one. One of them is either covered in blood from the murder, or deliberately smears themselves with it. Waits for Dominic to give up and go back to his car. They deliberately bump into him, grab him, pretending it's to steady themselves, and make sure there's some blood transfer. There's next to no lighting in that car park, which is maybe why they chose it, so he wouldn't realise immediately what had happened."

"I've been thinking about that," Ashby said. "Dominic apparently chucked the jacket straight in the washing machine without realising what was on it. But what if he *had* realised? What if he'd told Lizzie and she'd reported it? Then Rob's body is found and it's established as his blood. Is Dominic still a suspect?"

Dan turned it over in his mind. "I don't think it necessarily gets him off the hook. You can still dismiss it as a cock and bull story – Dominic trying to look all honest and also explain away any evidence he might have left on the body, or the primary crime scene, if they find it. If you choose to think Dominic's capable of killing—"

"We all are, Dan."

"I know. I know. And if you think the evidence points that way, then his explanations sound like—"

"Some pretty desperate arse covering?"

"Yeah. But you said your man mentioned a *couple* of bits of evidence. Is there anything else?"

"Yep. The murder weapon. A slim-bladed knife, apparently. Do Lizzie and Dominic own anything that might fit the bill?"

"I'd have to ask. Even if Lizzie says no, doesn't mean there isn't one she's not aware of. I suppose he could have bought one somewhere, or maybe fashioned one out of something. They're no closer to finding it?"

"Nope," Ashby said, "but here's a happy thought. If Dominic's charged, it'll make it a bit easier for us to follow up the other theories without technically interfering."

"Maybe," Dan was doubtful. "I wonder if the distinction would carry any weight?"

"It might, so long as we don't actually pretend it's part of the official investigation. Okay, show a warrant card, be polite, but…"

"I still think my best bet for questioning the Upmans would be if there were forensics tying them to the fire at Lizzie's house. She had some idea about having another go at Cameron Connolly, but I don't know what was in her mind. If it came to anything, I think she'd have said by now. I hear what you say, but we can't 'unofficially' arrest someone or 'unofficially' apply the rack and thumbscrews."

"Especially for a case where it's been all over the news that someone's been charged," said Ashby.

"Quite. The Connollys would probably lodge an official complaint."

There was silence on the line for a couple of beats. "You know," Ashby said, "maybe we're falling into the same trap we think Smith is."

"What trap?"

"Well, if we discount the possibility that Dominic actually did kill this guy, it's obvious enough that he's being framed. But then we go and focus on the two people who made threats against Lizzie. But there's another possibility."

"Well, yes, she must have other enemies."

"Bound to have," Ashby said. "We're not all about winning friends and influencing people, are we? But no. I'm wondering if maybe someone has it in for *Dominic*."

"Just as Rob's in town stirring it up? Quite the coincidence."

"I know. Thing is, I have two rules about coincidences. Rule One: there's no such thing."

"And Rule Two?"

"They still happen. Now look. First chance Lizzie gets to talk to Dominic, she asks him to think about who might hate him enough to want to do this to him. And she tells him to call his lawyer and tell her. He's allowed to call his legal advisor, and those are the only calls the screws don't monitor."

"You're thinking more clearly than me or Lizzie," Dan admitted. "Okay, I'll talk to her, tell her what you've suggested. It might just give us something new to dig into."

After they hung up, he sat for a while, mulling over the conversation. Ashby was indeed a changed man. Or, at least, that was how it seemed.

But suppose he wasn't?

Because Dan had suddenly thought of two other people who might fancy a bit of revenge on Lizzie. A very long time ago, Steve Ashby and Lizzie's predecessor as DCI – Paul Gillingham – had wrongly suspected one another of involvement in a serious crime. Instead of raising their suspicions, each had attempted to cover for the other. It the process, the real culprit had gone undetected until the case had resurfaced and Lizzie had uncovered the truth.

Ashby had subsequently claimed that his demotion, and his guilty secret coming out, had been a sort of blessing. But what if that was a smokescreen? What if, instead, it had been a new grudge, gnawing at him more than the old guilt?

And Gillingham had been bound to Ashby by the same mistake. He'd chosen early retirement, a career cut short. For him, the guilt had been more personal, impinging on his family.

Was it possible that one, or even both, of them had blamed, not themselves, but Lizzie, for their misfortunes? And decided to do something about it?

Now he really was letting his imagination run away with him, he thought. Could they really have murdered an innocent man in their quest for revenge?

Or had them murdered?

Because the young guy Dominic had claimed to have collided with the night Rob died didn't sound much like Ashby. Even less like Gillingham.

But Ashby had always been about networks and contacts, he reminded himself. Dan could easily imagine him knowing someone who wouldn't think twice about committing a heinous crime or two if the price was right.

And Gillingham? Dan found that much more of a stretch. A devoted family man, would he really take the risk of throwing away all he still had?

Dan didn't think so. And then Ashby had talked about Amy, the woman whose love had done at least as much to save him from his demons as Lizzie's detection skills. He too had a lot to lose if he was behind a murder and got caught.

Dan sighed. The possible suspect list was ever-expanding, but not getting them very far. He decided not to discount Ashby – or Gillingham – yet, but to take Ashby's advice for now. He needed to speak to Lizzie.

He was about to call her when his phone rang.

"Are you sitting down?" Phil Gordon said without any small talk. "Because we've processed that car. Pulled out all the stops, and we've got something. Maybe not what you were hoping to hear, but something."

He didn't like the sound of that. "That second jerry can? What have you got?"

"A partial fingerprint."

"One of the Upmans? I'm sure they're all on the system."

"No, not them. That's the thing, Dan. There's no match for them at all."

He felt deflated. "So whoever handled that jerry can – and likely torched that car – hasn't been in trouble before?"

"Aye, well," Phil said. "I didn't quite say that."

30

Lizzie sat by the window of her bedroom. She'd been there a while, looking down through net curtains on the little brigade of paparazzi outside. The cars and people going by. A drizzle had set in, and windscreen wipers were going. Journalists and pedestrians had umbrellas or hoods up. She was indoors, warm and dry, but she still shivered.

The news that suspects in the fire at her house had been apprehended and confessed was good news. She *knew* it was.

Tony Noakes, the man whose wave of arsons had first brought Lizzie and Rob together, turned out to have confided in his sons – Rory, 23, and Michael, 21 – just a few weeks before his death from cancer that he'd love to get even with the policewoman who'd put him in prison. They'd seen it as something like a dying wish.

Both young men had been in some trouble in their teenage years. Lizzie didn't want to hazard a guess as to whether growing up without their father had played a part in that; it felt too much like amateur psychology. But they'd worked together to track her down and find out her address. They'd stolen a car, which Rory had used for the attack on Lizzie's house, then Michael had met him at the Ivinghoe Beacon car park, where they'd burned the vehicle and, they'd assumed wrongly, any evidence.

The fact that the arsonists were in custody, and that she should be safe from any further attacks of that kind, should have been something to be pleased about. But she had a strange sense of anti-climax, especially as they'd been asked specifically about, and produced pretty unshakeable alibis for, the time of Rob's death, with over a dozen people prepared to swear, and back it up with pictures on their phones, that the pair had been in a London club the whole evening.

So solving the arson felt bittersweet. Noakes, who might have also wanted to harm Rob, appeared to be one name she could cross off her list of enemies.

Several more remained.

She wondered how Dominic was feeling. Scared, most likely. Another night in a police cell and an appearance at the magistrates' court some time tomorrow to hear the charges against him and enter a plea. The court would then formally pass the case on for trial at a Crown court.

She knew Adina Walker would do her damnedest to get him out on bail, and she also knew her chances of success weren't great. That meant the time left to stop the process and keep him out of prison was growing frighteningly short.

Any fears she might have briefly entertained that, against everything she knew, he might yet be Rob's killer, were long gone. She wasn't so naïve – especially in her line of work – not to be well aware that anyone was capable of murder in the right circumstances. But she refused to believe that Dominic would have been willing or able to deceive her about it. She'd still like to know why he'd never told her about his past brush with the police, but it had been an altogether different matter, and an awfully long time ago.

Meanwhile, her boss had been sympathetic, but had made it clear he didn't want to see her around the station for a while, at least until it was one hundred per cent clear that she wouldn't face any charges herself. Josh Stowe had urged her to take some leave. The threat of suspension, albeit on full pay, had hung in the air like fog.

"I'm sorry, Lizzie," he'd told her. "It's a matter of perception. I trust you, but sections of the media might ask why you're still working with all this hanging over you. And could you even focus properly?"

The truth was, she was more than happy to be free to focus on the shadow investigation into Rob's murder. She would have no difficulty focusing on that.

She'd asked if he'd be appointing an acting DCI, but he'd said he'd just be more hands on for the moment. At least neither Dan's nor Lara Moseley's noses would be out of joint for now.

She tried to draw comfort from the willingness of Dan and the team to try and find the real culprit. She had her laptop set up with her webcam ready to call into the meeting at Dan's and was counting down the minutes now.

Her phone rang. She checked the screen. There had been a few calls from unknown numbers this afternoon, and she thought it wasn't just her address that the journos had winkled out. But the name on the screen was a familiar one. She accepted the call.

"Jason," she said.

"Hi, boss," said Jason Bell. "We decided having you on a video link wasn't good enough, so I've been sent to pick you up. I'm outside."

She groaned inwardly. "That's sweet, but drive away. I don't want any of those media types following us to Dan's and then making a nuisance of themselves there."

He chuckled. "They can try to follow us. I didn't do advanced police driving training last year for nothing."

His predecessor had benefitted from the course before his arrival in the Vale, and she'd occasionally made use of those skills. He'd managed to make the car feel like it was flying while at the same time making her feel totally safe. When Jason had been promoted into Amir's post, he'd surprised her by asking to do the training, 'to fill a skills gap', as he'd put it. She'd agreed, hoping it would be another booster to his growing self-confidence, and here he was, offering to vindicate her trust.

He met her on the drive and hustled her to his car, both of them ignoring the microphones thrust their way and the bellowed questions. One or two journos piled into their cars to follow, but Jason had lost them within a few minutes.

"I thought about showing them my warrant card while I was waiting for you," he said as he slowed down, "and daring them to try and keep up with me. But I thought that'd just provoke some negative press."

"You're probably right," she said. "I'd have loved to see their faces though."

She was impressed at how Dan's study had been set up as a mini-briefing room. Karen had decided that one whiteboard wasn't enough, had purchased a second, and both were balanced on the desk, leaning against the wall behind them. Dan and the rest of his team, plus Karen and Charlie, were already assembled. She moved among them wordlessly, receiving hugs and pats on the arm as she made for the seat Dan had indicated for her.

"It's good to see you, boss," he said, "even if the circumstances aren't the best. Do you want to lead?"

"Nope," she said, "it's your team, Dan. I'd just like to say..." Her eyes misted and there was another constriction in her throat. *Get a grip!* she admonished herself as she swallowed. "... none of you has to do this. I already tried to forbid it, but it seems this team has turned into a democracy in my absence and I'm outvoted. So thank you. If there's any comeback, I'll say you were following my orders—"

"Oh, no you—" Joan began.

"Oh, yes I will," she said. "But there won't be any comeback, if we can find out who really killed Rob Thomas, however much the brass might not like you lot going all maverick. And, if anyone can do it, this team can. So, DI Baines, where have we got to?"

With eight of them in the room, it was a bit of a squeeze, but there was still enough space for Dan to stand by the board and kick things off.

"Here we go then. Will, Karen and Charlie between them have found images of potential suspects on the Internet, as well as one of Rob," he told Lizzie. Rob's picture sat in the centre of the display, the others fanned out around it, names noted underneath: Cameron Connolly; Gaynor Upman; John Mitchell; Anne Bright; Tyrone Barron. "We were wondering whether we should add the Noakes boys too?"

"Not if their alibis are as cast iron as it sounds, no. Funny thing is, when I found Tony Noakes had died, I assumed whatever grudge he might still have carried had died with him."

"Of course, what the boys did in revenge for their dad could widen the suspect pool," suggested Will. "You know, friends and family of enemies."

"It could," she agreed, "but then those two had their dad's death as a catalyst for their actions. The chances of relatives of other people I put away finding themselves with a similar motive at the very same time seems vanishingly unlikely. So let's concentrate on the five names in front of us for now."

"Makes sense," said Dan. "Before we get into that though, Steve Ashby said something that might be worth considering."

"Go on."

"So far, we've been focused on people who might have it in for you. But what about Dominic? What if, instead of hurting him to get at you, they just want to hurt *him* for some reason? Does he have any enemies?"

Her instinct was to say no immediately, but she knew the question deserved more consideration than that.

"I'm struggling to think of anyone," she said finally. "I mean, he can be tough when he needs to be but, even then, he really doesn't do nasty."

"What about that..." Dan tailed off, looking awkward. She remembered that, although she'd told him about Dominic's caution, she hadn't said he could tell anyone else. It wasn't really something she wanted widely known about her husband, especially as he'd never even mentioned it to her.

And yet, these people, her colleagues and friends, were going out on a limb for her and for Dominic.

"It's all right, Dan. They all deserve to know."

So she told them about that scuffle years ago, that ended with a man in hospital and a caution for Dominic.

"This guy who got hurt," Jason spoke first. "Sounds like Dominic was doing the right thing, protecting his girlfriend. But was there any permanent harm?"

"I don't think so. I can't be sure." She wasn't about to tell them she'd not long heard about it herself. "I don't even know if Dominic knows, to be honest, but it was such a long time ago. I'll ask him when he's allowed to call me, and I'll ask if there's anyone else we should be looking at. Let's park it for now though."

"Fair enough," Dan said. "We're also all familiar with Gaynor and Cameron, so what say we park them too? I know Will's done some digging on the other three…"

"Me and Natalie, actually," Will said. "Quicker that way."

"So why don't you give us a quick résumé of your dealings with each of those three, boss?" Dan suggested. "Then Will and Natalie can update us."

She nodded. "Let's start with the nastiest then, Tyrone Barron. Up to his neck in organised crime in London. Started in Edgware, moved in on St John's Wood, selling drugs and women to young men with too much cash and too much sense of entitlement. Anyone who owed him money or tried to stiff him for a few grams of coke off the top got dealt with harshly. He had a couple of muscle men who lifted offenders off the street, but Tyrone liked to administer the punishments himself.

"One day, he went too far. The kid he'd picked on died and was dumped in a bin and fell out when the rubbish was collected. It was an easy case to solve. Lots of big talk from him when we nicked him, and more in court after he was sentenced. How he got off with just manslaughter, I'll never know. But I do know he's out. Couple of years ago now."

"I asked around," said Will, "and it looks like he's back with a dodgy crew, but not running the show. Doing okay though. Nice flat, drives a fancy BMW. Girlfriend with supermodel looks. I can't imagine why he'd choose now to target you."

"The whole frame-up thing, too," Joan put in. "I don't know, it somehow feels too… *sly* for someone like that. Tell me if I'm wrong, boss."

Lizzie pondered. Thinking out loud really helped to focus her mind. "I agree," she said. "He liked to use his fists, and on people he felt wronged by. The personal touch. Even if he did have a reason to carry out those threats he made years ago, he'd have taken it out on me, not Dominic, and he'd have itched to do it in person. He'd have wanted to be there when he got his revenge. Although I suppose people change."

"I spoke to a couple of the guys who police his current patch," Will added. "Their intelligence isn't bad, they reckon.

There's no suggestion he's got a bee in his bonnet about his arrest back then."

"What about John Mitchell?" Lizzie said. "As far as I can see, he's on the side of the angels now."

"I had a look at him," said Natalie Chen. "You're mostly right. At least, it *looks* that way."

She looked at her askance. "What's that mean?"

"He was certainly a model prisoner. Did you know he was in a documentary shown on a couple of small time streaming channels? You can see it online. Kept his nose clean, worked in the library, got some qualification, found God. Says he's dedicated his life to helping young people not to make the same mistakes he did."

"Sorry," Jason interjected. "What were those mistakes?"

Lizzie held her hands up. "No, *I'm* sorry. I should have said. He was a crackhead who stole to pay for his habit. People who tried to stop him got hurt, a couple of them pretty badly. That would have included the cops who arrested him, given half a chance. Anyhow, when I gave evidence against him in court, there was so much foul-mouthed, threat-ridden heckling from him that, in the end, the judge had him removed from the court until he gave assurances about his future behaviour."

"How seriously did you take the threats?" asked Joan.

"I couldn't decide at the time. I think he would have been having drug withdrawal issues, and his addiction had made him aggressively self-centred anyway. Did I think he wanted to harm me there and then? Absolutely. Did I imagine he'd ever come after me? Not really. To be honest, I wasn't sure he even had the attention span for it."

"Did you know he'd written a book?" Natalie said.

"No." She was astonished.

"A memoir. About how prison, and a priest who used to visit, changed him. Gave him the help, and the strength to get off the drugs, educate himself, work in the prison library. He met a couple of his former victims through a restorative justice programme and apologised. As soon as he got out, he got involved in a charity that helps young offenders get a second chance. Now he's one of their paid staff and runs courses.

Married with a kid, too. I mean, I don't know, boss, but he might be the real deal. Or he might be *too* perfect?"

"In what way?" asked Dan.

"Oh," she said, "call me a cynic, but a squeaky clean façade like that would be ideal cover for something more nefarious, wouldn't it? Grooming the bad boys and channelling them into organised crime, for instance. But I must admit, if there's anything like that, it's well hidden."

"And this was about fifteen years ago. Why would he start settling age-old scores now?"

"Well," Jason interjected, "say he hasn't changed his spots so much, deep down. He's still self-centred, but getting clean has made him cunning. Maybe he's always been cunning. Maybe he's kept a list of people he reckons have wronged him all this time, and only now does he feel secure enough to start ticking them off."

"Were you able to track his movements over the past few days, Natalie?" Lizzie asked.

"A bit. I've looked at what I can see on his social media. As a matter of fact, he wasn't a million miles from here the night Rob died. A conference in Hertfordshire. Sounds like a full-on day, and he was on a panel in the evening. I suppose if Jason's right and he's got some of the kids he's worked with under some sort of spell, maybe…"

"Maybe he didn't need to be here?" Lizzie closed her eyes and summoned up the thin, pale, shell of a man, long hair all over the place, his eyes wide, screaming invective and spraying spittle. "He'd have had to be pretty charismatic. But then, I suppose he could have been before he tried crack. Not that he found any character witnesses to speak at his trial."

"Am I allowed to say anything?" Karen asked tentatively. "I now I'm not police…"

"Doesn't matter," Lizzie said. "This isn't *official* police business."

"Well," she continued, "there's something about this whole 'old enemies' thing that bothers me. I can just about buy them having some reason why they come at you ten-fifteen years after you first pissed them off, but that all starts to unravel when you remember Rob only showed up a few days ago. And next thing you know, they're framing your husband for his murder? That's a pretty quick and convenient route from plan to execution."

"It is," Dan agreed. "But remember, we suspected that, if Gaynor Upman or Cameron Connolly were at the bottom of it, they'd have to know what was happening with Rob. If they were watching Lizzie's house, that row was pretty public. Anyone who meant her harm could have been watching her, have seen the argument, and seen a chance for something more satisfying than attacking her physically, even killing her."

"He's right," Lizzie said. "If you put Dominic behind bars for something he didn't do, you hurt me more, for longer. And, if something happens to him inside..." A lump rose in her throat and she couldn't continue.

"Okay, look," Will said. "Natalie and I will try and find out who Mitchell has worked with through the charity. I'm thinking of his success stories."

"There are a few of them on the charity website," said Natalie. "Some are involved with the charity themselves."

"So we should see what we can find out about them. What they've been doing. Where they've been lately."

"I can see what I can find on Tyrone Barron along those lines," Joan suggested.

"I can help," Charlie said. "You might have to tell me where to look."

"He's not big on Facebook or Twitter," Will said. "I can see if his girlfriend is. Blonde, gorgeous – I'd be surprised if she can resist Instagram. I'll fish out some details. I should have looked before."

"So there's one face on the board we haven't discussed," Dan said. "That woman. Anne Bright."

"Yes," Will said. "I looked at her too. Just to recap, for those who don't know, Anne caught her then fiancé messing around with another woman. Now you might think, if she was going to get violent with anyone, it'd be her man, who 'done her wrong'."

"I take it she didn't?" Charlie said.

"No. She followed his lover home from work, forced her way into her flat, and beat the crap out of her. Broke half the bones in her body, ruptured spleen and brain damage."

"I'd have thrown the key away," Lizzie said. "She went down for grievous bodily harm with intent. Eleven year sentence that included time served. And she didn't serve all of that. She's been out six years."

"Yeah," agreed Will, "but there's a twist in the tale."

"Really?"

"Would you believe the fiancé got in touch with her in prison and they *stayed* in touch? They were married six months after she got out. All pretty low key, but you can find it if you look. Got two kiddies now, four and two."

"So she's a changed person too?" Lizzie said dryly. "Evidently getting nicked by me will do that to you. I didn't know I was a social service."

"That's not all," said Will. "She's befriended her victim. Contributes to her care."

"How do you know all this?" Lizzie demanded. "I searched the Internet too."

"There's searching and searching," he said with a wink. "I found it tucked away in an online women's magazine. Look, boss, I know we shouldn't dismiss anyone..."

"No," she said, "you're right, Will. She seems the least likely, even if she's the only one who actually hurt me when I arrested her. Bit me on the hand, and I had to take antibiotics." She paused. "In all fairness, she wrote to me about a year later, apologising, saying jealousy had made her crazy. She didn't have to. Maybe she was sincere. Still, is there any way we can trace her movements recently?"

"Why don't Charlie and I look at her and Tyrone's girlfriend?" Karen suggested. "Two heads better than one and all that?"

Charlie gave her a thumbs up.

"Which brings us back, almost inevitably, to Cameron Connolly and the Upmans," said Dan. "Lizzie, you had an idea for tackling Cameron?"

She started to recount her coffee meeting with Grace Connolly.

"Was that wise?" Dan asked. "Meeting with his sister is bound to antagonise him."

"You think?" She laughed mirthlessly. "I don't give a toss. If he's behind Dominic being about to be charged for murder, he's already done about the worst thing he could do to me, short of actually killing him. I can't imagine him thinking up anything worse just because I had coffee in Rumsey's with his sister and talked about putting a piece of her art on my wall. Which I might, by the way."

"So did you learn anything?"

"Not really. Seems Cameron and his brother are locking horns over who should be the head of the family business now Murray's gone."

"So..." mused Jason, "shouldn't *that* be Cameron's priority right now, rather than revenge on you?"

She thought about it. "That's a fair point, actually. You know, the first time he threatened me – when we first nicked Desmond – he told me then how patient he was. That he'd bide his time and I wouldn't see it coming. Although he now insists those threats outside my house were in the heat of emotion after the funerals," she admitted.

"But he would say that," Natalie said.

"With most people, yes," she agreed. "But that's probably the nearest thing you'll get to Cameron Connolly backing down. If he wants revenge, he won't rush it. It's a scary thought, but..." Her shoulders slumped. "Christ almighty. *Someone* must have done it."

"And we'll find out who," Dan insisted. "We will. It's just taking time."

"Yeah, well, Dominic hasn't got time. He'll be in a cell in Newlands this time tomorrow. And I reckon that's right where the real killer wants him."

31

Dominic's appearance at Aylesbury magistrates' court had been short and to the point. As he walked in, his eyes had searched for Lizzie, and he'd sketched a wave when he saw her. He hadn't quite managed to muster a smile.

He'd confirmed his name and address and pleaded not guilty. The magistrates had, inevitably, decreed that the charge was for an indictable offence and thus a matter for a Crown court. Adina Walker had applied for bail, the prosecution lawyer had opposed it, and the court had refused.

As Dominic had been led away, he'd mouthed 'I love you' to Lizzie, and she'd mouthed back, 'I love you too,' before her eyes were blinded by tears.

Neither Dan, nor any of her team, had accompanied her. She'd insisted that it wouldn't be a good look for them. But members of Dominic's family were there, sharing her agony. More importantly to Lizzie, Adam had come, and he squeezed her hand now. She'd never been so glad to have her brother with her. Yet, at the same time, she'd never felt so alone.

Adina found them outside the court building after she'd finished the formalities for the time being.

"How is he?" Lizzie ventured.

Adina shook her head. "Not great, I'm afraid. I think a part of him was still hoping this would all turn out to be some sort of bad dream. That the prosecutor would withdraw the charge, or the magistrates would chuck it out. As if being innocent is all it takes. Now, maybe for the first time, it's all too horribly real. And, not surprisingly, he's terrified of prison."

"Of course he is. He doesn't belong there."

"I know, and I wish there was something I could do. But we both know there isn't, and we need to talk practicalities now.

He'll need a barrister for his trial, and he's said he's happy for you and me to decide who to approach."

"Don't look at me," Lizzie said. "I've seen a fair few in action, obviously, and some have managed to get people off who I was certain were guilty. But this case?" She shrugged. "Is there anyone you'd suggest?"

"There's a chambers I've worked with a lot, and one of their guys would be ideal, I think. Quick on his feet, nothing gets by him…"

"Bit like you." Lizzie knew her smile must look as forced as it felt.

"What's his name?" Adam asked.

"Guy Miles. KC, obviously. He's expensive, mind."

"Don't worry about that," Adam said, before Lizzie could respond. He looked at his sister. "Nic and I agreed last night. We're not short of a few bob, so any financial help you need with this, it's covered."

"That's not right—" she started to protest.

"Listen. I'm not allowing my brother-in-law to get convicted for something he didn't do. So that's that."

Not for the first time this week, she felt herself tearing up. She'd probably shed as many tears over people's kindness as she had over the misery of this situation. She mentally berated herself. If this went on, she'd turn into a total wuss.

"I've had offers from Dominic's dad, too," she told him. "But this means a lot. Thank you. We'll repay every penny, obviously."

"Let's not fuss about that now." He looked at Adina. "Do you reckon you can get him? I'd imagine these guys are in demand."

"I'll get him," she smiled. "I've put some good cases their way, and this is a cracker, from their point of view."

"I'm glad someone will enjoy it," Lizzie said acidly. "Anyhow, I'm still hoping it won't get that far. Not if I have anything to do with it."

Adina's smile never wavered. "I'm going to have to pretend I didn't hear that," she said. "At least, not officially. Privately, good luck."

*

"We turned out to be in more luck than we thought," Alec McGivering told Dan. "The people who bought Duncan McNeil's house in Aberdeen happen to be the world's biggest hoarders. Not only did they keep some of the furnishings, but also a few items that match the ones we suspect McNeil took from his victims' houses."

"Not a flour grader figure, I suppose?"

They couldn't get that lucky. Could they?

But there was a glint in McGivering's eye. "The very same. Pride of place on a window ledge in the kitchen. Altogether, we can tie four items, each depicting a man in some way, to our crime scenes. I'm not saying we're anywhere near linking all our eleven cases – or that all of them even *are* linked – to Duncan McNeil, but we're on the way to building a case."

"Well, that's..." Dan made triumphant fists with his hands, even though his heart wasn't in it. "That's great. Doesn't mean my son was involved, of course."

"It doesn't," McGivering agreed, "and, if it puts your mind at any sort of rest, I can tell you we won't be busting a gut to prove he was, just on the word of a psychopath who likes to play mind games."

Dan relaxed a little. But only a little. It couldn't be that simple.

"I appreciate that."

"That's not to say," McGivering continued, "that we'll ignore evidence if we find any. Or if McNeil presents us with some. But why would he do that, given he raised Peter as his son?"

"The same reason he hinted to me that Peter had helped him kill in the first place. You said it yourself. He likes mind games, especially with the police. Especially with people like me. And, just because he was Peter's dad for all those years, that doesn't mean he loves him like a normal dad. Messing with us – with me – might actually mean more to him than any feelings he has for 'his son'." He sighed. "I'm not even sure he's really capable of feelings."

His phone rang. He checked the name on the screen, apologised to McGivering, and accepted the call.

"Yes, Joan."

"Dan, sorry to interrupt your meeting, but I think you'll want to come. There's a body."

"Where are you?"

"In the office. I mean, I can go with Jason, if you'd rather."

"No, we're more or less done here. Give me five minutes."

*

The village of Prestwood lay about two miles west of Great Missenden, where Cameron Connolly lived, and six miles north of High Wycombe. Back in the nineteenth century, its location on the road between London and Birmingham had made it an important place for travellers to rest, with several inns springing up to meet the need. Today, even the original Travellers' Rest had been demolished to make way for new homes and only three pubs remained. The village population numbered a little under 8,000.

The chalk grassland of Prestwood Local Nature Reserve had been a dump for motor vehicles until 1976, when it was acquired by Wycombe Council, who in turn leased it to the Chiltern Society in 2013. It was home to a diverse range of wildlife, but Dan and Joan hadn't come to spot birds and butterflies. They stood in the site's car park off Hampden Road, watching the CSIs at work. Phil Gordon had just joined them.

"Well," he said, "Dr Carlisle will have to confirm, I suppose, but if that gunshot wound to the head isn't cause of death, it certainly didn't do him much good."

"So what can you tell us?" asked Dan.

"I've no idea exactly what the time of death was, but it has to have been in broad daylight. If he was killed overnight, someone would surely have noticed sooner than they did."

"Maybe he knew his killer? They lured him here, waited until the car park was quiet, then came over to him."

"Broad daylight? Risky."

"Silencer?" Joan suggested

"Perhaps," Dan conceded. "I wonder if there's CCTV."

"I've already asked," said Phil. "Vandalised overnight. Kid in a hoodie and a Covid mask. Last thing on the tape."

"Sounds too coincidental to me," Joan said. "I'll get hold of the footage."

"But you think close range?" Dan put to Phil.

"Again, I'll leave it to the doc to confirm, but it looks like it to me. I'd say he was parked here, rolled his window down, either for ventilation, or more likely to speak to somebody, and they shot him."

"Does the wound tell you anything about the likely murder weapon?"

"I wouldn't want to go out on a limb at this stage and send you on a wild goose chase. Hopefully the projectile's somewhere in the car, and then we'll have a better idea. I'm thinking hand gun though – easier to conceal. But, if the shooter arrived by car, maybe that wasn't an issue and a rifle would do as well. If we get really lucky, we'll find the gun's been used for other crimes. Might help, might not."

"Fair enough," Dan said, not really surprised. "Any indication who he was?"

The corners of Phil's eyes crinkled. "Thought you'd never ask. He had his driving licence in his wallet. One Calvin Dougan."

The name clicked at the back of Dan's mind. A heartbeat later, he knew why.

"As in *Cal* Dougan?"

"I also managed to check the car's registration number. It's registered to—"

"Cameron Connolly?"

"Yes," Phil confirmed. "You obviously know – or knew – the guy?"

Dan conjured up a mental image of Connolly's assistant-cum-enforcer. He hadn't had much to do with him, but he remembered the shaven-headed black man, fairly unremarkable to look at until you made eye contact. There was something reptilian going on behind the eyes. He wasn't a lunatic like 'Mad Willie' McMurdo, who'd had the job before him, but Dan had found something about him infinitely more scary.

"Are we all right to come and have a look?" he asked.

"Seeing as you're already both suited up, I don't see why not."

There wasn't much to see. Not much more to say. It was Cal Dougan, all right. In death he seemed smaller, diminished. He might have received only a single gunshot to his temple, but his head was still a mess.

"What are we thinking?" Joan tore her gaze away. "Murray Connolly dies, Cameron and his brother are apparently squabbling over who's going to be top dog. Unless we're thinking the falling out has turned violent, and Dougan was collateral damage, you have to wonder if someone's seeing this as a perfect moment to muscle in on their turf."

He mulled it over. "Okay, say I buy it. But why take out Cal Dougan? Why not go after one of the brothers? Or both of them?"

"He's small beer," she admitted. "But isn't he part of the glue that holds everything together here? Protection for Cameron when he's out and about… gone. The guy who keeps the organisation in line… gone. Sort of like taking out a keystone from a building. It starts to crumble."

He cast a last, long look at the dead man.

"I've seen enough."

And they were probably cramping the CSIs' style. They moved away from the car.

"Shit," he said. "Why now, when we're trying to make time to find out who really killed Rob Thomas?"

"I guess poor Dominic must be spending his first day inside by now," said Joan. "I hope he's okay."

"Me too. But we have to do our jobs, rubbish though the timing is. So I'll brief the Super, then let's get the team together and we can get this investigation started."

32

Lizzie hadn't expected Dominic's permitted two-minute phone call to come especially early. She knew a little too much about the mechanics of getting a prisoner into the system. Sometimes ignorance really was bliss.

Located south-west of Bletchley, not far from Milton Keynes, Newlands Prison was relatively new, holding remand and sentenced prisoners aged eighteen and above. A section of the prison was designated as a Young Offenders Institute, and it was also one of the nine national high-security prisons that held Category A prisoners, some of them in the Close Supervision Centre.

Lizzie was acutely aware of reports expressing concerns about long-term staff shortages and way too much reliance on agency and temporary staff. Assaults on both staff and inmates had risen in recent years, and Newlands had one of the highest suicide rates in the UK prison system. The tendency, for prisoners to remain locked in their cells for over twenty hours a day, plus increasing use of psychoactive drugs, added to stress for prisoners with mental health issues and made them more inclined to violence and self-harm.

Dominic would have made the forty-five minute journey from Aylesbury magistrates' court to the prison in a large white van, aptly known as a 'sweat box', a three-ton truck containing fourteen small lockable compartments, each of them about three feet wide, three feet deep and seven feet high. Unless things had improved lately, which Lizzie doubted, it would have been filthy and stank of piss and worse. He'd have felt every bump, swerve and stop, and – with no seat belt – he'd have been in danger of shooting forward and bashing his head whenever the driver slammed on the brakes.

The actual processing of a new arrival at the prison would have felt interminable, a series of holding cells, paperwork, medical staff, and a humiliating strip search, followed by a session in a 'BOSS' chair, whose purpose was to check that nothing had been concealed inside his body.

She knew he'd want to talk about all that, but she also knew time was too short, and there were things she needed to say to him while she had the chance. Whatever he was feeling, he was wise enough to shut down his own narrative and listen.

"What are the chances you'll get a cell to yourself?" she asked. On completion of the formalities, he'd be taken to the induction wing and locked into a cell for his first night. Tomorrow he would be moved onto a regular block. In theory, remand prisoners wouldn't normally be expected to share a cell, and certainly not with a convicted prisoner but, with prisons so overcrowded, she guessed that might not be possible.

"All Adina would say was, if I didn't, the staff would at least try to ensure that I'm not put in with anyone unsuitable," he said. "It all sounds a bit vague for my liking. For all I know, I'll be put in with a psychopath, or a sex offender who takes a fancy to me. They say as a remand prisoner I'm allowed to wear my own clothes, rather than those hideous grey sweatshirts and trackie bottoms. But maybe not wearing prison clothes would flag me up as a newbie."

"They'll spot a newcomer anyhow. Just keep it vague what you've been charged with and, for God's sake, don't let slip that you're married to a police officer."

"Adina says, if the word does somehow get out, I'll be transferred elsewhere as soon as possible. Assuming I live long enough."

He said it like a joke, but she could hear the fear in his voice.

"Just do your best to keep your head down," she said. "And your chin up. I think you're being framed, and Dan's team are working off the books to find out who did it. It could be someone trying to hurt me, but can you think of anyone who's got it in for you?"

"Only Rob, and we know it's not him."

"I know about your caution," she said.

"What?" She knew her bluntness had shaken him. "Look, Lizzie—"

"I'm sure you've reasons for not telling me. But he wound up in hospital. Could it be him?"

"After all this time? I doubt it. He recovered okay, as far as I know. Oh, Christ, time's up!"

"His name?"

"Jake Sloane. I love you."

His voice broke, and that did for her.

"I love you too," she sobbed, and then the call was abruptly cut off.

She sat holding the phone, sobs racking her body. She felt as if she was watching some sort of Shakespearian tragedy happening to somebody else. If only she'd been able to talk to Dominic for longer. Try to reassure him, instead of just warning him and questioning him. But there'd been so very little time.

The one thing she knew for certain now was that tonight was going to be the longest night of both their lives.

*

Cal Dougan had lived in High Wycombe with his husband, Hugh Hutchins-Dougan. Joan picked up Natalie Chen and headed over there to break the news and question Hugh. Dan took Jason Bell with him to see Cameron Connolly.

As usual, they were buzzed in and directed to his office.

In spite of his loathing for the Connollys, and Cameron in particular, he knew Cameron must have worked closely with Dougan, and he delivered the bad news as sensitively as he could. He watched as Cameron's eyes widened.

"Dead?" he repeated. "No, that can't be right. He's out... running a few errands for me." He paused, looking perplexed. "Although I was wondering where he'd got to."

"We'll need a list of those errands," Dan said. "But I'm afraid there's no mistake."

"What happened? A car crash?"

"I'm afraid he was murdered."

There was no stunned shock. "Are you sure?" was all Cameron said.

The image of what was left of Cal Dougan's face flashed through Dan's mind. "Pretty sure, yes. We're not releasing any more information at this stage but, if we're going to catch the person or persons responsible, we'll need all the help we can get. So I hope you can cooperate with us."

Cameron Connolly didn't blink. "Of course. Always happy to help the police."

"Of course," Dan agreed, ensuring there was no trace of irony in his voice.

"And in this case... Poor Cal. Oh, God, Hugh'll be devastated. His husband. Does he know?"

"Someone's with him now, breaking the news. May we sit?" He and Jason were still standing.

Cameron's initial response when they'd arrived had been frosty. Now he shook himself and gestured to the two chairs in front of his desk. He went and sat opposite them.

"Look," Dan said. "This'll go a lot quicker if we don't have to waste a lot of time dancing around what you do and what Cal used to do for you. So let's both pretend our questions are in the context of you being an honest businessman and Cal being your..." he made quotes with his fingers, "...assistant."

A phantom smile flitted across the other man's face. "All right."

"Good. So, first of all, can you think of anyone who might have wanted to harm Cal? Either him personally, or because of his work?"

Cameron reached a hand forward. It hovered above the granite block that had held his Excalibur paper knife. The knife wasn't in the block, but he picked it up and began passing it from hand to hand, as if it aided his thinking.

"Of course," he went on after a moment or two, "this is a difficult time for me and my family. My father's death has left a temporary situation where a bit of restructuring in the hierarchy is necessary."

"Or, to put it more bluntly, you and your brother, Fraser, are squabbling over who controls what." Dan made it a statement, not a question.

Cameron raised an eyebrow. "Where did you hear that?"

Dan felt a flush to his cheeks. He'd misspoken. Whatever internal family squabbles might be taking place, he doubted if many people saw them. Did Cameron know his sister had met with Lizzie? Dan was willing to bet he did. Even if Grace had kept it to herself, her brother had boasted to Lizzie about 'knowing things', and Dan was more than willing to believe it.

He hoped he hadn't put Grace in the path of Cameron's wrath.

He recovered quickly, "Just a calculated guess. One you just as good as confirmed, by the way."

"Yeah? Well, so what? My point is, I suppose there might be some especially unscrupulous competition out there who might think they perceive a weakness and think they can exploit it at any price."

Jason chimed in. "I seem to remember something like that going on a few years back. It didn't end well for the Meredith brothers, did it? Nor Dragos Lupu."

Cameron sighed. "Full marks for being informed, Sergeant. I assume you also know that was nothing to do with me. We only buried my brother Desmond last week, and I hate to speak ill of him, but he was an idiot. And, as I keep having to explain to you and your colleagues, he was an idiot who had delusions of becoming some sort of gangland kingpin. Somehow he roped poor Willie McMurdo into his crazy scheme. But that was his private enterprise. Not mine."

Dan made a show of scratching his head and stroking his chin. "Mr Connolly, I don't pretend to know much about business but, whenever I read in the news about hostile takeovers, the action seems to be in the boardroom. Companies don't generally seem to start shooting each other's employees. At least," he added with a grin, "not legitimate companies."

Cameron shrugged. "You're right, of course. Although stranger things have happened. Maybe someone a bit unhinged is sending me a message. Or maybe it's more personal to Cal than that. I'm not his keeper. I don't know who he may or may not fall out with."

"Hang on, though," Dan said. "You as good as acknowledged that you and your brother have, shall we say, differences over the future of the business. Could *he* be the one sending you a message?"

Cameron barked a laugh. "*Fraser?* I told you, whoever killed Cal must have had some balls. I love my family, and Fraser's no exception, but that really doesn't sound like him. Unless Cal was spreadsheeted to death."

"We'll need to speak to him, if he's around."

"Of course." Cameron replaced his granite block on the desk and drummed his fingers on the surface. "I'll get him in and you can use my office. If you're done with me?"

"One more thing," Dan said. "Mr Dougan's body was found in your car, so it's being kept for processing."

"The Merc? Yes, Cal uses it when he's out doing jobs for me. I'll let you have that list, by the way. I might not show it, but I'm angry and upset about what's happened, so process away."

"And what have your movements been today?"

"Mine? I drove over to my shooting club for a bit of practice and a drink."

Dan looked at him. "You belong to a *shooting* club?"

Cameron chuckled. "God, Inspector, you sound as scandalised as a Victorian lady catching a glimpse of a table leg. It's a popular sport. The club's just outside Amersham and has, I think, about a hundred and forty members. I like it. Just me, a gun and a target. The focus is relaxing."

"You keep guns at home?"

"Yep. In a gun safe."

"Can we see it?"

Cameron considered this. "No," he decided. "Not without a warrant."

"Something to hide?"

"No. Just being bloody minded. But why are you suddenly all excited... oh." His eyes widened again. "Cam was shot?"

"I'm not commenting on that. Did you take your own gun to the shooting club?"

"A rifle."

"You have any other guns?"

"Yeah, I've got a pistol and a couple of machine guns."

"Really?"

Dan didn't expect such a frank admission. But then Cameron scoffed. "Obviously not, Inspector. That would be illegal."

"Mr Connolly, if you've nothing to hide, I suggest you voluntarily turn that rifle over to us. We'll give you a receipt. Otherwise, we will come back with a warrant and we will take this whole house apart."

He shook his head. "Christ almighty. You do that, then. Now, is there anything else?"

Dan looked at Jason, whose headshake was almost imperceptible.

"Not at the moment. If you can get your brother for us?"

33

After speaking to Dominic, Lizzie had set about trying to arrange to visit him. She knew that making the booking by phone, despite the long wait for someone to answer, was quicker in the long run than online methods. When she got through, she was able to confirm that she was on Dominic's visitors' list, but tomorrow's visiting times were already fully booked out. She had more luck with Thursday, managing to get a morning slot.

Next, she wanted to see what more she could find out about Jake Sloane, the man who'd come off worst against Dominic. Suspecting that a sexual predator might actually be emboldened after a few days hospitalisation that ended with no charges, she'd entered 'Jake Sloane offences Harrow' in her search engine, and a string of results came up, spelling 'Sloane' with and without an 'e'.

She didn't actually know the date of the incident, but recalled that Bill Smith had told her it had occurred when her husband had been in his twenties. She reasoned that, if he had re-offended, it was most likely he'd have been caught at some time after that altercation.

He'd been easier to find than she'd imagined. She'd found a twenty-eight-year-old Jake Sloane receiving a high-level community service order for sexual assault in Harrow. Armed with a rough idea of his year of birth, she'd scrolled back and found a tiny report from a Harrow local paper three years earlier, headlined 'Man taken to hospital after pub altercation'. Although there was so little detail that she couldn't be absolutely certain that this was the same man, his name was Jake Sloane, and his reported age also fitted perfectly.

Moving forward two years from the sexual assault, she'd found the same offender being jailed for three years for rape.

He'd be on the sex offenders' list.

She continued to search for him, but unearthed no later results. She supposed Sloane could be going by a different name now. Even so, she phoned Will Tyler and asked him to see if he could find out what had become of him. She was doubtful that this would amount to anything, but being targeted by Tony Noakes' sons had been unexpected.

As she mulled over what to do next, her phone rang and Charlie's name flashed up on the screen.

"How are you holding up, Lizzie?" she asked. "I saw he'd been remanded. I know you were prepared for it, but…"

"Yeah. Nothing can quite prepare you for it happening for real."

"Well, for what it's worth, Karen and I have been poking around online as we promised. Will gave us enough to get started. We looked at Anne Bright and, really, there's nothing at all to suggest why she'd start trying to get even now. She's got a happy family life and a job at a local café. She still helps with her victim's care. Nothing to see here, folks."

"And Tyrone Barron? You were going to see if you could find his girlfriend on social media?"

"Oh, yeah, she's on everything. Works in a night club, even does a bit of singing there. Online persona looks like an airhead, but that might just be the public image she wants to cultivate. Big on hairdos and manicures and showing off her figure in the latest designer gear. Oh, and she's pregnant and she and Tyrone are getting married."

"Christ, no! Really? I nick them, they make dark threats, they do time, they come out, and suddenly they're all the bloody Waltons." She pondered. "Okay, so Tyrone's personal life is going through some big changes. What if he wants to settle some scores before he becomes a respectable family man?"

"Hardly respectable," Charlie reminded her. "It's pretty obvious he's moving in the same sort of circles as before, meaning he's almost certainly slipped right back into the underworld. But yes, there might be something in that. It would sort of explain the timing. Except…"

"Except?"

"Well, I suppose these changes might explain why now. But not why not sooner? If he came out of jail full of rage and went straight back to his old ways, why take so long over targeting you? It's not like he doesn't have the connections."

"Maybe I'll go and see him," Lizzie said. "Ask him to his face."

"That doesn't sound wise to me."

Her shoulders slumped. "Probably not. But this whole thing's so frustrating. Being low key is all very well, and I know we're doing good work, but I really feel like getting in someone's face."

"Yeah, well. I'd feel angry in your shoes. Especially as it must all feel so personal. When did Rob first show up, out of nowhere?"

"Hang on." She cast her mind back. "Wednesday."

"So, a week tomorrow. And that was the same day as the Dougie Upman trial finished and Gaynor Upman made threatening gestures? As Cameron Connolly issued verbal threats?"

"Yeah, but—"

"Then you've had someone set fire to your house, Rob – someone you once had feelings for – has been murdered." She imagined Charlie ticking off events on her fingers. "You've been arrested. Dominic's been charged. Bloody hell, that's seven things in seven days. Seven pretty big things, and none of them good. Look, I'm not a psychologist, but what I went through was three years ago, and I'm still not over it—"

"That was altogether different."

"I know it was. And it was a huge thing in my life, it probably always will be. My point is, you must feel like a punch bag. You're bound to want to hit back. But we're going about this the right way. Try to be kind to yourself. You don't always have to act the tough guy."

"I know." She'd always been a woman making her way in what had traditionally been a male culture. Dinosaurs like Bill Smith and, still to an extent, Steve Ashby, were still there. She was about to say as much, but something undefined was suddenly ticking away at the back of her mind.

"Say that again," she said.

"Which part?" asked Charlie. "I made a bit of a long speech there. Sorry about the lecture."

"No, no. The last bit. Something about tough guys."

"What? Oh, yeah. Look, I work in a male-dominated profession too. It's easy to put on an act for so long that you forget—"

"Yeah, that was it." She closed her eyes, trying to recapture a fleeting germ of a thought. "An act."

Silence stretched out.

"Lizzie?" Charlie prompted. "You still there?"

"Yeah. Just what you said. It didn't exactly ring a bell, but something…" She sighed. "It's gone. It'll come to me if it's important."

"What about the lad who collided with Dominic in the pub car park? The one we think smeared the blood over his clothes in the first place? You said the police had looked at CCTV footage, didn't you?"

"Apparently it shows two people bumping into each other, one grabbing at the other for support. Bill Smith says it's useless for identifying anyone, and he's sceptical the other person did it deliberately. In fact, he thinks Dominic might have engineered it as part of his alibi."

"Will the pub have retained the footage?"

"Almost certainly. Most CCTV footage is kept for at least thirty days. Pubs generally keep it for six months or longer, partly for security reasons, partly for just this sort of reason: the police asking to see it. And it's almost certainly stored on a hard drive, or at least an SD card. But only the police can ask for it normally. Data protection. You're thinking we should ask to see it ourselves?"

"You know this DCI Smith better than we do. If he's already convinced he's got his man, would he do a lazy job trying to track down this person?"

She thought about it. "I'd say not," she decided. "It could actually strengthen his case against Dominic. But you've made me think of something else. Maybe the face can't be seen, but there's the build? And there's gait analysis too. *If* we have something to compare it with. If only the guy had a wooden leg and a hunchback..."

"Could you, or one of the team, ask the pub to show the footage? I don't know, maybe imply without actually saying as much, that you're working with Smith?"

"Why, Charlie. What an improper suggestion! I couldn't possibly ask one of my team to do that."

"No?"

For what felt like the first time in ages, Lizzie grinned. "Definitely not. So I'll do that little job myself."

34

Dan's interview with Fraser Connolly had yielded even less than the conversation with his brother. Afterwards, he'd contacted Steve Ashby, who'd promised to ask around in case a new underworld turf war was about to break out in the Vale. Right now, it was as feasible an explanation as any for Cal Dougan's murder.

He was considering what to do next when Alec McGivering rang him.

"You're not going to like this," he said, with no small talk whatsoever.

Dan sighed. "Thing is, Alec, there's less and less that I do like at the moment. So don't hold back."

"I wanted to speak to Duncan McNeil. Confront him with our new evidence. Hell, I wondered if he might crumble, confess to the lot. Nothing really to lose."

"Yes, I see the sense in that. I can't see it happening, but worth a try."

"So I rang the prison, the governor has apparently spoken to him – straight away."

"He knows what we've got?"

"I didn't get into that. Just said new evidence had come to light."

"So did he agree? I bet there's a catch, if he did. He'll want his lawyer present, for sure."

"You'd think so, but no. He doesn't. Dan, it's like he's been expecting this. He says he'll speak to the police. But on his terms."

Dan felt the hairs rising on the back of his neck like a premonition.

"What terms are they?"

"No lawyers. Not me, either. He'll talk. But only to you, Dan. Just him and you."

*

Lizzie returned from the Five Birds pub not much wiser, but with a few things nagging away at her. The pub manager hadn't seemed fazed by being asked to see CCTV footage already in possession of the police.

"I just need a quick glance at the original footage," she'd offered by way of explanation. "When you copy it, the picture can get grainier, and the machine we view it on isn't the best in the first place. It's just a couple of things I need to make sure about."

That had been good enough for him. As she sat viewing it, she'd hoped she'd conveyed the impression that she'd seen it all before.

Helpfully, the manager had been able to quickly locate the section of the film she was interested in. She'd watched it through once, and seen exactly what Bill Smith had described. Dominic, instantly recognisable, even in a poorly lit car park, came into view, the pub building behind him. Then a second figure, shrouded in a dark hoodie, entered the screen, approaching him. They collided, sort of grappled, then the second person had extricated himself, appeared to utter a couple of words, and then gone on his way.

To Lizzie's eye, it bore out the notion that the second man had bumped into Dominic and not the other way around. She asked herself if this was simply biased wishful thinking and asked to watch again. This time, she noticed something else, something that made it more than mere wishful thinking.

The second man had weaved towards Dominic, like he was under the influence of something, and had staggered away afterwards, giving the same impression. But this time she'd studied him from his first entry into the frame until he disappeared out of shot. However unsteady he'd appeared during the main action, his initial arrival had been somewhat brisk and purposeful, as if he was hurrying to be in the right place to stage the collision scene. It was the same afterwards. He'd staggered away from Dominic but, as soon as he was well away from him, he'd straightened up and lengthened his stride. Lizzie was struck by the notion that the whole act had been for Dominic alone, and not for the cameras. She'd half-wondered if the other man had given a moment's thought to the possible presence of cameras.

It hadn't been the work of an accomplished professional criminal, but she supposed that didn't rule out someone simply following orders, with one job to do – the grappling coming together – and with not too much attention paid to what happened either side of that.

Driving home, she'd wondered if there was any way she could urge Smith to view the footage again for himself, to see what she had seen. She wasn't afraid of getting herself in trouble if it undermined the case against Dominic, even at this late stage.

The trouble was, she knew in her heart that Bill Smith was a competent copper. DI Nancy Fleetwood too. She couldn't imagine for a moment that they hadn't viewed the footage several times over, nor that they'd missed what she thought she'd seen.

The reality, she knew, was that you only needed to put her interpretation on the scene if it suited you. The deliberate collision could disturb Smith's narrative, but only if it was an inevitable conclusion to draw from the footage. It wasn't she knew, the only one. She imagined someone slightly pissed, or drugged-up, or both, trying to keep it together, losing concentration, blundering into somebody and, having almost lost their footing, making another determined effort to remain upright as they walked away. If Smith and Fleetwood chose to see it that way, they were hardly going to hold up their hands to a terrible mistake.

Not for the first time today, there had been something else about the footage, something that rang the faintest of bells, but something she simply couldn't put her finger on. She hoped it would come to her. She wondered if it would prove important.

Indoors, she'd fed Barney and had something to eat, and a cup of strong coffee, while she willed Dominic to call her. She wanted to know how his first night had passed, and how he was doing on the block.

She was halfway into her second coffee when she got her wish.

Dominic's hope of passing his first night in Newlands alone had been dashed when his cell door opened and a prisoner who had travelled with him in the sweat box was ushered in to join him.

"Could have been worse, I suppose," Dominic said. "Guy called Toby, younger than me, and at least as scared. I simply said I was on remand and didn't want to talk about the charges. Toby can't *stop* talking. Seems he mounted a pavement in his Audi whilst blind drunk and mowed down three teenagers. You might remember it. Two dead, and the third had life-changing injuries. Both legs amputated below the knee. A female footballer on the verge of the Chelsea first team."

Lizzie did remember the case. Her own outrage. Her devout hope that the driver would receive the maximum penalty the law allowed, never dreaming her husband might find himself locked in a cell with him.

"He's full of remorse," Dominic said. "Self-pity too. Went on about how he was pleading guilty, deserved everything he got. Reckons he'll get a life sentence, talks about topping myself."

"Nice that you're making friends." She tried for a light tone that she wasn't feeling.

"Yeah, well. They've moved me onto 'B' Wing now. It's where the more run of the mill offenders are, and at least I'm not in with the most violent or dangerous."

"Be careful," she said. "That doesn't mean the inmates there will all be gentleman burglars, nor that none of them has committed violent crimes."

"I know. But I seem to have struck lucky with my cell mate here. Brad Hepworth. He must be in his fifties, and he's like a character in a 1980s TV show. You know, always on the fiddle, but a likeable rogue. He's showing me the ropes, doesn't ask too many questions, and has a fund of stories. I've spent half the time in stitches."

"I'm glad." It must feel good to laugh.

"Over lunch, I met his mates – Ronnie and Graham. They seem okay. Toby joined us, and they shut him up as soon as he started talking about what he was in for. Told him to say he was in for fraud, or cons, or anything that doesn't involve kids getting hurt."

"I'm glad someone seems to be looking out for you. No trouble so far, then?"

There was a short silence on the line.

"Dominic?"

"No real trouble. I mean, it's probably nothing, but…"

She felt cold. "Tell me."

"There's this one guy seems to keep staring at me. I noticed him at dinner last night and again at lunch. Never seen him before. Maybe I'm imagining it, but…"

With creeping dread, she asked him what had happened.

"As we were leaving the dining hall today, the same guy man who was looking at me was suddenly right there. Crossed right in front of me and slammed me aside. Then he stopped and gave me a look. Somewhere between mocking and furious. Told me to 'Look where I'm fucking going,' then stalked off. A bit like a school bully. I hope that's all it is."

"Yeah." She tried to help him shrug it off. "Just like school. Pick on the new boy."

And maybe it was nothing more sinister. But dark imaginings came crawling into her mind. Things she daren't share with him, because he was probably more than terrified enough already.

"I'm afraid I'm going to have to go," he said, "and I haven't even asked how you are. I miss you so much."

"Me too," she said, tears pricking her eyes, "but you hang in there. We're still working Rob's case, and we won't give up."

35

Much as Dan was on tenterhooks for the lab analysis of the items found in the car – Cameron Connolly's car – that Cal Dougan had died in, he knew the service was backed up and that, even with the fast tracking Phil Gordon had ordered, the results wouldn't be back until some time tomorrow. He'd asked Joan to keep him updated, made some calls, and then set off for a long drive north.

Wakefield Prison in West Yorkshire had been dubbed 'Monster Mansion', a reflection of the number of murderers, high-risk sex offenders and other dangerous inmates held within its walls. Alec McGivering had smoothed the way for Dan's visit, but he knew it was still going to be a very long day: a round trip of around three hundred miles, plus the inevitable bureaucracy involved with getting him in and out.

Traffic had been kind, though, and he had enough time to pull off the A1(M) for coffee and something to eat. By the time he was face to face with Duncan McNeil, he was already tired. He hoped this wasn't going to be a waste of time.

The Scot's face creased into an all-too-familiar genial smile when he was brought into the room where Dan already sat.

"Laddie! Well, well, well. And I thought our little bromance was over." He sat down.

The face, the smile, the twinkling eyes, the voice, all belonged to a man who Dan had once counted as a friend and mentor. A man who had killed eleven people for certain – five of them children – and whom he now believed was responsible for God knew how many more deaths. Even if the Scotland and Northumberland murders he was suspected of could all be laid at his door, there could easily be yet more.

Harold Shipman, reckoned to have been one of the most prolific serial killers in modern history, was believed to have claimed around two hundred and fifty victims. Mac's tally was unlikely to be in that ball park, but he was still one of the scarier monsters in the mansion, not least because killing seemed to have always been nothing more than a sport to him. An ex-detective himself, he especially loved the idea of the police trying in vain to find anything at all that might help their attempts to solve yet another murder.

Dan himself had been lucky not to be yet one more statistic on Mac's list of victims. If he hadn't been stopped, how many more might have died by now?

"It's the emotion, isn't it?" Mac was saying. "You're so overwhelmed to see me, the cat's got your tongue."

It was emotion, all right, that had temporarily paralysed Dan, but not of the kind Mac was implying.

"Sure, Mac," he said. "It's been a while."

"And you must be a daddy all over again, by now. It must be lovely. I've had a lot of time to think about it, and I'm glad you, Karen and the bairn are still with us."

"No, you're not." He managed to say it without betraying any of the feelings squirming inside his gut.

Mac laughed out loud. "No, you're right. I'm not glad at all. That would have just been perfect – me and Peter together, killing off his father, his mum's twin sister and his own unborn half-sibling. But there we are, and here you are. You've got questions, and I've got answers. I wonder if we can marry them up."

"I wonder."

Mac leaned forward a little. "So maybe we can move it along? I've got a busy schedule today."

"Then let's come to the point. You asked to see me."

Mac tutted. "Let's at least be accurate, laddie. Someone from Police Scotland asked to see *me*. I declined, but I said, if someone wanted a chat, I didn't mind catching up with you."

"This is supposed to be about a string of murders we think you committed in Scotland and the North East. You know that. You said you'd talk to me about *that*. I didn't drive all the way up here to talk about the weather. Or is this just another of your piss takes?"

"That's up to you. If you want to talk about anything more interesting, what's in it for me?"

"For you?" Dan knew he was still being needled. "What did you have in mind?"

"Maybe a visit from our boy? From Peter?"

Dan shook his head at the absurdity. "You know that's not going to happen. Even if there was the remotest chance I'd want him within a million miles of you, it would never be allowed."

"How about a nicer cell, then?"

"Nicer in what way?"

"Oh, I don't know... I've always fancied some of that William Morris wallpaper."

"William..." Dan stood up. "Are we wasting each other's time here?"

"Och, sit down, laddie." Mac gestured at the seat Dan was walking away from. "You've got to allow me a bit of fun. This place is deadly boring. I mean, you'd think, the calibre of psychopath we have in here, there'd at least be some interesting conversation, but no. And I know I'm in here for keeps. So sit down, and let's get to it. No more fooling around, I promise."

His tone bordered on contrite. Suspecting more joking around, Dan sat again.

"So," Mac said. "Police Scotland. If they suddenly want to see me, I have to conclude they think they've found something."

"You did rather imply to me that there were victims after your Invisible Man phase."

Mac guffawed. "Invisible Man phase. I like it. Makes me sound like a real artist."

"Yeah, well. It doesn't take a genius to work out that, if that was the case, you'd have probably been operating north of, or not far south of, the border."

"So I'm guessing they've broken out cold cases for both. And I know all about cold cases."

This was true. After his early retirement from Thames Valley, Mac had returned to his native land, secretly taking Dan's son with him. In due course, he'd started working cold cases up there. On one occasion, Dan had even picked his brain about cold case methodology.

"So what do they think they have?" the Scot asked.

"If I told you we know about your invisible men? And that they recovered some of them from your old home?"

For a moment, Mac looked surprised. Then a grin split his face.

"Aye, well, I was careless, wasn't I? Taking them was one thing, but hanging onto them... Maybe I was a bit too clever for my own good."

"You admit it?" Was it really this easy? "How many?"

"I don't know. I'd have to tally them up. Tell you what, I'll make a list. If your mate from Scotland wants to come in, I'll go through it with him. Who knows? There might be a few he's overlooked."

Much too easy, surely? "You mean that? No tricks?"

"Why not? Like I said, I'm never getting out of here. I might as well be as notorious as possible. Knowing I did what I did, and no one else knows, loses its appeal after a while. I'll sign as many confessions as you want. Only for ones I did, mind. I'm not going to help them clean up any I didn't. I think that's more than fair."

It was, if he kept his promise.

"Hold on, though," Dan said, as something struck a chord. "No one else knows? You tried to imply Peter had a hand in at least some of them, and he's never denied it. Are you saying he knew nothing of it?"

"Well. I can't deny I raised him to think we were different. Special. We were entitled to live by a different code. Even then... well, you saw. It took a lot to get him to help me when we tried to kill your Karen. I didn't think he would. I still think he might have drawn back, even without your intervention. That's not a hardened, experienced killer, is it?"

"So you're saying..."

"That was the only time, yes. By the way, have you seen him?"

"Only once. A few days ago."

"And how did it go?"

He knew the other man must be taking some weird, twisted delight from this, but Dan supposed it was a small price to pay, all things considered.

"Awkward. I think he's mixed up. Loyal to you, but maybe ready to engage with his birth family. I don't know what will come of it. If anything."

"Do something for me, laddie."

"What?"

"Tell him, in spite of all that I've done, what I tried to make him do, I do love him. He's still a son to me. Can you do that?"

It was a tough ask. But Peter had a right to hear it, he thought.

"All right," Dan said. "I will."

Mac held out a hand, his expression sad now. "Will you shake on it?"

Dan thought of all the lives cut short by this man. The pain he'd suffered personally because of him. And then he thought of all those cold cases, murder victims whose families still had no closure.

He reached out and shook the hand of a monster.

36

On the long drive home from Wakefield, Dan spoke to Alec McGivering on hands-free, feeding back his conversation with Mac. He was already having his doubts about the king of mind games keeping his word. Perhaps he'd just wanted to raise Dan's hopes in order to dash them again. Dan could imagine McGivering making the trip to the prison, expecting to come away with signed confessions, only for Mac to tell him he had no idea what he was talking about.

"You might be right," McGivering had said. "But what can we do? We have to play the hand we've been dealt."

"I know. And I got no sense, for what that's worth, that he *was* pissing around. He seemed... I don't know. Tired. Sad. He mentioned a few times that he's never getting out of that place, so maybe he figures he has nothing left to lose. He's never appealed against his conviction or his sentence, and I think he really does love Peter, in his own twisted way."

"Maybe he regrets now that he tried to implicate him in other crimes. Wants to take it back, if he can. Anyhow, I'll make an appointment for me and someone from Northumberland to go and take statements, and we'll see what happens. I hope it works out, Dan. For us and for you."

"Thanks, Alec."

He had no plans to call in at the office at the end of the day. A six or seven hour round trip, plus a stressful meeting in the prison, would be more than enough. Joan had promised to ring him with anything that wouldn't wait, and he had little hope of anything from Phil Gordon today. It would be nice to spend a quiet evening with his family and put thoughts of work aside for a while.

He was just passing the Nottingham turnoff when the phone rang. Five minutes later, he knew that quiet evening wasn't to be.

*

There was little of his usual smoothness about Cameron Connolly when they descended on him. He stood on his front doorstep, arms folded and face like thunder, taking in the number of officers Dan had with him.

Getting everything in place had taken a while, and Dan had half-expected Superintendent Stowe to tell him to leave it until the morning. Instead, the boss had rolled up his own sleeves and mucked in to help set up the raid, including getting the search warrant fast tracked.

There had been no shortage of eager volunteers to come along, but with a Police Search Advisor team, Phil Gordon's CSIs and several uniforms, it was already quite a deputation, so there was only one other detective in the party.

"Back again," Cameron said after allowing a silence to play out. "You might have given me some warning."

"Apologies for the discourtesy," Stowe drawled in a voice that said exactly the opposite.

"We only just finished dinner."

"Sorry if we're keeping you from the washing up."

"Funny. And what's *she* doing here?"

"Oh," said Lizzie, "this is one show I wouldn't miss for the world."

"I imagined you were suspended."

"No. I am supposed to be on leave but, to be honest, I was getting a bit bored."

"How's that husband of yours? How's he enjoying life inside?"

It was an obvious attempt to hurt her and to provoke. Considering how she'd been quietly falling apart these past days, Dan was impressed with her poise and coolness.

She inclined her head. "It's not what he's used to, obviously. But I don't expect him to be there long."

"Cam?" a woman's voice called from the depths of the house. "What's going on?"

"They haven't said yet, darling," he called back. "I'll take them over to the office."

"No, you won't," Stowe said. He turned to Lizzie. "DCI Archer, would you like to do the honours?"

"Love to," she replied. "Cameron Connolly, I am arresting you—"

Cameron's jaw dropped. "*What?* Is this a joke?"

"...Arresting you in connection with the murder of Calvin Dougan. You do not have to say anything. But it may harm your defence if you do not mention when questioned something which you later rely on in court. Anything you do say may be given in evidence."

"Meanwhile," said Dan. "We have a warrant to search your premises."

Cameron Connolly looked like he didn't believe what was happening to him. "You're making the biggest mistake of your lives. This is harassment."

"We're going to take you to the station now," Stowe said.

Fraser Connolly appeared, with two women behind him – his wife and, Dan suspected, his sister, Grace.

"Cam?" Fraser demanded. "What's going on?"

"I'm under arrest. Can you believe it?"

Mrs Connolly's right hand strayed towards her throat. If she'd had pearls, Dan suspected she'd have clutched them. "Oh, God..."

"Lizzie?" Grace's eyes were wide.

"Hello, Grace," Lizzie said. "Sorry to ruin your evening."

"They're going to search the house too," Cameron snarled. "Fraser, would you mind calling my solicitor and getting him to meet us at Aylesbury police station? And make sure they don't break anything or make too much mess."

37

Cameron Connolly's solicitor, Robin Monk, had the same man-mountain build as the late rock star Meat Loaf. The effect his expensive-looking haircut, exquisitely tailored suit and beautiful silk tie should have made was ruined by his beefy, sweaty complexion. It wasn't as if the station was anything like overheated, yet beads of the stuff kept breaking out on his forehead and dribbling down his cheeks.

At this hour, there was quite a choice of interview rooms. Lizzie took a mean delight in recommending the pokiest one, which also happened to be most in need of refurbishment. She could almost read Robin Monk's mind as he tried to keep his sleeves out of contact with the grotty tabletop. Lizzie, Dan and Josh Stowe sat opposite them. Lizzie shouldn't strictly be here, and it was made clear she was only observing.

"All right," Cameron said, after they'd all identified themselves for the recording. "So what's this rubbish about?"

"Straight to the point," Josh said. "That's good. DI Baines?"

"Let's start," said Dan, "by talking about what we've found in Calvin Dougan's car. *Your* car, more accurately. We've got some pictures here, if I can show you?"

"If you must." Cameron made a show of looking bored. "Let's get this over with. What have you got?"

Dan had brought a folder in with him. He opened it and fanned out a number of photographs on the table in front of Cameron.

Cameron shrugged.

"What am I supposed to be looking at?"

Dan tapped one. "This is a black hoodie top, recovered from the boot of that car. You'll see traces of what look like blood on it. Luminol has already confirmed that's what it is, and the crime lab has confirmed whose blood it is." The rush job had

241

been expensive, but Josh had seemingly cast the budget to the wind on this one. The wearer had also left a single hair inside the hoodie but, whoever they were, the DNA wasn't on any database.

Cameron's gaze flickered between the image and Dan's face. "Cal's blood?"

"Not Cal's, no." Dan tapped another photograph. "Here's a pair of gloves. More blood. The same as on the top. Oh, and there are traces of the same blood in the boot. Not much, but enough."

"I don't understand, Inspector," said Robin Monk, mopping his forehead with a handkerchief. "You seem to be saying *Mr Dougan* has – what exactly? – killed someone? Been involved in a murder?"

Cameron chimed in. He was making a very good job of looking bemused. "But I know nothing of this. What had he been up to? Is this what got him killed?"

"All of the above," said Dan. "Yes. But you're asking the wrong questions. Neither of you has asked whose blood it is."

"So enlighten us, please," the solicitor said. "It's late."

"Does the name Robert, or Rob, Thomas mean anything to you?"

"Can't say it does," Cameron said, a tad too casually.

"Oh, come on," Josh said. "You know very well who he is. You referred earlier to DCI Archer's husband being in prison, and I'm sure you know why. We'll make greater headway if you don't tell us obvious lies."

"Oh," he said, theatrically slapping his forehead. "*That* Robert Thomas. But why would Cal want to kill *him*?"

"Again, Mr Connolly, come on. Even if – *if* – you insist this is nothing to do with you, I'm sure you know where we're going with this."

"Suppose you spell it out, anyway, Superintendent," Robin Monk suggested.

But the Superintendent had no intention of doing so, preferring to switch back to Dan again. Lizzie had never seen him interview a suspect before. For a fast-streamer without a great deal of hands-on policing experience, she had to admit he was damn good.

"Calvin Dougan was your man, Mr Connolly," Dan said. "Give him any title, any job description you like, but that was the long and short of it. He worked for you. Did your dirty work, some would say. And you bore a grudge against DCI Archer. You blamed her for two recent deaths in your family and swore revenge. You said you'd exact it through her loved ones."

"And I apologised. Heat of the moment on an emotional day."

"But you've never denied saying it."

"I'm sorry," Monk said. "Maybe it's too stuffy in here, or maybe I'm being dim. You're accusing the deceased Mr Dougan of murdering this Robert Thomas, but then saying my client murdered Mr Dougan. I must say, it's all quite a leap."

"Sadly, Cal wouldn't be the first of my legitimate employees to branch out into some private criminal enterprise," Cameron said. "We do seem to have some bad luck in that area."

He was smirking. Lizzie could see he was recovering confidence and cockiness.

"So, I don't know," he continued. "Maybe Cal was killed in some gangland tit for tat. Who knows? Maybe after he killed one of theirs, whilst wearing that top, those gloves."

It was so preposterous, Lizzie had to resist the temptation to roll her eyes.

"The blood's Rob Thomas's," Dan said. "He wasn't a criminal."

"To the best of your knowledge," Cameron persisted. "Maybe he was in the area on nefarious business. None of this is to do with me."

"All right then," Dan said, "but that brings me to the third item recovered from your Mercedes. This time from the glove compartment."

He indicated a third photograph.

Cameron's eyes widened. "What? But... in the glove compartment? Why?"

"You recognise this, don't you?" Dan said. "It belongs to you, doesn't it? A fancy letter opener, made to look like a sword. It normally sits on a granite block on your desk, like Excalibur in the stone—"

"Do you think you're King Arthur, Mr Connolly?" Josh asked.

"Don't be ridiculous. I'd lost this. No one has admitted to taking it from my desk."

"Yes, I've seen you twice in the past week," Dan said to Cameron. "The first time the sword was in the stone, the second time, it looked like you'd lost or mislaid it. You reached for it, and it wasn't there."

Josh stepped in. "Now, we happen to know Rob Thomas was stabbed with a thin-bladed weapon. Something very much like this, in fact. And there's dried blood around the hilt."

"And I suppose you're saying *that*'s Rob Thomas's blood too?"

"Exactly what we're testing for now. As well as fingerprints. Unless you think Dominic Newman could have smuggled the knife into your car, he's off the hook and Cal Dougan would appear to be on it."

"And it works, doesn't it?" Dan said. "You blame DI Archer for your brother's and your father's deaths. You want revenge, and you've boasted about how good you are at..." he turned to Lizzie, "...what was that phrase, DCI Archer?"

"Knowing things," she happily supplied.

"Knowing things. And you get to hear that a man you know to be her ex-boyfriend from a long time ago has turned up in the area. Has in fact been involved in a row on her doorstep."

"You're making it up."

"Are we? We know you followed her home the day of your family funerals, after seeing her with Rob Thomas. You'd have made it your business to find out who he was, and it wouldn't be that hard, nor to find out what their relationship had been."

"And," Josh added, "the reason you know things is you have eyes and ears everywhere. If you were having DCI Archer watched—"

"*If,*" he sneered.

"Or maybe someone simply saw the altercation, knew for whatever reason that you'd be interested, and fed it back to you for a financial consideration."

Lizzie suddenly wondered about the uniformed constable who saw the whole thing. She knew the Connollys had a few coppers in their back pocket.

"Supposition," Monk said contemptuously.

"Stronger than that, when you put it all together," said Dan, "but hear me out. Cal Dougan, acting on Mr Connolly's orders, kidnaps Rob and puts him in his car boot, alive. He makes a call on a burn phone to Dominic, posing as a potential client and luring him to a pub. He's parked somewhere out of the way, and there he stabs Rob to death with the letter opener."

"Why that?" Cameron protested. "Why something that could come back and bite me?"

Lizzie could contain herself no longer. "You couldn't resist. If you weren't going to get your own hands dirty, then using your lovely letter opener was still a personal touch."

"DCI Archer." Josh held up a hand to silence her. "Please."

She subsided.

"You must admit, though," said Dan, "it's a good explanation. Only you were supposed to get it back. Anyhow, after the killing, I reckon Cal puts on the hoodie top and gloves and then waits in the car park. Dominic gives up waiting, as Cal knows he eventually will, and leaves the pub. Cal intercepts him, makes it look like an accidental collision and gets a decent amount of blood on Dominic's jacket, trusting the darkness to hide it. Maybe he does a passable impression of a younger man's voice, saying sorry."

"That's a lot of maybes, Inspector," Monk said.

"But plausible. Very plausible. You know it is. Next day, he drives the body to the Northfields estate and dumps it, making sure he leaves the burner phone with the body, knowing it'll lead the police to the only person the phone has communicated with. Dominic Newman."

There was silence for a moment, then Cameron gave out a low chuckle.

"It's a great story," he conceded. "But it raises too many questions. If it's as you say, why does he keep the hoodie, the gloves, the letter opener, knowing they'll incriminate him and me?"

"Maybe he just forgot about the letter opener," suggested Dan, "and you forgot to ask. We've all done it. Keep meaning to do a silly little thing, forget, intend to do it next time…"

"Last week I drove around with a letter in my car for three days," Josh said. "Kept forgetting to post it."

"Except it isn't a letter, is it?" retorted Cameron. "It's a so-called murder weapon. You're describing a clever, elaborate plan to kill a man and then fit Lizzy's hubby up for the murder, all undone because Cal gets himself shot with all the evidence still in his car. It's preposterous. You should be embarrassed, Superintendent."

Lizzie found that she was holding her breath. When he put it like that, it did sound ridiculous. She found herself doubting, as if a balloon of hope had been punctured. Maybe Josh would actually find it less plausible than the case against Dominic.

But Dan was having none of it.

"Maybe you put too much trust in Cal," he said. "The clothes, maybe the knife too… I'm guessing it was Cal's responsibility to get rid of them, and he was still deciding on the best way to do that. Who knows?"

"Still just a fantasy," said Cameron, "but suppose we go with it for a moment. Why would I want to kill *him*? Cal?"

"Well," said Dan, "I'll admit I'm speculating now, but maybe he turned around and asked for a nice fat bonus for what he'd done. Implied he'd talk if he was caught, unless you really made it worth his while. I can't imagine you like being blackmailed. Or was he simply a loose end?" He shook his head. "The casebooks are full of clever people being caught because they've done stupid things."

"Or, as I said at the outset, why can't it all still be some sort of gangland thing that I know nothing about?"

"Now *that* sounds like a convenient reach. More to the point though, Mr Connolly, you own at least one gun that you'll own up to. It's being seized even as we speak. Without getting too boring and technical, we can see if it, or any other weapon we might recover, matches the bullet that killed Cal. If I was a betting man, I'd put my shirt on it. With all the other evidence…"

"It's still all circumstantial," Monk protested, but Lizzie heard no conviction in his tone.

"We'll let the DPP be the judge of that," said Josh Stowe with a happy smile. "And then a jury."

Cameron's last vestiges of arrogant confidence drained away. He turned pale, his face seeming to fall in. He looked at Lizzie with appeal in his eyes.

"Lizzie," he said, "you have to believe me. I know what you think of me, but *I did not do this*."

"I *have* to believe you?" she scoffed. "Why? Because you're such an honest man?"

Her heart was pounding so hard, she feared it might burst. Not only could this exonerate Dominic, but it might actually finally get Cameron put away.

Clever people doing stupid things, Dan had said.

The original Teflon man, Cameron had been full of anger and grief and had made some rare mistakes – getting caught, not for the fingers he had in so many underworld pies, but for what had turned out to be a clever enough frame up, but then a disastrous attempt to silence the only witness.

So out of character.

It should have felt so delicious.

So why did it still feel too good to be true?

38

Lizzie had wanted Josh to go in with all guns blazing this evening, to get Dominic out. But he'd resisted that.

"We've got to draw a line between justice and special favours somewhere," he'd said. "If it was another innocent person, not related to the force, we both know the whole system wouldn't drop everything to make this happen."

"This isn't *anyone else*," she'd protested, despite knowing he was right. He'd advised her to speak to Bill Smith and Adina Walker.

If Bill Smith was disgruntled to receive a call from Dan, asking to see him urgently, that was nothing to his reaction when he laid eyes on Lizzie. He'd agreed, 'as a courtesy', to meet Dan in his office, even though it was out of hours and the station was like a ghost ship. Now he stood up behind his desk, jabbing an index finger in her direction.

"What's *she* doing here? *She* can't be here."

"Keep your Y-fronts on, Bill," she retorted. "I've come to stop you making a bigger bloody fool of yourself than you have already."

"Look," he growled, "I've followed the evidence, built a case, and the DPP agrees. Your hubby has done his thing in the magistrates' court. It'll go to trial when it goes to trial. It's out of my hands and, frankly, I resent—"

"You *resent*?" She shook her head pityingly. "Wow. Whatever I thought about you before – and not much of it was good – it never included 'pompous'. Until now."

"Sir," Dan said, "you should hear us out. I don't make a habit of interfering in cases, especially something like this, but something's come up that turns the Rob Thomas case on its head."

"I doubt that," he said, "but like I said, I'll do you the courtesy. You," – he jabbed his finger in Lizzie's direction again – "were not part of the invitation, and I take a dim view of you tagging along. But you're here now. Sit down and keep quiet."

Having dismissed her, he turned to Dan. "DI Baines? You've got five minutes to say what you came to say, and then I'm off home."

Swallowing her fury, Lizzie took a seat.

"Sir," Dan began, "you might have heard we have a new murder case in the Vale."

"Yet another." Smith smirked. "Careless. Must be the standard of policing around there."

"One Calvin Dougan. He worked for a local businessman, Cameron Connolly, who is in reality a kingpin in organised crime around our way. Shot to death in a car park near a local nature reserve."

"What's that to do with me?"

"What's to do with you, *sir*, is what we found in his car. I've a couple of pictures, if I can show you?"

Smith made a huge show of various negative emotions, principal of which was bored irritation.

"If you insist."

Dan took out his phone and carried it over to the DCI's side of the desk.

Lizzie came too. Smith glowered. "I told you to—" He threw up his hands. "Fine. What am I looking at?"

Dan showed him the photographs of evidence bags they'd confronted Cameron Connolly with: the black hoodie top, the gloves, the Excalibur letter opener. He explained how all the items bore Rob Thomas's blood.

"Hang on," Smith seized on something he'd said. "You said that letter opener's blade was similar to the Rob Thomas murder weapon. That information hasn't been released, so how could you possibly know?"

Dan simply smiled. "I think what's more important, sir, is that you're not denying it."

"So what's your point?" But Smith's belligerence was already turning to petulance.

"I think you know very well what I'm saying, sir. Dominic Newman didn't kill Rob Thomas. Cameron Connolly had Cal Dougan kill him and make it look like Dominic was the murderer. We know only too well that Cameron blames Lizzie for his brother's and his father's deaths, and this was his revenge. I think he'd been watching her or having her watched from the moment his dad died. So he'd have known about the row with Rob on Lizzie's doorstep, and a plan to hurt her through her husband dropped into his lap."

Smith sighed. "Go on, then. Tell me what you think happened."

Dan ran through the scenario he'd described to Cameron, from that first telephone contact with Dominic, through to Cal Dougan's own murder.

"Well," Smith said when he'd finished, "no question that it's a great story. There seem to be a few ifs, buts and maybes."

"The letter opener is pretty compelling," said Dan. "It will tie Rob's death straight back to Cameron Connolly."

Bill Smith drummed his fingers on his desk, looking decidedly unhappy. He must know there was a chance of some egg on his face, but he was still a detective, with a detective's instincts.

"All right," he said finally. "The missing link is proving Cal Dougan was killed with Cameron Connolly's gun. If that stacks up, then so does your story."

"It stacks up even without," Lizzie said. "Cameron may have got rid of the actual gun that killed Cal, or he might even have ordered the killing, although he might not have wanted anyone else in on his conspiracy. Everything else still points to Dougan as Rob's killer, and his own death being aimed at shutting his mouth on the subject forever."

He chewed his lip. "Okay, I concede it does sound convincing."

"So you'll drop the charges against Dominic?" she urged.

Bill Smith blinked. "I don't want to rush into that. Let's wait and see what those tests on the guns turn up."

"Wait?" She was ready to explode. "What do you mean, wait? Those tests could take days."

"Lizzie, I know you've been having a bad time, but think. This scenario, this very plausible scenario, still needs all the evidence you can muster. Now, I'm happy to come to Aylesbury in the morning and take part in questioning this Connolly character, but the gun is still important. Where's the harm in waiting?"

"My husband's in a prison," she said through gritted teeth. "A detective's husband surrounded by convicted criminals, many of them will hate coppers, some of whom will see him as an extension of me. Every second he's there increases the risk that his identity will get out. God knows you didn't make a great job of keeping me out of the media, did you?"

"Even so."

She finally erupted. "Here's a promise, Bill," she said. "If anything happens to him, then that's my whole life screwed. I'll have nothing to lose. My career? Who gives a shit? I'll come after you, Bill, and I'll take you down, one way or another."

She knew what she sounded like, yet she couldn't seem to stop the words coming out of her mouth.

Dan squeezed her arm. "Lizzie..."

She shook him off. "No."

Smith chuckled. "Well, well. All that high and mighty talk about people threatening *you*, and now you're at it too." His eyes narrowed. "Well, I won't be intimidated. If... *if* these tests suggest Mr Newman might be innocent, then I *might* consider applying to release him on bail. Until then... let's let DI Baines's investigation take its course, shall we? And Lizzie?"

"What?" She was trying to regain some modicum of control.

"I've never seen you so het up." He actually winked. "It looks good on you."

She had never wanted to hit someone quite so much. She might have done so, had Dan not spoken.

"That was really inappropriate, sir," he said icily.

"Really? Well it's you two in cahoots, against my word. Now piss off, the pair of you. I thought your investigation was urgent."

*

She phoned Adina Walker once they were back in Dan's car.

"Regardless of whether Cameron's formally charged with something like conspiracy to murder Rob," she argued, "which would be the motive for silencing Cal Dougan, the DPP will surely see there's already enough evidence to get the charges against Dominic dropped. So how long would it take to get him released?"

"It would be either a discontinuance or a formal acquittal," Adina said. "I would hope it would be the former. It's not the same as a not guilty verdict, because, in theory, the case can be picked up again. But in practice, in this case the charges are dropped and it's like they never happened."

"How long does it take?" Lizzie repeated.

"Longer than it should but, if the police no longer think Dominic's guilty – well, if that wouldn't fast track it, I don't know what would."

Lizzie had hoped that, instead of visiting her husband in prison tomorrow, she might be bringing him home today. That might not be going to happen. Not knowing how fast things would move was maddeningly frustrating.

"Okay," she said. "DCI Smith seems minded to drag his heels, but my Superintendent said he was happy to speak to *his* boss in the morning, and to escalate it to Chief Constable level if necessary. So hopefully the ball will at least be rolling by lunchtime tomorrow. I guess it's the best we can hope for."

As she ended the call, she tried to tell herself it was all good news today. They finally had the goods on Cameron Connolly. And, even though Dominic wasn't out of Newlands yet, it was just a matter of time. She should be upbeat, but she couldn't be until Dominic was out of that place.

No one knew who'd stabbed Desmond Connolly to death in Newlands. She'd have thought his family, with all their connections, could have found out, but no one had been charged, and there was no sign of any unofficial justice being meted out.

Even the motive for Desmond's murder was unknown. Most likely someone didn't like his face, the way he talked, the way he acted. Every moment Dominic was there, the same could happen to him. She kept telling herself it would be so unlucky as to be improbable, but the nagging fear just refused to go away.

Another night without him awaited. Another night of dreading the phone ringing.

39

Bill Smith duly rocked up at Aylesbury police station early, but not necessarily bright, in the morning, so Superintendent Stowe didn't need to get him leaned on at a higher level. Maybe he'd realised that, one way or another, he was going to have to engage with the Cameron Connolly case. Maybe he'd taken his head out of his backside and seen how it would look for him if something befell Dominic in prison while he pissed around.

Dan didn't much care, so long as he was here.

Ballistics testing was under way after Stowe had secured funding to fast track it. Although he was still wary of anything that looked like special treatment for the police, he'd apparently argued that Dominic *wasn't* police, but his marital status made him more vulnerable than the average prisoner. If it could be confirmed that the gun that had killed Cal Dougan was Cameron's, that would clinch the case they were building and point to Dominic's release.

Dan vehemently hoped that the bullet had been fired from Cameron's rifle. No other guns had been found at his home, and Cameron had already confirmed that no one but him knew the combination of his gun safe. The numbers had been passed on to the PolSA team to save them breaking in, so it would be challenging for Cameron to say someone else might have used his weapon.

The only thing that worried Dan was how relaxed Cameron was. He'd been rattled last night when he'd first been arrested, but now he was playing it as cool as only he could. Most likely it was an act. Or did he know things about the evidence that he wasn't saying, things that made him confident he'd be released without charge?

Again?

But, if that was the case, Cameron's confidence was shattered around lunch time, when the ballistics report came in and he was confronted with the results.

Every bullet had 'rifling' marks, caused by spiral grooves located inside the gun barrel which caused the bullet to spin, producing a more stable flight path. By identifying the bullet calibre and its rifling marks, experts could identify the type of gun used. And wear around the inside of the barrel could give a gun a unique rifling signature.

The report was damning. Cal Dougan had been shot with a rifle belonging to Cameron Connolly.

"No," he'd protested when confronted with this. "No, that just can't be right."

To be fair, he made a pretty convincing show of being confused. But then, Dan knew the man was a consummate liar. He must have known he was in trouble and that there was a strong possibility of evidence being turned up that would nail him. Maybe he'd decided that feigned bewilderment was his best approach.

He'd been stupid to keep the gun but, as Lizzie had suggested, grief had unhinged him enough to make reckless threats against her, and now it seemed to have finally led him to make a series of bad decisions. Decisions worthy of his fool of a brother, the late, unlamented Desmond.

"You're sure no one else has access to your gun cabinet?" Dan asked. "Nobody else knows the combination?"

"No one knew it but me. And, before you ask, no, it's not based on some obvious date, like a birthday and, no, it isn't written down anywhere. I know what kids are. I don't want them getting at the gun and larking around with it."

Dan folded his arms. "Well. If you're the only one who could have got at the guns, how do you explain one of them being used to kill Cal?"

"I can't. Obviously. There must be a mistake. Or, more likely, someone is trying to set *me* up."

"Like you set up Dominic Newman?"

"That nonsense again? Oh, I must admit, the original idea doesn't sound bad, but shooting Cal with my own gun and leaving a ton of evidence in the car for anyone to find? I mean, come on."

"The only mistakes have been yours, Mr Connolly," said Stowe. "Evidence is evidence and, by your own admission, no one else could have accessed that gun."

Bill Smith had kept silent until now. "For what it's worth, you're right. You framed Dominic Newman brilliantly. You had me fooled. If you hadn't got messy, it would have played out just as you intended, and you'll have had your revenge." He shook his head. "Whatever it would have taken to buy Cal Dougan's silence, maybe you should have paid it. Instead, you got your own hands dirty for once, and you messed up."

Dan wanted to punch the air. Smith was convinced, and singing from the same hymn sheet at last.

"Didn't happen," Cameron said sullenly.

Dan smiled. "Don't believe you."

*

Dan still didn't like Bill Smith, but the Bedfordshire DCI's disposition had transformed and things were moving fast now. All were agreed that, at the very least, Cameron Connolly could be charged in relation to both killings – Rob Thomas and Cal Dougan – although, in the former case, they might have to settle for conspiracy to murder. Josh Stowe thought there was probably enough to go for murder in the case of Dougan.

This time, they all agreed, all the fancy lawyers on earth wouldn't be able to save him.

There was paperwork to be done, but Dan was hopeful that Dominic might be home with Lizzie by tonight. He couldn't wait to tell her.

Meanwhile, Dan wondered what this might do to the criminal balance of power in the Vale. Would Fraser Connolly try to take a more active grip on the territory, when their father's death had already signalled a possible weakening at the top? Would he promote from within the local network? Would other gangs, scenting blood, try to move in and stake their own claim?

That had always been the fear: an out and out turf war in a traditionally quiet part of the country.

"We'll cross that bridge when we come to it," Stowe said. "Let's go back in and tell Mr Connolly he's facing charges. Then you can call Lizzie with the good news, if you like."

"And you can tell her I'm sorry," Smith added. "For what it's worth. I know she probably won't believe me. But this bastard set him up nicely. Made a right fool out of me."

"It *was* a nice set up," Dan agreed. "Yet, as soon as we tugged a loose thread, the whole thing fell apart. I'm still surprised."

"Don't let's look a gift horse in the mouth," Stowe said.

As they headed back towards the interview room, Dan's phone rang. He checked the display.

"Sorry," he said. "I really need to take this."

The call was short. When it was over, it was evident that the others could see the shock on his face.

The Superintendent closed the distance between them. "Dan? Are you all right?" He nodded towards the phone, still in Dan's hand. "Bad news?"

"Pretty bad, yeah." He could scarcely believe it. "The worst."

40

Dan had shaken off his shock quickly, as best he could, going in with the others to break the news to Cameron Connolly of the charges he would be facing. The news he'd just received had taken the shine off it, but not so much that Dan didn't still feel pleasure – especially at the disbelief on Cameron's face.

Apart from the late Desmond's ham-fisted schemes, no copper had been able to lay a glove on a Connolly up until now. Knowing that his usual attention to detail had failed him and made his own downfall all too easy must have been a very bitter pill for Cameron to swallow.

He'd hoped to catch Lizzie before she left for her own prison visit, to Dominic, but she'd just been contacted and told it was cancelled.

"Why?" he wanted to know. "What's happened?"

"They wouldn't tell me much, but there's been a pretty serious incident, so the visit's cancelled while people are interviewed and statements taken." Her voice broke. "Shit, shit, shit."

"Well," he said, deliberately casual, "you might be picking him up later and bringing him home."

"There's news?"

"The best. Lizzie, Smith is satisfied that Cameron connived to frame Dominic for Rob's murder. The charges are being dropped."

There was a long silence.

"You still there?" he prompted.

"Sorry, yeah. Just taking it in. You're sure?"

"Definitely."

He was almost deafened by a squeal of pure joy.

"Oh, I wish I was there. I could hug you. I could even hug Bill bloody Smith. Well, almost."

"Obviously, there's all the bureaucracy hoops to jump through, but he'll be released without a stain on his character."

"Apart from the damage done by announcing his – actually *our* – arrests."

"You know, that's strange," he said. "The Super took him to task over that. Smith absolutely insists that neither he, nor any of his team, leaked it to the media. All that was put out was that arrests had been made."

"Steve Ashby's source, Woodger?"

"Maybe. But I half-wonder if Cameron got someone to make an anonymous call, supplying the names. Once one outlet went with the story and it hadn't been denied, it snowballed."

Another pause. "You know, I can see that," she said. "That way, if he gets Dominic put in prison, he's painted a target on his back too. His life is made a misery and I suffer."

"We'll probably never be able to prove that one. But the sooner we get him out of there, the better."

"Yes, please. Still," she said, something of her old bounce in her voice, "not a bad day, eh? Two murders solved and Dominic's coming home."

"Yeah," he said, his own mood suddenly taking the opposite turn. "It's great."

"What's wrong?"

"Nothing." This wasn't a good time to put a damper on things.

"I can tell it's not nothing."

He hesitated. He hadn't even told Karen yet, but he had to tell *someone.*

"Okay, then. It's not all good news," he said. "Mac's dead."

"Mac? Invisible Man Mac?"

"Alec McGivering called. He'd got halfway to Wakefield – to see if Mac would keep his promise about signing confessions – when the governor called him. Mac hanged himself with his bedsheets this morning."

"Oh, Jesus. I mean, I can't say the world isn't better off without him, but still…"

"I should have seen it coming when I went to see him myself. He asked for *me*, Lizzie. Now I'm thinking it was his way of making his peace with a world he didn't intend to occupy much longer. He talked about how very boring prison life was, a life stretching out in front of him for as long as he lived. He said he was ready to confess to his other crimes. And he even asked me to tell Peter he loved him. Now I see why. He was saying goodbye."

"Yeah, well," she said, clearly not so impressed. "It would have been nice if he'd given everyone some proper closure first."

"He sort of did. He left a note, which the governor read to Alec. He listed murders he was admitting to: nine of the eleven cases McGivering was investigating, and four more not previously connected to him."

"Thirteen? Bloody hell. So what about Peter? Where does that leave him?"

"The note was apparently adamant that his 'son' had no involvement in, nor knowledge of, any of the crimes."

"Oh, Dan, what a relief. You believe him, right?"

"Ninety-nine per cent. More importantly, so does McGivering. I just hope, when Peter knows about the note, he won't feel inhibited about confirming it. Although I'm dreading telling him. He might be my son, but he still sees Mac more as his father than he does me. I think he'll be devastated."

"And what about you?"

"You know, I should be elated. I thought I hated Mac, but my feelings are more mixed than I'd have expected. He was my friend once – at least, he seemed to be – and he's done right by Peter in the end. He's also left whatever he still had by way of an estate to him and – you won't believe this – he's named me as his executor, trusting that I'll do what's best for Peter."

"Maybe this is a good day for both of us in the long run, Dan. Maybe, once the dust settles, you can move to more of a father-son relationship."

"Who knows? Will it bring him closer to me? Or drive him away?"

"It won't drive him away. You said he was curious. About you, about Louise and Karen. About Ellie. You're the only family he has left. And maybe, if he doesn't feel so much need to be loyal to Mac, we can help him get as early a parole as possible."

"That'll be in about two years' time. But you said 'we'?"

She smiled. "I can talk to my new best mate, Adina Walker, about how we lay the ground."

"That's what we need," he said. "Thanks. If only we had the lawyers Cameron Connolly has access to. They'll be looking for ways to wriggle him out of it even as we speak. When do you think you'll be back at work?"

Silence.

"Lizzie?"

"Oh, sorry. Just thinking about something. What you said about Cameron and the lawyers. Best have no loose ends. Can you do something for me?"

"Sure," he said, intrigued.

"See if you can get hold of any CCTV footage anywhere of Cal Dougan. Also, that footage of Dominic's car park collision. Then ask Will if he can get some gait analysis done. Be good if we could show the guy in the car park was most likely Dougan."

"On it. Good idea. Keep me posted on Dominic's release."

*

Lizzie ended the call with her emotions pulled in a dozen directions. The overwhelming one was elation that the nightmare was all but over and, unless life had another nasty twist in store for her, Dominic would be coming home.

There was enough evidence to tie Rob's murder to Cal Dougan, and Dougan's to Cameron Connolly. Some, maybe all of the details would emerge between now and Cameron's trial.

But why should she care about that now? Far more important that she concentrated her mind on how she and Dominic were going to put these past few bruising days behind them. Maybe a holiday was due. Some autumn sun?

And then there was Dan to be pleased for. No one was going to be prosecuting Jack – she still struggled to think of him as

Peter – in connection with Mac's later crimes. For them, the future was still full of uncertainties, but it was something.

But, even as she told herself all this, something still niggled away at her, like an itch she couldn't quite reach. It was an itch that had prompted her to ask Dan about that gait analysis.

She'd mentioned loose threads and, for her, there were still too many for her liking. So what, she reproached herself. The DPP seemed to think the case against Cameron was robust enough. The main thing was that the man who'd thought he was untouchable was looking at a life sentence. Soon he'd be in Dominic's position, in prison and awaiting trial.

What was not to like?

So why did she still have reservations? Just because the case against Cameron seemed too perfect didn't mean there was anything wrong with it. She kept telling herself that grief and anger had made Cameron careless. But a voice in her head kept whispering, '*that* careless?'

It was ridiculous. Here she was, fretting over whether they were mistaken about Cameron Connolly. After all the times he'd avoided justice, why should she care?

Because you care about justice, even for him.

Because, if her gut was right, then there was a chance that the real killers of Rob, and of Cal Dougan, could get away with it. She didn't give much of a damn about Cal, but real justice for Rob mattered to her. For Dominic, too, who'd gone through hell as a result.

She sat back in her chair, closed her eyes, and did her best to clear her mind. She cast her mind back to the evening when Cameron Connolly, his sister in tow, had turned up outside her house, issuing threats against her and everyone she cared about. She attempted to play back what he'd said, and found something that jarred. A phrase that had sounded a slightly wrong note at the time, but which she'd all but forgotten with all that had happened since.

As she ran through subsequent events, she found there were a lot other little things that had lodged at the back of her mind. None of them of much consequence by themselves but she

found that, putting them together they might just add up to...
something crazy.

She could let sleeping dogs lie, but that had never been her
way. She wasn't going to start doing that now, not with this
case.

41

If Dan had been taken aback when Lizzie had asked him not to dismantle his unofficial incident room just yet, he'd been amazed when she'd ask if he and the other conspirators could meet her there this evening. The call had come just before she'd set out for Newlands to collect Dominic, and Dan had questioned the need for a wash up meeting when, surely, she and her husband would want to be together. Wouldn't Dominic resent being left on his own on his first night home?

"He might," she'd conceded, "and I'll call it off if he does. But I don't think he'll have a problem when I tell him why I think it's important."

"Care to share with me?" he'd asked her.

"Not yet. I'm either on the right track, or I've finally lost my mind. I'm waiting on one more phone call to be returned, then I'll know for sure."

It wasn't like her to be cryptic, especially with him, but he trusted her enough to know she never did anything without good reason. Now, a few hours later, six detectives, plus Karen and Charlie, were again seated around his study. Lizzie had assured him that Dominic was happy enough being home with Barney the cat for a while. He'd not slept wonderfully in Newlands, so he was planning an early night in any case.

Now she had the floor.

"Thank you all for coming," she said. "Dominic thanks you too, for your support the last few days. It makes me feel all the more awkward about what I'm about to say, but I wanted you all to hear it. You deserve nothing less."

"Whatever it is, we're listening," said Joan Collins. "But I think we're all a bit mystified. Dominic's out, Cameron Connolly's in, and all's right with the world. Isn't it?" she added.

"Well, that's been my problem. I'd have made a case against the Dalai Lama, if I could show he, and not Dominic, was behind Rob's murder. But we all thought we had Cameron almost *too* bang to rights, didn't we? And, try as I might, I couldn't get past it. I've spent years wanting to see him put away but, more than anything else, I wanted Rob's killer to pay the price – not someone else who'd been set up."

"Set up?" Dan's head reeled. "Cameron?"

"You're joking," added Joan.

She massaged her temples. "I know, I know. But I've spent a fair bit of this afternoon trying to get my head round what doesn't add up, trying to see what we – *I* may have missed. I came up with something so ridiculous that it made everything else seem entirely plausible. But then I made some calls, and now I'm not so sure."

Dan tried to ignore the sick feeling in his gut. After Mac's death, he wasn't sure he could take any more shocks today. But Lizzie looked anything but happy.

"I realised this whole thing… Cameron's threats, Rob's death, Dominic being framed, Cal Dougan's murder, and finally Cameron being arrested… it all really started with Desmond Connolly being killed in prison, didn't it?"

She walked up to the board and added Desmond's photograph at the top.

"I guess," Dan agreed. "If that hadn't happened, then the shock wouldn't have killed Murray Connolly, and Cameron wouldn't have been looking for someone to blame." He shrugged. "But what of it?"

"Well," she said, "as far as I knew, Desmond's murder hadn't been solved. I mean, I know there's a code of silence in prisons, but the Connollys are supposed to have contacts everywhere. I'd be amazed if they hadn't been paying a prison officer or two to keep an eye on Desmond."

"If that's so," Jason said, "and someone in there had a line back to the Connollys, they'd have known soon enough who was responsible and arranged some retribution."

"You're right," Dan realised. "But there's been nothing, has there?"

"No, exactly. So I phoned my opposite number at Milton Keynes, who I'd assumed would be investigating it. He wasn't."

"Why not?"

"Because the National Crime Agency has come in over their heads and taken the case off them. Our old friend DCI Sheppard, to be precise."

He stared at her, recollections and emotions kaleidoscoping in his head. *"Catherine?"*

"Yep."

"Jesus. Last time I saw her was when I got shot. To be fair, she did save my life." He thought about it, shuddering at the memory. "But she did have an interest in all things Connolly, didn't she?"

"Still does. I phoned her. Much as she hasn't lost a wink of sleep over Desmond and Murray checking out, she wanted to know who'd have the temerity to attack a member of that family. And, more to the point, why they were still alive."

"And?"

"And she did find a few things out. Some from the local force, some through her own intelligence. The first is that Desmond was always playing the big man inside."

"That's hardly a revelation," observed Joan. "I seem to recall he always did fancy himself. So do they reckon he pissed off the wrong person?"

"It's possible. Except, as Jason says, you'd have thought payback would have been pretty swift for some lowlife hothead stupid enough to mess with a Connolly. Family honour, plus a warning to others. And it gets more interesting. I don't know, maybe Desmond didn't think he was getting enough respect, but even some of the prison officers were surprised about how freely he'd started to talk about family business, using it to big himself up, apparently oblivious to the dangers of such indiscretion."

"I'm still not seeing what this has to do with who killed Rob," Dan said.

Lizzie smiled. "So let's fast forward a little. NCA has a tad more leverage than local forces enjoy. They can do deals. No one would state categorically who'd killed Desmond but, when they could get someone to at least drop hints, the same few names kept cropping up. Three potential suspects."

"I'm betting they didn't get a confession," said Will.

"No such luck. But they also did pretty thorough searches of their cells. One of the three, a bottom-feeder by the name of Jamie Keynes, had a shiv hidden inside his toilet cistern. There were traces of blood on it. They left an identical-looking replacement there, so Keynes wouldn't know it had been discovered, and they set about testing the blood."

"Desmond Connolly?" Karen suggested.

"In one. Meanwhile, they'd been looking into the three suspects' backgrounds. Keynes's crimes included a bit of county lines stuff, some violence…"

"County lines?" Natalie Chen said. "Organised crime then. So he was connected to a rival gang?"

"He had gang connections, yes. He also had a wife and three kids who've been struggling financially with him inside. The last few weeks, things seem to have got a little easier for them. So DCI Sheppard had her watched. She spends in cash."

"People on low income often do," Dan said.

"True. But a few discreet enquiries showed that she'd been maxing out her credit card previously. Suddenly she's paying cash and using her bank account to pay the card off. Conclusion?"

"She's come into some cash," Jason said. "Do they know from where?"

"They asked neighbours for any CCTV – you know, doorbells and the like. They captured a guy dropping a thick brown envelope in Mrs Keynes's bin. You see her looking furtive when she recovers it. Catherine sent a couple of clips to my phone."

"I don't suppose they've identified the courier?" Dan asked.

"Another gang member, just a bit higher up."

"But what gang?" he pressed.

"Okay," she said, smiling again. "I've teased you enough." And she told them.

Dan stared at her. "What the fuck?"

"Oh," she said, "and that incident that put Newlands into

lockdown earlier today? Someone has got to Jamie Keynes. He's dead."

42

Two weeks later.

A gap finally opened up in the traffic and Lizzie hurried across the road and took a closer look at the small gallery in a fashionable, arty corner of Glasgow.

Peering inside, she could see Grace Connolly talking to a customer. Today was one of three days a week when, according to her website, 'The artist will be in the gallery from 10 am to noon.' Lizzie checked her watch. It was one minute past eleven.

She pushed the door and walked in. Another woman, of similar age to Grace, who was manning the till, said hello. Lizzie nodded to her and wandered around, looking at the pictures on the walls, Grace's distinctive style.

Grace's customer, male, ruddy-faced and probably pushing seventy, was doing most of the talking. Lizzie didn't pretend to understand all of what he was saying, but she wondered how long her patience would last before she just marched over and interrupted.

Grace must have felt Lizzie's gaze upon her, because she glanced over, looked again, and registered surprise. Hastily excusing herself, she stalked over, her pink jacket eye-catching, her stride brisk as ever in leggings and tall black boots. She wasn't smiling.

"Well," she said, "this is a surprise. I'm not sure we should be talking."

"After I came all this way?"

"What do you want, Lizzie?"

Lizzie held up her hands. "Look, I'm in the area with my husband, and I remembered I never did get that print I liked."

Grace wasn't buying it. "The least you can do is not take me for an idiot. This is no more about a print than it was last time we met. All that's happened the past few weeks and you decide to take a city break *here*, of all places? Why don't we go in my office and you can say whatever you came to say. Although it'd be a long way to come to gloat over Cameron."

"This isn't about gloating, I promise," she said. "But lead the way."

The other woman apologised to her red-faced customer, told her colleague she wouldn't be long, and led her into a surprisingly tatty and untidy office. There were only two chairs. Grace sat on the one behind the desk and told Lizzie to dump the boxes piled on the other on the floor.

"So, if you're trying to pin something else on my family, just come right out with it," said Grace. "You'll get nothing out of me."

"Let's just see how this goes, shall we?" Lizzie replied. "Quite a lot's happened since Cameron's arrest. I thought you'd like to know that the person who killed your younger brother was himself murdered in prison a couple of weeks ago."

"Really?"

"It's not common knowledge yet."

Grace nodded. "Well, that's something, I suppose. Thank you for telling me."

"Conveniently for whoever was behind that, no one has yet been arrested for it."

"Why does someone have to be behind it? There are so many scumbags in prison, and I dare say half of them are a bit quick to anger. Unfortunately, Des was one of them, but he still didn't deserve what happened to him."

"Hmm," said Lizzie. "We'll have to have a long chat some time about what Desmond deserved. Don't forget he was in jail because a lot of people died the last time he tried his hand at being a big gangster. But here's the thing. His killer was involved in organised crime, and it seems he murdered your brother in exchange for cash payments to his family. But his paymasters should have found a brighter assassin. Maybe there wasn't time to be choosy."

"Hang on. If they know who did it, why is this Keynes person dead? Instead of under arrest?"

"Because whoever killed him was evidently under instructions to make sure he never talked. As soon as the police were on to him, he became a liability. A bit like Desmond."

Grace raised an eyebrow. "What's that supposed to mean?"

"Well, poor Desmond was, by all accounts, so indiscreet that even the prison officers noticed that he'd started making rather too free with his mouth about the family business." She smiled. "I'll bet word got back to Cameron. As you know, what you witnessed on the day of the funerals wasn't the first time Cameron threatened me. I had similar threats when Desmond was first put away. Funny thing is, I've never known Cameron show much more than contempt for his younger brother. I thought his anger back then seemed more about family honour than any love lost."

Grace regarded her with a steady enough gaze, but Lizzie thought there was tension on her face.

"I thought even then that he was capable of losing the plot," Lizzie continued.

"If you're saying what I think you're saying, then *you're* the one losing the plot," Grace said, her mask of equanimity finally slipping. "You seriously think Cameron would have his own brother killed?"

"I'm not sure I'd go that far. Maybe Des wasn't supposed to die. Just a warning. But, as I say, they sent a dimwit to do the job, so he likely bodged it."

"Okay, this is ridiculous. Cameron was a long way from perfect and, yes, Fraser and I did think he might have lost… let's call it a sense of perspective… when Des and Dad died. The way he came round your house, ranting… But—"

"The trouble with a rant is you can let things slip. I remembered much later that he specifically said he hadn't seen *his father's* death coming. It was a bit odd. Almost as if Desmond getting at least hurt had been foreseen. Only later I started to think perhaps he *had* foreseen it because he planned it. What he hadn't reckoned with was the shock taking your dad too."

"I think you'd better leave."

"And I think you should hear me out."

"Make it quick, please."

"We were working on the theory that someone heard we'd rowed publicly with Rob Thomas and concocted a plan to frame my husband. He was lured to a pub by a phantom 'client' who never turned up. As he left the pub in the dark, someone barrelled into him and got Rob's blood on him. I'm sure you know all this. That and some supposedly clever stuff with an unregistered phone, and everything pointed to Dominic having killed Rob. Except the murder weapon and other evidence turned up in Cal Dougan's car after he was shot."

"Yes, I do know that, thank you. Evidence supposedly pointing at Cameron."

"That's right. Plus Cal was shot with Cameron's own gun, supposedly to silence him, or perhaps because he started demanding extra money. I take it you knew Cameron had a gun?"

"What?" Grace looked startled. "Oh. Well, I knew he went shooting."

"You never saw it?"

"Once, first time I went there after he joined the club. He wanted to show it off. Typical Cam. I wasn't interested, but he was insistent."

Lizzie chuckled. "That gun safe, eh? Pretty secure, with that complicated combination lock. I mean, even if you'd seen him open it, you'd need a good memory for numbers..." She snapped her fingers. "A bit like you. When we had coffee in Rumsey's and you had the two bills totted up in your head."

Grace was looking wary now.

Lizzie continued. "Cameron isn't the only one with eyes and ears inside prison, is he? I'm pretty sure Fraser got to hear that Jamie Keynes was responsible for Desmond's murder, and was astute enough to work out where the order had come from. Maybe the two of you confronted Cameron. Maybe he admitted it. Or maybe that conversation never happened, but you'd worked it out anyway and wanted an opportunity to pay him back. And, by pure chance, one came along." She leaned back in her chair. "Feel free to jump in at any time, if I'm getting it wrong."

"Oh, no. This is fun." Grace seemed to have recovered just a little composure. "You should have been a writer. Fiction, obviously."

"Oh, no, Grace. You're the creative one. From what I know of Fraser, he's very clever, but not necessarily that imaginative. But then I always thought killing Rob and fitting up Dominic was a two-person job. Two people acting alone, trusting absolutely no one. Putting me through hell for putting Desmond inside in the first place, then punishing Cameron for two deaths in the family. *And* putting him away where his increasingly unstable behaviour would do a bit less harm."

"Can you prove any of this fairy tale?"

"We'll get to that. Here's another thing. Dominic thought he'd been bumped into by a youngish man wearing a hood, in the dark. When the bloody hoodie and gloves turned up in the car with Cal's body, we imagined it was an unidentified foot soldier in the Connolly network. Then I viewed the car park footage myself, quite a few times. And it's interesting. What you actually see is the person walking normally into and out of frame. It's only when they're on stage, so to speak, that they weave about and blunder into Dominic."

"So? If that's a fact, they were putting on an act." But her mouth was set in a grim line now.

Lizzie leaned her elbows on the desk. "Nice choice of words. A bit like me saying 'on stage'. Someone else talked to me about 'putting on an act' only the other day, and it rang a faint bell. Later I remembered you talking about how you'd dabbled in some other arts. Dance, a bit of poetry, you said. And acting. So let's talk about the acting."

Grace said nothing.

Lizzie sat back in her seat again. "I had a look on the Internet. You called it dabbling, but I see you did some TV work, some provincial theatre... pretty decent stuff."

"Not really. The TV roles were always pretty small. Waitress, barmaid, that sort of stuff. One scene, half a dozen words tops, usually."

"Impressive stage CV, though. Even played a bloke a couple of times. Hamlet once, for goodness' sake. Challenging?"

"Not particularly." Anyone else might have missed the glance away, the slight falter.

"But you have to do the voice convincingly," she pressed. "Right? I mean, is it just putting on a deeper voice?"

"That and inhabiting the character, yeah. If you must know, I think of it as like putting on an outfit."

"Yes," Lizzie said thoughtfully. "The actual outfit must be important too. Or should I say 'costume'?"

"Call it what you like." Grace rose. "I think we're done here."

"Sit down," Lizzie said sharply. "We're done when I say we're done. And it's in your interests to listen and to cooperate. It might just shave a bit of time off your sentence."

"My sentence?" she scoffed, but she sat back down. "You're throwing accusations around. Do you have a shred of actual proof?"

"Well," Lizzie said. "We have motive – vengeance for your father and brother, plus getting a liability off the scene. We have means – you could easily have memorised the combination of Cameron's gun safe, and I'm sure you or Fraser could have got into his office and taken that fancy paper knife. I've no doubt either that Cal Dougan would have been off his guard when one of you approached him in the car park you'd lured him to, distracting him while the other one sneaked up on him with the gun. I haven't worked out how exactly you managed to kidnap and kill Rob Thomas. Maybe you can help me with that."

"I'm still waiting for your so-called proof."

"Heard of gait analysis?"

"What do gates have to do with anything?"

"Gaits. How you walk. Everyone has their own. Yours is quite distinctive, and it's there to see in a nice little film clip on your website. You're strolling down Sauchiehall Street, with a nice voiceover, talking about your art and your influences. As I said, I've seen the CCTV footage from the pub car park where someone smears blood on Dominic's jacket. The person's normal walk. I knew it was familiar. It's just like you in that clip. Right height and build, too. And the acting... Dominic was fooled, even up close."

"And that's it? A *walk*?"

"We've had an independent forensic podiatrist look at the clips, and she came to the same conclusion. It's still regarded as a bit of an emerging science, and each case is treated on its own merits, but a trial judge is entitled to rely on it, if they choose."

"Yes? We'll see what my lawyers make of that."

"That and a single hair inside the hoodie you left in Cal's car. Whoever thought they'd been careful wasn't quite careful enough for our CSIs. Oh, I know you're not on any DNA databases. You're the good one. But it's your colouring. I'd be amazed if it didn't turn out to be yours." She shook her head. "Nice, artistic Grace. I'm betting you hatched the whole clever double-frame once word had got back to Cameron about the falling out with my ex. He probably had a good laugh about it, but you saw it as something you could use. You just got a bit *too* creative with the evidence trail. It really was too good to be true."

"Just suppose," Grace said carefully, "any of this actually happened. Why couldn't it have been Fraser's idea?"

"It could," Lizzie agreed, "but he's more the buttoned up accountant type, isn't he? Ruthless, of course. I would never be surprised if he carried out the actual killings. I wonder what he'll say when we confront *him* with all this. Maybe he'll deny all knowledge. Make out it was all you."

"Yes, well," Grace said. "If you seriously thought you'd come here with all this and I'd make a big confession, you're off your head. Show yourself out. I've heard enough."

"So have we," said a male voice, the Scots burr thick.

Lizzie turned more slowly than Grace, who whirled around. DI Alec McGilvray of Police Scotland, happy to help smooth the way north of the border, stood in the doorway, flanked by two uniformed officers. Jason Bell, always up for a trip to his home city, stood behind them.

McGilvray tapped the earpiece he wore and pointed to Lizzie, who casually showed her the little microphone behind her lapel.

Grace recovered fast, shrugging expansively. "So you recorded it? Big deal."

"Big deal indeed," McGilvray agreed. "I think a jury will find the bit where you name Jamie Keynes as Desmond Connolly's killer, without DCI Archer actually mentioning his name, especially instructive. Now, if you'll kindly keep quiet while I caution you, these officers will escort you to a police car."

"And I'll get onto my colleagues in the Met to pick up Fraser," Lizzie said. "I wonder if he'll throw you under the bus. If he does, don't forget I gave you a chance to cooperate."

"You bitch," Grace hissed at her.

Lizzie looked at her, then burst out laughing. "I've been called that before."

*

Questioned under caution, Grace Connolly had changed her tune considerably. It seemed she'd been happy to ally with Fraser in the commissioning of two murders all in the interests of a clever, but ultimately clumsy plan to stitch up their brother – but less willing to take the fall for it alone.

She was astute enough to understand that all the evidence that had been gathered pointed strongly to her, but there was little or nothing to positively incriminate Fraser. She'd asked if cooperation was still a possibility and had made a full confession that spread the blame around. She even tried to make out she'd acted under pressure from her brother.

It had emerged that Cal Dougan's murder hadn't just been a convenient part of the setup. Cameron had admitted to his siblings, in a rare moment of candour, that he'd asked Cal to arrange a little scare for Desmond, to warn him to keep his mouth shut. Thus the order to Jamie Keynes had come through Cal. The fact that Keynes had been a fool who'd gone spectacularly beyond his brief had been enough for Cal's death to be part of the plan.

She had seemed at least a little mollified that, whilst the charges against Cameron would now have to be dropped, he would be facing fresh charges in connection with Desmond's death. It wasn't yet known who had killed Jamie Keynes, nor who had given the order. Grace was still denying knowledge of that.

All in all, though, Lizzie reflected on her way home, it was a satisfactory end to her leadership of Aylesbury Vale's CID. She hadn't been sure she'd still be in the running for Josh Stowe's job. Even though she and Dominic had been entirely exonerated, she'd feared that mud might still stick, especially to her. But in a couple of weeks she would be starting, back in uniform, as Superintendent Archer.

Lara Moseley, as the more senior DI in the division, would be acting DCI until a substantive replacement could be secured. She wasn't sure yet if Dan would apply. He seemed content that his son hadn't rejected him after Mac's death. He'd even said it was okay to call him Jack.

In so many ways, Lizzie's life was settling down again. The first few days after Dominic's release hadn't been easy, but his resilience had surprised her. Now, if he alluded to it at all, he joked about being an 'old lag'. She sometimes wondered if Dominic was painting over his true feelings. She worried that he wasn't quite as over it as he made out.

He'd raised the matter of his old caution without Lizzie needing to prompt him. As she'd half-suspected, he'd spent too long waiting for the right moment to tell her about it. It had got to the point where he'd simply decided the best policy was to keep quiet. They'd had a heart to heart about the need for no secrets between them and, if anything, she felt they were even closer than before now.

As far as the house was concerned, it was already as if the fire had never happened. The front door had been replaced and the hall redecorated. The insurance company had made everything gratifyingly easy. They'd decided to have Adam and his family over for Christmas lunch – a thank you for their support during some dark and difficult days. Inviting them had been Dominic's idea, and he'd made it clear he'd be taking charge of the cooking. Which, Lizzie thought, was probably just as well.

As for Gaynor Upman, it appeared that her brand of vengeance had begun and ended with a nasty piece of car vandalism. Even after a respray, Lizzie had found she didn't like the car any more. She now drove an electric Mini.

The only possible dark cloud on the horizon was how the underworld would respond to the sudden removal of the entire Connolly clan from the scene. Would their lieutenants continue to manage their interests, taking their instructions from men behind bars? Or would a vacuum inevitably occur that other organisations would be eager to fill, not only in the Vale, but in London? It was a fear DCI Catherine Sheppard had articulated when Lizzie had updated the NCA officer on the arrests that had been made.

She found it wasn't something she could bring herself to dwell on for now. All she wanted was to get home to Dominic and Barney. The future, and whatever it might hold, would have to wait.

THE END

ACKNOWLEDGEMENTS

As always, huge thanks are due to the many people who have played their part in helping me make this the best book I can. Lisa Cutts, Clare Heron, Ruth Mancini and others have been extraordinarily generous with their professional expertise. Any inaccuracies are either intentional in the interests of the story, or my mistakes.

I am ever grateful to my brilliant and insightful beta readers, Chris Sivers and Debbie Porteous; their sometimes painful critiques are always an essential part of my writing process, and this novel is dedicated to them. The gimlet eyed Helen Baggott has again helped me to give the book a final polish.

Thanks to individuals who lent their names to characters in *Price to Pay*: Archer and Baines 'veteran' Lara Moseley, and Bill Smith, who made a generous donation to charity to have a character named after him. I hope he likes his namesake. I should point out that he's nothing like Bill the detective.

The support and friendship of all my mates in the crime writing business – too many to name, but they know who they are – as well as the Oxford Crime Writers, Chiltern Writers, and my friends and followers on social media – all help to keep me going.

Last, but anything but least, my thanks and love to my wonderful wife, Chris, who supports, encourages and loves me every day. I couldn't do this otherwise.

Buckinghamshire, 2024
www.davesivers.co.uk
X/Twitter: @davesivers
Facebook: @davesiversauthor1

Printed in Great Britain
by Amazon

38649641R00162